THE OLD
CAPE TEAPOT

BARBARA EPPICH STRUNA

B.E. Struna

Cover Designers: Loretta Matson & Timothy Jon Struna

Edited by Nicola Burnell

This is a work of fiction. Names, characters, places, brands, media, and incidents are either the product of the author's imagination or are used fictitiously. Any resemblance to similarly named places or to persons living or deceased is unintentional.

PRINT ISBN 978-0-9976566-1-9
Library of Congress Control Number: 2014918193

"Fans of Barbara Struna's *The Old Cape House* will warmly welcome this delightful sequel. Familiar characters from both the past and present return and find themselves enriched in new mysteries spun from the legends of Cape Cod pirates. Struna's historical research and exquisite plotting will keep both new and old readers captivated and wanting more."

—James Lang, Author of *Learning Sickness: A Year with Crohn's Disease* (Capital Books, 2004 and *Cheating Lessons: Learning from Academic Dishonesty* (Harvard University Press 2013)

"The legend of the pirate Samuel Bellamy grows with each retelling, and because the real man left no paper trail and little verifiable history, the legend takes on a new shine with each author's voice. In The Old Cape Teapot, Barbara Eppich Struna brings legends and folklore to life through the discovery of artifacts from the past, and reunites them with her own version of this unique Cape Cod story. It's an excellent read for those who enjoy a contemporary treat—with some history on the side."

—Elizabeth Moisan, author, *Master of the Sweet Trade: A Story of the Pirate Samuel Bellamy, Mariah Hallett, and the Whydah*

*To my husband Tim, my soul mate and partner
in love, laughter, and eternal optimism.*

Present Day
LONDON

ALEXANDER DAMIEN ended his day in the study with the same ritual. He required a crystal goblet filled with the finest sherry and a tufted Corinthian leather chair in which he reclined to admire his 'beauties.' He gazed upon six small alcoves built into a long wall lined in rich oak wood. Each one glowed with soft lights, highlighting his priceless collections.

With the flick of his wrist and a light push on a button, the middle niche slowly moved towards him then stopped a few inches from his knees.

"You are exquisite," he said as he gently spoke to the Fabergé egg, now at eye-level. The oval treasure depicted a sapphire-studded Cherub pulling a two–wheeled, silver-gilded chariot carrying a diamond-encrusted gold egg. Mr. Damien studied it for several minutes, almost as if he expected the cherub to move across the small platform that it rested upon. He sipped his sherry as the beautiful egg retreated backwards into its protected environment, nestled in the strong oak wall.

A second button brought another glass enclosure forward. "And you, my beauty, will soon have a friend, perhaps to discuss the intricacies of the diamond process or the pleasures of the royals from whence you came." He so enjoyed admiring the star and badge of the Order of Saint Patrick. The rubies, emeralds, and Brazilian diamonds mounted in silver were magnificent. The fact that he owned them was even more satisfying. Another button and the front glass disappeared with a swoosh. He carefully lifted the bejeweled star and caressed its dazzling points, then returned it to the display.

As he savored his sherry, each treasure within the alcoves presented itself to their guardian.

There was a slight rap on the door before an elderly gentleman entered. "Sir, will there be anything else?"

"No. Thank you, Stewart. You may lock up and set the alarm."

"Has there been any word from Antigua?"

"Very little, but things seem to be in place."

"Yes, sir. Good night, sir." Stewart poured a drop more sherry and dimmed the lights.

Alone again, Mr. Damien smiled with relish as he thought of his secret treasures. Over the centuries, everyone had assumed they were lost to the world, never to be found. His eyes moved towards the only light in the now darkened room, which came from the sixth alcove. It was empty.

1

Present Day
BREWSTER - CAPE COD

THE FRONT PARLOR of the old Cape house had become my office. It suited my needs and even had a pocket door in case I wanted to hide from everyone. A manila file holding a hard copy of my manuscript was stored in the top left drawer of my desk. My writing was coming along; I was about half way to the finish line. The big question was whether it was memoir or fiction? I was confident that I'd have time to figure it all out on the plane.

I looked around one last time at the framed pictures of the kids, me exploring the woods of Cape Cod, sailing on a replica of the 17th century Elizabeth Tilley, and posing for the newspaper wearing the antique necklace that I'd found among the pirate treasure. The room looked clean enough. I was only going to be gone a week.

I yelled into the foyer, "Martha, make sure Molly gets to camp on time."

The sound of Danny's five-year-old bare feet echoed in the foyer as he slapped them against the wooden floor. "Do you have to go, Mommy?"

"I won't be gone long. Your brother misses me just as much as you would if you were in a far-away place." After one last check in the mirror, my light blue linen blouse looked nice against my prematurely grey hair and navy blue cotton skirt. I grabbed my bag and hurried out of the office, ready for a comfortable journey ahead.

"Why did Brian have to go away?" Danny asked as he followed close behind me.

Over my shoulder I said, "He wanted to help people, so he joined the Peace Corps."

Martha filled the open doorway wearing a bright red paisley top and black stretch pants that covered her huge derriere. She stared out into the driveway looking for my ride. Within seconds she yelled out, "Your taxi's here!"

"Thanks, Martha."

As I turned to give Danny one more hug, Molly came running down the stairs with a big smile on her face and her eight-year-old arms swinging like a windmill. "Give Brian a big hug for me when you get there."

Another squeeze for Molly and I was out the door.

Paul emerged from his studio to meet me at the end of the deck. He put his arms around me. "I hope I don't get any paint on your new clothes. You look wonderful in that color blue."

I smiled. "Thanks. I'm really going to miss you."

He picked up my suitcase and put it into the waiting open trunk.

I turned to wave at Martha who was now holding Danny.

She called out, "Bye, Nancy. Make sure you don't get involved with any pirates on Antigua!"

I found myself laughing at her comment as I climbed into the back of the taxi.

Paul leaned his head into the window for one last kiss. "Nancy Caldwell, please try to have a nice, quiet visit with our son."

I straightened my skirt, took a deep breath to relax, and sat back in my ride to the airport.

Stately homes and ancient trees flew by me like a movie in fast forward. I thought of how much I loved living on Cape Cod as I touched the antique locket around my neck for good luck.

2

April 28, 1717
CAPE COD

THOMAS DAVIS took off to Samuel Harding's house, eventually convincing the old man to hide him and his salvaged treasure for payment in more gold. Within the hour, Davis returned to Maria Hallett's shack, along with a wagon to load his share. As he left, he saluted his shipmate, John Julian. "Better days ahead, mate." His last look was to Maria, who was caring for Sam Bellamy as he lay unconscious beside her. "May good fortune attend you and the captain, ma'am."

Maria said nothing as she turned her attention back to Sam.

By the time the sky darkened into black night, Julian had secured his riches to a short pole stretcher, covered it with a blanket and tied a shovel across the top. It was a struggle to pull the heavy chest across the rough terrain but he was determined. When the sky turned to early dawn, he'd finished burying his cache beneath the largest rock in Eastham. Wasting no time, he piled stones and rocks on top of the freshly dug dirt to hide what was buried. Julian smashed the rustic stretcher and heaved the shovel as far away as he could to further elude anyone from his nocturnal secret. He took only a small pouch of gold coins with him. Now he needed to hide through the daylight hours and run through the night to safety. Then it was on to Antigua.

*   *   *

1722
THE ATLANTIC OCEAN

Thomas Davis never dreamed that he would be sailing again to Antigua, in the West Indies, especially after his ordeal with the pirate Captain Sam Bellamy. Davis had sailed with the captain five years ago, but not of his own choice, and the courts of Boston had agreed that he was innocent of piracy. Today, he was sailing as a gentleman traveler from his home in Yarmouth on Cape Cod. He stood tall, not wanting to get his fine clothes dirty from the rough wooden rail under his hands.

Isaac Smith, at 18 years and on his maiden voyage, stood to Davis's right, pale-faced and leaning on the railing of the ship. Davis would give the young man not more than a few hours before the motion of the sea would make Isaac lose the contents of his stomach. Sadly, he proved to be correct. As if on cue, the sound of someone hurling vomit broke the stillness of the cool evening air as the young man leaned over the rail. Davis thought it humorous as he retired below for his dinner.

Later, within the same hour, Davis enjoyed one last smoke in the night air up on deck and noticed his ailing fellow passenger was still against the rail. He approached him. "Just let it all come out, son." He patted Isaac on the back. "You won't die, and in a few days, you'll be just fine." He filled his clay pipe and took a sniff from a gold inlaid snuffbox.

Spittle dangled from Isaac's lips as he glanced over to Davis. "Thank you, sir. Your words are reassuring but not plausible based on the way my insides feel."

Thomas Davis chuckled to himself. He looked up to the stars and rested his hand on a letter in his breast pocket that he had received a few weeks prior to his departure from Cape Cod. He remembered its words well.

Dear Thomas,

The time has come for us to talk. I seek your assistance in matters of our past together. I have information that would be of benefit both to you and I. Your presence is needed to reap great rewards.

J.J. Island of Antigua

Davis knew the initials stood for John Julian, the navigator and pilot on the pirate ship *Whydah*. He and Julian were shipmates together when the *Whydah* went down in a nor'easter, just off the coast of Cape Cod, on April 27, 1717. Davis shook his head, still in disbelief of how lucky he was that night. The other pirates had perished in the sea or were captured upon making it to shore. He pinched another snuff. He, Julian, and Captain Bellamy had eluded the soldiers that night by hiding in the shack of the young girl, Maria Hallett. In the early morning hours, the three had managed to salvage treasure from the wreck, then separated to hide their share of the booty until it was safe to return for it. Davis had almost lost hope when he and Julian were quickly spotted and captured, becoming prisoners of the King, then sent to Boston for trial with seven other pirate survivors. He had been found innocent, along with Julian, by reason of coercion; the rest were hung. They never saw Sam Bellamy again. Davis sneered with satisfaction and stroked the diamond encrusted gold ring on the smallest of his fingers.

3

Present Day
ANTIGUA

THE GLASS PANELS of the airport exit slid sideways, and I stepped out onto the island of Antigua. A sweltering 90-degree heat hit my body, as if I had just opened a hot oven. I saw Brian driving a dark brown, open Jeep looking for an empty space in the small airport's lot. Waving, I watched him finally find a space and park. As he walked closer to me, I noticed his peculiar attire. His shorts seemed odd paired with a black button down dress shirt, black socks and black tennis shoes. A funky Khaki jungle hat was tied under his chin, making him look like he was on a safari expedition. But it didn't matter what he wore, I was just happy to see my son.

I gave him a big hug. "Hi, honey. It's good to see you."

He grabbed my paisley suitcase from the curb and planted a quick kiss on my cheek. "How was your flight?"

"Okay. It's great to be on land again, even if it is a little hot for me. How've you been?"

"Fine, Mom. It's been good."

As he carried my bags I followed him, hoping to talk more, but he was my quiet one…a man of few words.

When we pulled away from the airport, my hair took off with a mind of its own, flying and swirling around my head. It felt good across my face. As the road continued, bumpy and curvy, I grew edgy about the rough ride and kept turning to the back seat to make sure the bags hadn't fallen out. Holding the side of the doorframe with one hand, my billowing skirt with the other, I felt like I was on an amusement park ride. The noise of the open Jeep made it difficult to talk, but I managed to get in a few simple questions: How far is your house? Do you have any meetings today? What's with all the black clothes?

Brian grinned at my teasing. "I try to stay away from white clothes; the water here turns everything yellow."

I returned a smile as he sped up around a bend and onto a two-lane highway. "Have I told you that I love you and am very proud of your work here?" I noticed another smile grow across his face. "Your brothers and sisters all say hello."

He quickly turned to me. "Thanks, Mom. I love you too."

Almost completing his second year in the Peace Corps, Brian knew his way around this little island in the West Indies. From his recent phone calls, I also knew that his work was finally becoming satisfying. Most people never see the tremendous poverty that exists behind all the posh resorts. Brian was right in the middle of it.

We passed several fancy hotels on the highway and then turned off and onto the back roads again. A group of houses came into view along a dirt road that led to the water.

"Here it is," Brian announced. He drove down to the end to show me the ocean and its white sandy beach.

"I can hardly wait to explore the beach," I whispered in awe, admiring the cool colors of the sky and water.

"Yeah, we should go for a walk tomorrow morning."

"Sounds good to me," I said as we turned around and drove back up the small incline to the houses that were all clumped together. Brian's was the first near the road.

"What do you think?" he asked as we stopped uphill on a grassy area under three tall palm trees.

"It's nice and shady." It was all I could think of after noticing the laundry hanging on the veranda, broken screens, empty beer bottles in a pail, and bikes leaning against the stairway.

As I climbed the steep stairs to the front door I asked, "Where's your new roommate...is he around?"

Brian opened the door and carried my bag inside along with some milk and other groceries. "Nick had a meeting with the teachers in his school. He's joining us in town for dinner at Mrs. Jones's house."

I stepped into the cramped rental. "That's nice of her, although I just don't know how much I'll eat tonight. I'm a little queasy from all the travel...just tired maybe."

Brian turned on a fan in the dark paneled living room. "We won't stay out late. I've been up since six this morning."

The first thing I did was find the bathroom, which was adequate, if you discounted the rust stained tub-combo-shower. Its walls and corners were dotted with mold and a few token pieces of hair decorated the rest of the faded linoleum floor. It was obvious that two guys lived in the old house; the toilet seat was up, but it was clean. I appreciated that Brian had made a real effort to make the house nice for me.

The bedroom was down the hall on the left. My bed was opposite Brian's. The room was stuffy and hot. I wanted to unpack but left everything in the suitcase because there was no place to put my things. Undaunted, I changed into fresh clothes.

Thirsty, I looked for a drink of water in the kitchen. Closed plastic containers of food floated in the double sinks. I assumed it was for preventing ants from getting into the sweet staples. Poking my finger into the off–colored water I asked, "Does this really work?"

"Yeah, the old guy who lives next door told us about it. Ready to go?"

"Yup." I replied, grabbing a fresh bottle of water from my suitcase; the tap water didn't seem very inviting.

*   *   *

Mrs. Jones, a native of Antigua, worked in the Peace Corps office and fed the volunteers once a week, becoming the designated mom for most of them. As I entered her small, stucco-walled, pink-colored home, she greeted me with a lilting Caribbean voice, "Welcome! It's so good to meet Brian's mom! What a nice boy he is. And so polite." I felt proud to hear her words. She disappeared into the tiny kitchen before I could reply.

Brian left my side for a moment to talk to a few of the Peace Corps people in the sitting room then returned with Nick for an introduction.

"Mrs. C, it's great to meet you," Nick said. The next statement out of his mouth went right to the point. "Is it true you discovered old pirate treasure?"

He caught me off guard but I enjoyed his frankness. "Yes, it is. I assume Brian told you all about it?"

"No, not all the details; I've only been here a few days." He pushed his horn-rimmed glasses up onto his nose then leaned closer to me. "Of course, when he said you found it on your property, I didn't believe him, then he showed me pictures of you on the internet and some of the jewelry that was found in the chest."

Mrs. Jones interrupted his questions with a shout out, "Time to eat, my friends."

A large table held a smorgasbord of native food. The red, yellow, and orange dishes were all colorfully laid out on top of a piece of material under clear plastic that depicted birds of paradise flying through a jungle. I assessed the chicken, beans, rice, and pasta in front of me. Positive that they were seasoned with hot spices, and not being fond of spicy food, I took only small samples of everything, just to make sure I wouldn't be eating anything that I didn't like. My plate was half empty.

"Not very hungry?" the hostess asked as she watched me pick at the food.

I tried to be gracious. "No, not really." I was hungry, but held back on saying anything else for fear I would be obligated to eat more. As I nibbled, I discovered I was right in assuming the food was peppery. I quickly reached for a cool drink of soda to calm the heat in my mouth. With my plate in hand, I then sought refuge from the stuffy house outside on the breezy veranda.

The temperature had dropped to a pleasant 74-degrees and young voices drifted through the tropical night air, along with sounds of a football game from the States blaring from a large screen TV. As I settled into a plastic lounge chair Nick came over and sat down next to me. He wore black pants with a beige polo shirt. His glasses were definitely too big for his face.

Nick continued with more questions. "How did you happen to find the treasure?"

I smiled, always eager to tell my once-in-a-lifetime story. "After we moved from Ohio to an old 1880 house on Cape Cod, I wanted to dig a garden behind the barn. By accident, I dug up a buried root cellar and at its bottom was evidence that pointed to a famous Cape

Cod legend."

"You mean Sam Bellamy and Maria Hallett?" Nick asked.

I nodded.

"Is that one of the pieces you found?" He pointed to my good luck charm dangling from my neck.

"Yes, but not in the cellar. I found this later, in the woods." I held my locket in the glow of a streetlight that illuminated the front of the house so he could see it better.

Nick leaned closer to inspect the diamonds that surrounded the delicately engraved blue-green flowers on the tiny orb of ivory.

His eyes widened. "It must have been really cool to find all that treasure!"

"Oh yes. No one had ever thought to look in Brewster, where we live, because the *Whydah* had wrecked near Marconi Beach in Wellfleet."

"Would you like a beer?" Nick asked me as he stood up.

"No thanks, my soft drink is just fine."

He returned with a cold bottle of Wadadli, an island beer. "Then what happened?"

Leaning back in the chair I let out a big yawn. "An article appeared in the local paper about how we'd found the cellar, then two guys broke into our house looking for more treasure."

The effects of travelling and not much sleep were taking their toll on me. My words began to slur together. "If someone had told me that I'd become involved with Black Sam Bellamy and the mysterious Maria Hallett, I would've said they were crazy."

Nick's face beamed.

I ran my fingers through my hair and massaged my head, trying to get rid of the headache that was starting to surface.

Brian came out of the house and cut Nick's questions off with, "Mom, are you feeling ok?"

"I'm fine...just talking about my pirate treasure adventures." I crumpled up a napkin across my half eaten food, hopefully hiding what I didn't eat. "Are we leaving soon? I'm pretty tired."

Brian leaned back to stretch his back out. "Yeah, we should get going."

Nick stood to leave also. He said his goodbyes and then informed us that he was going to stay at another volunteer's house for a few nights, to give us some privacy. "Maybe we can talk later?"

"Sure," I smiled.

The air felt cool in the open Jeep. I closed my eyes for the ride home to Brian's. When my head finally rested on a pillow, sirens sounded and flashing lights circled the dark bedroom. Loud voices were arguing outside on the road.

"Brian, are we safe?"

"Yeah, don't worry. The police will take care of it."

I closed my eyes again and repeated Hail Mary's over and over until I fell asleep.

*   *   *

1722
ANTIGUA

The sun began to set in the west as John Julian, overseer of the Smith Sugar Plantation, walked home from the fields. He could still feel the heat on his neck. The benefits of his stature on the island of Antigua were many; one of them was enjoying the evening meal with his lovely wife, Elizabeth.

His wood-sided house with its thatched roof stood apart from the other slave houses on a narrow piece of flat land. The Smith's mansion had a stone edifice that looked down upon the crowded complex of shanties. Julian's path home took him through the workers' community and each person cordially greeted the man who controlled them. Julian looked around at the men, women, and children and appreciated that the fate of slaves on a Smith's plantation was far better than most after the British Royal African Company had captured them. He noticed a new boy, who'd recently lost his mother. She had been raped by one of the soldiers in charge of the new captives. Ashamed, she took her life by jumping into the crushing depths below Devil's Bridge. The orphan obediently moved to the side of the overseer's path. Julian patted his head and hoped the family that took him in was treating him well.

Thanking the heavens again for his position on the island, Julian walked on. He was well aware of the British Royal African Company's reputation for seizing human goods from tribal villages along the

Gold Coast of Africa. Upon arriving on Antigua or Barbuda, the captives were separated for work by gender, age, and ability regardless of family ties. They were then traded and sold among the British colonies, their destinies decided by white merchants looking for profit. Some slaves were shipped to the new colonies in America, others forced to labor on the sugar plantations that dominated the Caribbean. These poor souls had a bleak future or no future at all. Julian took pride in the fact that even though his skin was the same color as theirs, he was a free man and not indentured to anyone but himself.

Enjoying his casual pace home, he hoped that any day now word would come concerning the matter of a very important business transaction. Julian hoped that the letter he sent to Thomas Davis would have already found its way to Cape Cod and into the hands of his former cohort. All the recent overseers had been talking of the Smith family and the possibility that they were selling their fields. Julian began thinking of his future as a landowner and it included Davis's help. His plan was a long shot, but his gut instinct told him it was a sure shot.

He opened the door to his home and saw Elizabeth by the table rolling out the flatbreads. "Elizabeth, it's good to be home."

She smiled and her honey bronze face glowed in his presence. "How's your day?"

Taking his seat on a bench by the table, he leaned back against the wall. "As good as expected. Any letters?"

"No, I'm sorry, not today." She stopped her work, came closer to him, and sat on his lap. They held each other in silence. She kissed him lightly on his forehead and then returned to her work at the table. "Something will come soon, I feel it."

He rose to relieve himself out back and whispered, "My hopes are high."

4

Present Day
ANTIGUA

THE NEXT MORNING I awoke to the gentle whisper of palm trees rustling in the breeze. Brian was still sleeping. Long mesh netting encircled his bed. The netting around my bed was nicely tied to each side of the bedposts. I looked down on top of my chest to see a spotted green lizard staring back at me. "Brian!" I kept my head still, making eye contact with the creepy lizard. Then a little louder I repeated, "Brian! Wake up!"

He rolled over and looked at me through half open eyes. "What's the matter?"

"This thing's on top of me."

"What?" He squinted for a better view.

"Do something!" As I grew more impatient for Brian to rescue me, I decided that I was going to be my own rescuer. I quickly flipped the sheets up and away from my body. The tiny lizard flew into the air. I jumped out of bed just in time to see the creepy crawly thing skitter across the floor and through an opening in the wall. My sleepy son watched the whole thing from his bed. I got angry and yelled, "You never told me to tuck my netting in!"

He rubbed his face. "Sorry, I forgot."

"Is there anything else I'm supposed to know?"

He didn't answer as he adjusted the sheet across his chest and went back to sleep.

After showering, I got dressed and tried to dry my hair. Within minutes, I'd blown all the fuses in the house with my hair dryer. My annoyance with Brian concerning the lizard episode quickly subsided. I felt bad and should've asked about the power capabilities. Of course, he should've told me about the netting. I figured we were even now.

While Brian got the house running again, I went for a walk on the beach. In a few minutes, he was at my side, helping me collect conch shells for the kids. "Sorry about overloading the electrical system."

"No problem. It happens." He picked up a beautiful multicolored conch. "Molly and Casey are really going to like these shells."

It didn't take long before we were on our way into town. As I tied the straps to a new straw hat under my chin, I found it extremely practical as we began our sunny and windy trip for nine miles into St. John's. Brian's use of a funky hat back at the airport became perfectly clear to me.

Huge ditches flanked us on either side of the road. I glanced over to Brian and noticed a large cut with black and blue marks on his exposed thigh, just under the hem of his shorts.

"What happened to your leg?"

"I was riding my bike to work last week and someone ran me off the road. It's no big deal."

"What?"

"Don't worry. Some people here don't like us, it's typical...and I'm also a white American."

"It's like prejudice in reverse." I felt a twinge of fear for my son.

"I'm careful and always watching my back," he said, trying to reassure me of his safety.

It didn't work.

He added, "...and Mom, my landlady has arranged dinner for us tonight at her outdoor café. It's at the end of the sandy road near our house. Right on the beach."

"That's nice," I said, slightly apprehensive for another neighborly dinner of my least favorite: spicy food.

Brian sped up a little. "I want to show you Indian Town Point before we get into St. John's."

We drove past a vacation complex where Brian had crewed on a sailboat last month, and then we came upon a remote section of coastline.

It was flat, empty, and barren, ending in a sheer cliff straight down to water. "This is called Devil's Bridge," he said.

The bridge arched over the water to another mass of stony terrain, which shot upwards out of the sea, creating a rocky precipice. Its natural arch overlooked not a sandy coastline but a swirling mass of wave and foam that crashed against the sharp limestone ledges. We got out of the jeep and stood near the edge, choosing not to walk closer onto the bridge for fear that a trip of the shoe or loss of balance on the stones would throw us into the frothing mass of powerful waves.

"Why do they call it Devil's Bridge?"

"Legend has it that the devil lives here among the rocks. They also say the African people who were brought here, centuries ago, would hurl themselves off the bridge rather than live a life of torture and torment as slaves."

"How terrible." I shook my head in disbelief.

Brian leaned closer to one of the edges. "People still come here to commit suicide. Some young guy died here last week; it was in the paper. They think he was from the States."

I stepped back from the violent scene.

Brian whispered, "They couldn't identify the body. All they found were some limbs and a pile of shredded clothes."

"It's so sad and frightening. Let's go." We walked back to the Jeep arm in arm.

*   *   *

After we drove across town, we parked at the Peace Corps office and then took a short stroll for a quick tour of the city.

As we walked, Brian looked over to me. "Mom, do you have to wear that necklace?"

"What do you mean?"

"I'm uneasy with you wearing it around here. It looks really expensive. I don't want to give anyone any ideas…we have to be careful."

"You think I should take it off?"

"Maybe."

"Okay. I trust your opinion." I unhooked it and placed it inside my purse.

Vendors lined the edges of streets and stood under the stone archways that connected sections of buildings together. Bought souvenirs weren't for me; I would rather take home the big conch shells that covered the coastline for remembrances. Some people from behind the tables spoke to us as we passed by; I smiled even though I couldn't understand the local dialect.

Brian cautioned me. "Just look straight ahead and ignore whatever the vendors say to you. Don't acknowledge them."

"Why?" I asked trying to keep pace with Brian's long strides.

"They're actually cursing at you because you didn't buy anything from them."

"You're kidding!"

"No, do you want to know what that guy just said to you?"

"Not really."

The wide toothy smile of an elderly man hawking everything from deodorant to socks to postcards followed us as we passed him. I looked straight ahead and was grateful that Brian told me to keep the necklace out of sight.

As we rounded the corner of a large stucco building, a small freestanding lime-green eatery atop a cement block foundation came into view. It looked bold among the white and pastel painted houses on the small street. A sign was scrawled with scripted letters: *Julian's*. It was decorated with painted pineapples, bananas, palm trees, and huge white waves that encircled its rectangular opening. The wooden building had grass on both sides and a high, open counter facing the street from which customers could order sandwiches and drinks. A small basket of napkins rested on the counter. From behind it, the tall, middle-aged proprietor was smiling and greeted us with, "Hello, Brian!"

"Hi, John. How are you?"

"Fine. Who is this lovely young lady with you today?"

"My mom."

His black face lit up with a broad smile. "Well, I can see where Brian gets his good looks." After a quick swipe of the counter with a cloth, he asked, "What might be your pleasure today?"

The cheerful proprietor's name and the sign above his head made me stop dead in my tracks. I couldn't believe my eyes as the legend of Sam Bellamy and the Antiguan, John Julian, flooded my thoughts.

Julian was one of only two survivors of the *Whydah* pirate ship. Legend has him possibly returning to Antigua.

"I'll have the turkey on rye with a coke," Brian ordered, oblivious to my stunned stare.

I couldn't think about what to order; something far more exciting than turkey was on my mind. I elbowed Brian. Out of the corner of my mouth, I quietly asked, "Did he say his name was John? What's his last name?"

Brian reached for his sandwich and casually asked, "Hey, John, is your last name Julian, like on the sign?"

"Oh yes, I was named after my long ago grandfather." He stood tall and proudly added, "I am the seventh generation descended from the first John Julian."

I swallowed hard. With a timid voice, I ordered, "I'll take the turkey on wheat…with a bottle of water." Stepping back from the counter I took hold of Brian's arm. "Haven't you ever noticed his name?"

"What do you mean?"

"John Julian…?" No response from Brian. I repeated with more emphasis. "John Julian! One of the pirates who survived the *Whydah*?"

With his mouth full, he looked up at the sign, then to his friend John and back to me. "Holy crap!" He tilted his safari hat back on his head, let out a soft whistle and added, "I can't believe it!"

*   *   *

1722
ANTIGUA

Flour puffed into the air and circled Elizabeth's tightly woven hair. She always felt fortunate to have John Julian as her husband and never questioned him about his doings. He had told her of his past, and she paid no mind to what he'd been; she only cared about who he was now. As she prepared bread for the day, the bright morning sun reflected its light onto the tiny diamond orbs that dangled beneath Elizabeth's earlobes. They created flickers of rainbow colors that encircled her head and danced about the sparse room. She loved the small circles of ivory, painted with blue and green, from which the faceted diamonds swung. John had presented these earrings to her on their first night together as man and wife.

He had cautioned her to hide any sign of wealth from their neighbors for fear of retaliation or robbery and to be careful of who was near her when she wore them. So Elizabeth wore this gift from John in secret, only when she was alone during the day.

While the bread rose on the hearth, Elizabeth tended to her mending and spotted a few drips of black ink beneath the table. Perturbed, she tried rubbing them with salt and then vinegar to no avail. Wishing that John would be neater when he made his drawings, she passed over this small indiscretion as not worth her mention and went back to her sewing.

By sunset, John made his appearance at home. After their evening meal, he took a bottle of ink down from a high shelf along with the vellum papers that rested next to it. The prior week, he'd taken these items from the counting house for his personal use. He felt no guilt because he knew he was a good overseer and justly deserved occasional gifts.

Elizabeth sat reading the family Bible by the light of the hearth; she glanced over to John with each turned page. He seemed so intent in his drawing that she hesitated to interrupt him with concern over her coming late this month. Settling her mind with the thought of waiting a little longer, to be sure if she was with child, she continued her prayers. John, using his navigational skills, honed from his time at sea with Sam Bellamy, tried to recreate from memory a map of Cape Cod, carefully noting where his treasure was buried.

5

Present Day
ANTIGUA

WHILE I ATE LUNCH, I couldn't take my eyes off the living relative of the 1717 pirate, John Julian. My stomach churned with curiosity. I've always had an uncanny ability to solve mysteries and this was like a gift of a dozen roses. My leg bounced up and down under the picnic table with anticipation of finding answers. Suddenly the big wooden cover to the front of Julian's shack slammed shut. My whole body came to a screeching halt. Why was he was closing? I stared at Brian. "What's going on? It's only 11:30 in the morning."

"He always closes at this time."

"But I want to talk to him."

"I understand, but John has to pick up two of his kids from school. He'll open again at noon."

I folded the waxy paper around my sandwich. "So...how many children does he have?"

"Six in all: four of his own, two that are adopted, one of whom is handicapped and the other has Down Syndrome." Brian crumpled his sandwich wrapper into a ball and tossed it into the garbage barrel. "Don't worry, we'll come back later so you can ask him about his ancestors. Right now, we should leave. I want you to meet Ian."

"Okay." Disappointed, I turned and looked again at the name *Julian's* painted across the top of the lime-colored shanty. Ever determined to discover more information, I promised myself to return as soon as possible.

As Brian cautiously pulled out onto the road, I leaned back against the headrest. He started to talk to me, but I wasn't listening; my head was swirling with thoughts of pirates and treasure again. I did hear him say, "We better drive there; his neighborhood isn't the greatest."

Riding the back roads, I found myself appreciating the beauty of the less glamorous side of this island resort, the one a tourist never sees. My trip was not luxurious but was proving to have plenty of interesting new information about the Sam Bellamy legend. I was excited. Hopefully there'd be a chance to share an adventure with my son, maybe even solve another mystery.

We came upon Ian's house after a few quick turns and crossing several streets. It was in a closely settled section of St. John's where every house was painted a different color. Ian's was salmon colored. Brian pushed the door in.

Curious, I asked, "If it's such a bad neighborhood, why is his door open?"

"He wants to let his neighbors know that he's their friend and not afraid."

Ian's rented house was small, with the inside walls painted to match the outside. The main room included a full size couch, two leather lounge chairs, and a coffee table. The kitchen was to the rear of the house. Brian lay down on the couch and I sat on a leather chair while we waited for Ian to come home.

Brian's cell rang at noon. It was Ian. He said he might be another hour.

I noticed there were two bedrooms and a bathroom down a narrow hallway. I pointed to the closest bedroom. "Do you think I could stretch out on the bed in there?"

"Sure, go ahead. Ian won't mind." Brian settled back onto the couch.

A twin bed and dresser were the only furniture in the tiny bedroom. I lifted my legs onto the bed, dangling my feet over the side; being careful not to disturb the tightly tucked green blanket. My head rested on a clean white pillow. Almost immediately, something began to tickle my hands and arms. I sat up to see beige specks over the surface of the bed and assumed it was sand. I brushed my hand across the raised patterned lines of the blanket that ran lengthwise down its surface. The specks jumped. I jumped.

"Whoahhhh!!" I hurried out of the room and down the hallway.

Brian glared at me. "What's wrong?"

"The bed is covered in fleas!" I rubbed my hands all over my clothes, trying to brush off the little pests.

"Sorry. That must be where the dogs sleep."

Perturbed again, I asked, "How many other things are you going to keep from me?" He shot me a coy smile as I settled in the other crackled leather lounge chair in the living room. By now it was 12:30PM and there was still no sign of Ian. The house was quiet. "Brian, how did you meet John Julian?"

"He was one of the first people to sign up for my committee to study the problems of handicapped orphans on the island."

I looked over to him. "Your project...the special needs orphanage for Mariel. Will I get to see it?"

"Of course." Brian stood to turn on the kitchen faucet. "Want a glass of water?"

"No, thanks." I remembered the terrible smell of the water back at his house. I joined him by the sink. "Anything else to drink?" We both checked out the refrigerator. Three cans of Coke stared us in the face. "I'll split one with you," I said. We found two clean glasses, some ice, then leaned back against the sink and grew silent once more, enjoying our cool drink.

"Mom, it's been such a struggle getting the orphanage started, over a year now." He rubbed the back of his neck. "And there's so much more to do."

"I'm glad you persevered...you know... against all odds." I put my glass on the counter and gave him a hug.

At that, Ian opened the door. "Hey, what's going on in here?" He looked amused as he dropped his backpack on the floor by the couch.

Nick was right behind him.

Brian laughed. "My mom's catching up on all her lost hugs from over the last year."

Ian's short stature didn't hold him back from making his presence known. He bounded towards me. "Do I get some?"

Nick hung back by the open door, not like the other night at Ms. Jones's.

"Come on over here you two, there's always room for a few more in a mother's arms."

Ian wrapped his arms around me.

Nick came a little closer and gave me a quick but awkward hug, then asked, "Mrs. C, where's that beautiful necklace?"

I touched my neck. "Brian thought it would be safer if I didn't wear it out in public. It's in my purse. I'll probably keep it in my suitcase while I'm here."

"Oh." He took his seat in one of the leather chairs, picked up a sports magazine and said nothing more to the rest of us.

His behavior seemed odd to me. He'd been so curious before but... perhaps he was thinking of all the work that lies ahead of him. I understood his somber mood; everything must be so new to him here.

* * *

1722
ANTIGUA

After work, John Julian hurried home; he was almost finished with his maps. No word had come from Thomas Davis, but he knew a ship was arriving from Cape Cod tomorrow. Isaac Smith, the young son of his employer, was scheduled to be on the vessel and it was his job to greet him. John hoped Davis would also be aboard.

That evening, Elizabeth grew sleepy as she tried to focus on the words in her Bible. She glanced over to John at the table. "Will you be staying up much longer?"

He returned a contented look and said, "No. I'm finished."

Two pieces of vellum, displaying the same drawing on each, lay on top of the sideboard. Elizabeth got up from her rocker, carrying the Bible, and came closer to him. "They look like two bent arms."

"Yes, do they not?" Pleased with himself that he remembered it so well. "Wait and see, they will bring wealth and happiness to us." He folded each one into a square.

Elizabeth turned to stoke the fire and pushed a new log back into the hearth. Julian stood to replace the ink and extra vellum back on the shelf. Under a tankard on the table, he placed one of the folded vellums; the other he slipped into the back of the Bible. All was ready for the morrow. He was sure of his plan. Davis was his lifesaver, and his dream of being a wealthy man would soon become reality.

Elizabeth took off her earrings and put them in a wooden box that had an ivory carving on its lid. She slid into bed next to John. Leaning on her elbow she watched him before she finally spoke.

"John, are you awake?" She whispered again, "John?"

He opened his eyes. "Is everything all right?"

"Yes, I have something to tell you."

"What is it?"

"I think I am with child."

"Elizabeth, that's good news. Are you sure?"

"Yes. I have not bled in two months. I also spoke with the midwife and she agrees."

He pulled her close into his arms. "It's fitting that you tell me on the eve of the completion of my maps." Then he gently kissed her hair.

"I'm pleased that you're so happy," she said as she nestled in the crux of his elbow. "It will be a fine day when you write with your inks into our Bible the name of our first born."

A warm tropical breeze wafted through the one window of their small room and softly lulled them both into the night.

6

Present Day
ANTIGUA

THE NECKLACE matched my linen blouse perfectly; I couldn't resist wearing it down to dinner.

It was almost five o'clock before Brian and I were able to walk down the rutted dirt road to the ocean restaurant for dinner. Nick would join us later. We passed several cute goats tethered on the grass under palm trees. At the bottom of the sloped road, I could see the buildings' outside walls. They were painted orange and trimmed in turquoise, with palm fronds covering the roof.

We entered into an attached lean-to that opened onto a sandy beach. Heady smells of spice mixed with the salty air. Four round tables were positioned in front of a long polished wooden bar. Six high stools divided its length, inviting the casual beach stroller in for a drink. Two men were drinking beers at the bar as we made our way to a table. They looked out of place to me; sporting crew cuts, dark glasses, and white boxy shirts. I laughed at the thought that maybe they were on a break from guarding some celebrity.

Ms. Judith came out of the kitchen to greet us. She extended a slim, dark hand covered with gold rings. "Good to meet you, Brian's Mom."

Our hands clasped together. "Nice to meet you, too."

"I have prepared a special meal for you. I hope that it will bring you pleasure."

"I'm sure it will." I sat next to Brian at the table closest to the end of the lean-to's roofline, giving us a wonderful view of the horizon. "This is so nice," I said as balmy tropical breezes caressed our faces. "I guess we don't get a choice of food?"

"No, we just eat whatever she serves us."

"But you know I don't like spicy foods...."

"Mom, shhhh." Brian placed his hand over mine, trying to calm my fear. "Please, just sit back and relax."

I felt a little irritated with his attitude but realized that he was probably right. But even after a nice long breath of ocean air, I still kept wondering about my mystery dinner.

Nick finally showed up. "Sorry I'm late. Got held up in a meeting." He sat next to me. "Great to see you again, Mrs. C. Did you have a good sleep last night?"

"Not bad, except for the sirens and other surprises." I gave Brian a friendly glare.

Nick stared at my necklace. "Hey, I thought you weren't going to wear it out?"

"I couldn't resist wearing it tonight. It's perfect for a tropical evening on the beach. Besides, it's pretty quiet down here."

He smiled. "Well, you be careful with it; you don't want anything to happen to it that you might regret." He ordered a beer and leaned in closer. "You know, I'm still so curious about that treasure you found."

So the inquisitive Nick is back. Actually, it was nice to have someone who was interested in my story; everyone at home was tired of me talking about it. "What do you want to know?"

"Tell me everything."

He sounded enthusiastic. I leaned back, pleased to have a fan. "From the beginning, I never intended to be a treasure hunter. It just happened." I noticed that Brian seemed disinterested, as usual. He got up to look out onto the sandy beach. One of the guys from the bar went over to talk to him.

Nick scooted his chair even closer and distracted me from watching Brian. "It must have been unnerving to find the little baby's skull in the root cellar. Brian said that's when you also found the three pieces of gold?"

"Yes, and as soon as the discovery hit the papers, all the intrigue started."

Our waiter, a tall young man, dressed in white, about 17 years old, introduced himself as Junior. After serving our drinks, he waited to be dismissed but kept watching me or maybe the necklace. I wasn't sure. I thought again for a moment that I should've left it back in the house. My nerves began to ramp up higher on top of the anticipation of what I had to eat.

Brian returned to the table. "Mom, this is John Julian's oldest son."

That was a small relief. He wasn't anyone sinister, just a local kid and someone Brian knew. I smiled at him. "I met your father today. We had a great lunch at his eatery."

Young Junior bowed his head. "I'll tell him of your compliment. If you'll excuse me, I'll return shortly." Turning on his heel, he left to fill a pitcher of water for us.

Ms. Judith came out of the swinging doors that separated the kitchen from the dining area carrying two plates filled with a mound of multi-colored food and headed in our direction. "My specialty. Enjoy."

Decorating each white dish was a stew-like food that lay nestled on top of brown rice. A quick glance with wide eyes was exchanged between Brian and me as we scanned our dinner. Nick smiled and looked as if he could hardly wait for his serving. I stared at my plate and then over to Brian's and whispered, "What is it?"

"Goat stew," he answered under his breath.

"What did you say?"

"Goat stew!"

A cute, fuzzy, little face with big brown eyes popped into my head. I fell back against my plastic beach chair, not wanting anything to do with Ms. Jones's specialty.

With the arrival of Nick's plate, I had no choice but to begin eating the brown pieces of meat that were scattered among the vegetables. My fork timidly began pecking at the rice around the edges of the plate and then the utensil slowly found its way into my mouth. The rice was good and the sauce tasty. Confident, I ventured further into the middle and tried the bite-sized meat. It wasn't terrible, but I couldn't bring myself to eat any more. "I'm not sure how much I can eat of this."

Brian eyed his food and quietly said, "You better finish; it would be an insult to Ms. Judith. Remember, you get to go home; I have some more time here on the island."

"Can I give you some from my portion?" My plate inched its way closer to Brian's.

He placed his hand on the table, separating his dish from mine, preventing any chance of my food being deposited onto his plate. "Are you kidding, I can barely get it down myself."

Nick was quiet as he dug into his meal, ignoring our discomfort. There was no talking at our table, just careful, anxious eating.

When Nick was almost finished, he asked, "How did you connect the legend of Bellamy and Hallet with the things you found?"

I was happy for another question. "We found some old pieces of parchment at the bottom of the cellar. On them were dates and initials that, according to the state archaeologist and carbon testing, pointed to the 1700s and the Samuel Bellamy legend."

Nick took a quick drink and excused himself to use the restroom. "I'll be right back. I want more details."

"How come Nick is so curious?"

"Oh, he's harmless. He told me he's nuts for pirates, been that way since he was a kid apparently."

I smiled to myself, why not? My story is a great adventure. "What did that guy talk to you about before we got our food?"

"Not much. He just asked where the best sailing was. I told him that I was Peace Corps and had only sailed once on the island."

The unfinished meal sat in front of me. I racked my brain trying to come up with a solution as to how I could get out of this predicament.

"What if I asked to take it home?" I suggested to Brian.

"She'll know."

"I have to try; I can't eat anymore."

I got up and asked Junior for something to take the food home in for tomorrow's lunch, hopeful my fib would work. I offered many thanks and compliments upon Ms. Judith for her ability to combine interesting and tasty foods. My effort went well and she retired into the kitchen with a big smile on her face. As Junior handed me the tinfoil container, he asked, "I hope you don't think me forward, but I couldn't help noticing the beautiful jewelry that you're wearing."

I placed my hand on my neck, "Thank you, it's one of my favorites."

"It resembles earrings that belong to my mother."

"Really?"

"Yes, they've been in my family for many years, handed down from generation to generation."

My queasy stomach miraculously disappeared as my eyes widened with interest. "Do you know any history about them?"

"No, I just remember my mother always keeping them in a box under lock and key. She would only wear them for special occasions, like her wedding anniversary."

"Junior." A voice called from the kitchen summoning the teenager away from my next question.

I quickly returned to our table carrying the supposed lunch for the next day. "Brian, Junior just told me his mother has some earrings that look like my necklace."

"Oh yeah? That's nice. Shall we go? I'm kind of tired and don't feel so well."

Somewhat perturbed that he wasn't interested, I understood his ill feeling and tucked a mental note in my head to make sure to talk to him about Junior's information later. Brian did look a little pale.

Twinkling stars covered the black night sky. I felt a little better as we walked back up the hill to the house and it seemed that Brian did too. He smiled at me. "Did you enjoy your stew?"

"So…you think it was funny?" I tried to smack him on the shoulder but he was too quick and dodged my hand.

Nick caught up with us on the sandy path. "Hey, Mrs. C, I've got one more question."

I turned around. "Sure, what else do you want to know?"

"What about the big treasure?"

We continued walking up the hill. "I found that about a year later, beneath a huge boulder in our woods. It was in a rotted chest that was filled with gold and jewels."

Nick whistled. "Wow! Who would have thought you could find old treasure nowadays." He stepped in front of me, walking backwards. "How did you know it was Bellamy's treasure?"

"Based on the parchment found in the cellar and the initials of S.B. and M.H. on it, I just assumed it was his."

Nick wistfully looked up to the stars. "Bellamy must have been one hell of an interesting character."

"That he was! You know, when the *Whydah* was discovered off Cape Cod's coast in 1986, it made pirate Samuel Bellamy a national treasure."

Nick went into a pirate mode and jumped ahead of us. He yelled, "Shiver me timbers and avast, ye mates. 'Tis a fine night for a stroll!"

At the top of the hill, we laughed some more and then said our goodnights. Nick got into his jeep and disappeared down the dark road. Brian and I walked up the stairs to the house.

"I know what I'm going to do with this stew," I said, "throw it out!"

Before Brian could say anything sarcastic, he stopped in his tracks and held up his arm. "Hold it! Something's wrong here."

"What?"

"The door's open. I know I locked it. I always do." He placed his head close to the screen and listened. "You stay here. I'll go in and see what's going on."

I stood still holding the pungent remains of those sweet baby goats while Brian quietly reached in and flipped the light switch. I watched him scan the room. He turned and held his finger to his lips in a 'keep quiet' gesture. More lights went on as he checked the bedrooms. Within a few minutes he re-appeared.

"It's okay. No one's here now, but I think someone was…your suitcase is a mess."

I hurried to my bedroom to find my clothes strewn over the floor. I felt sick in my stomach. I couldn't stand the idea of a stranger rifling through my things. The memory of the night I'd been tied and gagged in my own home shot into my head. I sat on the edge of the bed and took some deep breaths, trying to clear my thoughts and bring myself back into common sense mode.

Brian scanned the other rooms. "The rest of the house seems untouched."

"I can't believe someone got in here," I said in a nervous whisper. "Do you think they were after this?" I touched my necklace.

"I don't know, Mom. Maybe."

"Should we call the police?"

"Not sure. I'll talk to someone in the office tomorrow."

I slowly got up and started to straighten my things. "Please make sure you lock the door tonight and maybe keep a light on in the living room."

"We'll be okay." Brian gave me a hug goodnight.

"Would you shove a chair under the doorknob?"

He moved over to the kitchen area and grabbed a chair. "Don't worry."

I felt a little relieved as I watched my son do as he was asked. While brushing my teeth I made a mental note to talk to Brian about Junior's comment that his mom's jewelry resembled my necklace. But by the time I was finished, he was already asleep. Grabbing my flashlight, I dropped the netting around my bed and crawled in. I fell asleep thinking that I wanted to go back and visit John Julian at the sandwich place. I'd leave early enough to catch him before eleven-thirty.

*   *   *

1722
ANTIGUA

Julian left in the early morning for the Smith's house to make sure that all was ready for the arrival of the plantation owner's son. With his own eyes, he confirmed that clean bedding and adequate food was prepared and that everything else was in its place at the sugar mill. When he was satisfied, he left for the harbor at St. John's, eager to find Davis and young Isaac Smith.

Within the hour, he was leaning against a black, oily barrel. John lit his clay pipe, hoping its spicy smoke would mask the putrid odors of dead fish, spoiled food, and the sweaty bodies of slaves as they loaded and unloaded cargo from the tall ships. On occasion, the sea air blew the stench away, but not today, it was calm and steamy. As he awaited the sight of the *Voyager*, he felt good; Elizabeth's news of the child was a pleasant surprise for him.

Isaac Smith had his bags ready on deck, keen to place his feet on land once more. Thomas Davis took his time below. Unlike Isaac, he enjoyed his sail, relishing his time at sea. As the *Voyager* entered the harbor, its hull skimmed across the glasslike water, headed for its docking.

Davis joined young Isaac against the railing. "We'll be on land soon. I suspect you'll be very happy?"

"Yes, I will that," answered Isaac.

The sun beat upon their heads and, as the ship slowed, the wind lessened its refreshing coolness.

"Are you staying with anyone, Mr. Davis?"

"No, but I'm meeting an old acquaintance."

"You're welcome in my house. I'd like to repay you for your kindness towards me while we sailed." Isaac scanned the dock for the plantation's carriage and its overseer.

"That's very considerate of you, Isaac," Davis said as he, too, looked towards the dock for John Julian.

As soon as Julian spotted the vessel, he straightened his shirt and doused his pipe. He was ready to meet Smith and, hopefully, Davis too.

The harbor at St. John's was wide and deep, enabling the ships to snug the land. Planks were drawn across the water and passengers began their exit, all looking for familiar faces. Julian recognized Isaac Smith from a portrait that hung in the great room of the big house.

"Welcome, Mr. Smith. I'm John Julian, the overseer for your father's plantation."

"Nice to meet you," Isaac said as they shook hands.

Isaac craned his neck to find Davis. "There's someone I need to locate. He was very kind to me on the voyage, and I want to offer him the hospitality of our house while he's here on the island."

Julian picked up the young man's bags, carried them to the cart, then looked over his shoulder to where Isaac was searching.

"There he is," Isaac said as he pointed to the last man to leave the ship.

Thomas Davis was dressed in gentlemen's clothing and had the airs of a wealthy man, but Julian knew his face immediately. Davis did not look desperate for money, which would be advantageous for John's plan. As Davis and Julian were introduced, they kept their alliance secret, greeting each other as strangers in front of the young man. They could talk later.

By the time they reached the Smith estate, poor Isaac was soaked with sweat from the heat; he had already loosened his shirt and shed his waistcoat. Wishing he were back on the ship in the cool ocean breezes, he asked as he dabbed his forehead with a kerchief, "Is there a place where I can lie down, somewhere a little cooler?"

"Of course, sir. Let me show you to your room," Julian said as he took the bags from the cart. Isaac followed him into the house.

Davis stayed behind in the wagon and called out, "Never you mind me. I'll be fine. I'm sure your overseer will take good care of me." He lit his pipe, leaned back, and was relieved at how easy it was to find his old cohort, John Julian.

7

Present Day
ANTIGUA

IT WAS MY last day on the island. I intended to make the best of it, despite the nerve-wracking break-in. All my things were laid out on the bed. I took into account my clothes for the day and what I would wear on the plane home the next morning, then jammed everything else into the travel bag. Several large knobbed conch shells that I'd found on the beach were strewn across the bed. I held one up to my ear; the ocean echoed back from deep inside the briny seashell. Molly and Danny would enjoy listening to the ocean sounds from these unique shells. I stuffed the large, chalky beach finds into a triple thick plastic grocery bag and tied them to my backpack.

Brian called out, "Before we see John, I want to show you the site of the new orphanage and stop at the Peace Corps office to see what we should do about last night."

"Great. Let's go."

The sun was already hot as Brian turned the jeep onto the road towards town. I couldn't stop wondering if Brian would be safe here anymore. And what about the earrings that might possibly match my necklace? I stared ahead, oblivious of where we were going.

We came across an open field of scrub and high weeds. The beginnings of a medium-sized house on the right slowly came into view. Two wheelbarrows, a small cement mixer, bags of powdered cement, and a pile of two-by-fours were stacked against its foundation.

Brian pulled to the side of the road. "What do you think?"

"You did this? All by yourself?"

"John and a friend of his helped me last week. We had to mix the cement by hand and push a wheelbarrow up a wooden ramp and dump it into the cement blocks. But it's almost done." He stood next to the underpinnings of the new home for Mariel and massaged the back of his leg.

"How's your leg feeling?"

"Better. You know, tearing my Achilles tendon from running on these bumpy roads, then landing in the hospital, was the only way I would have ever met Mariel."

I shook my head. "I wish I could have been here with you. I hated that you were hurt and I was so far away."

Brian walked the foundation with pride. "The first day I saw Mariel, in the children's ward, she was in her crib crying and banging her head on the mattress. The nurses were yelling and hitting her, thinking it would stop her from crying."

Brian's comment startled me. "You mean they were spanking her?"

He looked right at me. "No, they were hitting her on the head and face. None of them knew how to handle a special needs child." He carefully picked up a shovel from the dirt and placed it closer to the cement blocks.

I shielded my eyes from the strong morning sun. "God put you in the right place, at the right time and...you did the right thing." I knew it was good for Brian to talk about his feelings. Sometimes phone conversations are too quick, relating only a few bits of information.

He wiped his forehead with his bandana and then stretched his arms out to mark an area. "Now here's the veranda where the kids can sit outside in the shade." He fanned his hand in a semi-circle. "We can house eight children, with two live-in health aides." He moved to the back of the soon-to-be orphanage and pointed to where the bedrooms would be. Turning to me he continued, "The whole thing with Mariel bothered me so much that I couldn't sleep the first night after I saw her. That's when I decided to go back to the hospital the next day. I remember hobbling in on my crutches, past those nasty nurses, to find her crying again. I started to sit quietly next to her crib, so I wouldn't scare her. Then I started humming some of the lullabies from when I was little. By the following day, I was singing the songs. It got her to stop crying. Eventually she just watched me, listened, and swayed to the melody."

He sat down on the pile of cement bags. I sat next to him. "At the end of that week, little Mariel was reaching for my hand and then my face. Finally, she let me pick her up and we simply hugged."

His face grew serious. "No one in the hospital was pleased that I was making progress with her behavior. They got even angrier when I started asking questions about how they did things and about the care in general at the hospital. They didn't like it at all. And then I couldn't believe the people over me in the Corps told me that I shouldn't get involved, especially with the politics of the local government and their social service programs."

"They didn't appreciate what a good man you are."

We sat a few seconds in silence, both of us savoring the progress of the orphanage.

"Who designed all of this?" I asked.

"The plans were donated by a Peace Corps engineer working on St. Martin's. Next week some carpenters from Martinique are coming over and we'll start raising the roof and installing hurricane clips."

I patted him on the back. "It looks like it's all coming together for you." I picked up a little yellow wildflower from the field; it was just a simple weed. "When you told me that some disabled children on the islands are looked upon as a curse and are either abandoned or left to die when they're born, I was shocked."

"Mom, if these kids make it past the age of six or seven living in the hospital ward, they're then housed in a section of the local prison." Brian shook his head in disbelief and looked one more time over the foundation he'd built and then jumped into the jeep. "It's funny, now that the project is started, everyone wants to become involved and help out."

"I'm glad you stuck to your ideals and persevered, even in adversity." I glanced at my watch. "We should get going. John is going to close his shack soon and I don't want to miss him."

"Okay, but we better stop at the office first."

I sat in the jeep, waiting while Brian went in to find out if he should call the police. He re-appeared after only a few minutes.

"According to protocol, as nothing was taken or broken, they said I should just lay low for a while. They told me to keep the doors locked and watch my back. If any more suspicious things happen, they recommend that I find a new place."

"That's it?"

"Yes. The least involvement with the police the better."

"Maybe you should move."

"We'll see."

John was moving a large trash can towards the front of his stand. As he looked up, he saw the jeep and waved. Brian tooted the horn and pulled alongside the curb. We got out.

"Good Morning, mon," John said, then he greeted me with a tip of his baseball cap, "Good Morning, Brian's Mom."

I walked over to him. "I met your son last evening at the restaurant where he works."

"Yes, he told me."

"Did he mention that I had a necklace resembling a pair of earrings your wife keeps in a locked box?"

"Yes."

I took the necklace out of my purse and cradled it in my fingers to show him. "What do you think?"

John leaned over the counter and looked at the delicate piece hanging from the silver chain. "It is similar to the earrings, but I see them so few times a year, it's hard to tell."

"Didn't Brian ever tell you about what I'd discovered?"

Brian interrupted me, "I never mentioned anything. I need to keep a low profile as a volunteer." He stood with his feet apart and rubbed the side of his face. "I'm no braggart, Mom."

"I know...and you also never caught the connection between your friend John here and the treasure that I'd found."

The word 'treasure' spiked John Julian's attention, and he stopped filling the plastic containers of onion, lettuce, and relish on the counter. "Did you say treasure?"

"Yes, I did."

I rested my elbow on the wooden ledge and stared right at John. "If you have a few minutes, Brian and I would like to tell you some things that might be of interest to you."

The seventh generation grandson of the pirate John Julian stood listening to my words, taking in every nuance and inflection as I explained the story of the *Whydah* and Sam Bellamy. With each detail, his face contorted into quizzical expressions of surprise and then sometimes doubt. I was spinning a curious web of mystery, hoping to pull him deeper into my reality.

"Did you really find a pirate's treasure?' he asked.

I nodded yes.

"She's telling you the truth," Brian said, reinforcing my words.

John leaned back against the inside wall of the shack, took off his cap and rubbed his curly black hair. Turning, he asked, "So what you're telling me is that my great grandfather, seven times removed, was THE John Julian of the pirate ship the *Whydah*?"

"I believe so. And if you have anything of value that you've had in your family since the 1700s, those items might hold clues that could lead us to more treasure...for you."

"Mom, take it easy," Brian cautioned. "You really don't know what happened to John Julian, or if he ever got his hands on any treasure."

It bothered me that Brian questioned my supposition. I knew I was right. I stared at him and continued, "If the earrings that John's wife has in the locked box come anywhere close to resembling my necklace, then we can make an assumption that he did have some treasure."

"Wait a minute." John stood tall behind the counter and interrupted us. "You must slow down and let me get my head around this whole idea." He began to close the front of the shack. "I need to leave now."

I thought he was angry with me but then I remembered it was 11:30. "After you pick up your children, may we follow you to your house and see the earrings?"

"You both seem to be very serious about this whole mystery. I suppose it wouldn't do any harm for you to look at the earrings. But we must be quick. The kids will be getting out soon."

When we got into the Jeep to follow him, Brian looked over to me. "Mom, try not to get everyone all riled up about this. It might be nothing."

"Oh, for heaven's sake, I just want to look at the earrings."

Once at the school, we parked to the side of the road and waited. We watched John carry a little girl in his arms from the building's entrance to the back seat of his car. She was maybe five years old; her hand was curled close against her chest, her thin legs hung loose in front of John. Her good arm was wrapped around his neck, and as he turned to place her in the car seat, I saw a big smile on her face. A young boy was trailing behind him. He too, seemed happy, hindered only by a limp.

Brian whispered, "Rolanda has some sort of paralysis in her legs."

I smiled. "She's a cutie."

"Anthony has Down Syndrome. He's a nice little guy; one leg is shorter than the other."

When the kids were settled, Brian pulled the Jeep behind John's car, ready to follow him once more.

The Julian's white stucco house was only a short drive down a rutted road. It sat in an open field and behind it were other houses dotting the hillside in the distance. His wife, Angel, came out onto the veranda to greet the little ones. John held Rolanda in his arms as he carried her up the wooden stairs. "Here you go." He kissed the little girl on her head and handed her over to his wife.

Angel noticed us in the Jeep. "And who might be visiting us, John?"

We climbed out and walked over to the stairs.

John hurried down the stairway and helped little Anthony exit the car. As he closed the car door, he smiled at Angel, then gestured to us. "This is Brian, he's Peace Corps, and his Mom is visiting from the states."

"Nice to meet everyone," Angel said as she opened the screen door with Rolanda in her arms.

John followed close behind her with the boy in tow. He spoke to Angel, "Brian is the one that got me involved in the new orphanage being built in the heights area."

She smiled back at us.

He waved for both of us to come inside. "Angel usually substitutes at the high school, but not today, a lucky occurrence for your visit."

The house was typical for the island in its layout; we entered into the living room, which was connected to a dining area and a kitchen to its side. A railing alongside some steps led to the upstairs. I wondered about John's six kids and where they all slept.

Another quick glance around the room revealed a small mahogany curio cabinet standing against the wall next to a long couch. Within its glassed confines were small figurines, miniature framed photos and decorative shells. On the middle shelf, a wooden jewelry box was highlighted. It had an oval white piece inlaid on its top.

"Angel, remember Junior talked of a necklace that looked like the family's heirloom earrings?"

"Yes, I do," she said as she poured some juice for the kids.

"Maybe you could take a look at it?" John asked.

I came closer to the dining table and held the necklace in my hands for her to get a better look.

"Oh, it's beautiful. It does have the same colors and delicate findings," Angel agreed. "John, would you grab the kids' sandwiches out of the fridge while I get my key?"

"Certainly."

She disappeared into a room off the dining area and appeared within seconds with a small silver key attached to a black ribbon. Everyone watched as Angel opened the cabinet door. She carried the smooth wooden box to the clean end of the table. I could see that the white oval on top of the box was a piece of ivory. The ancient technique of scrimshaw was used to artfully scribe black tinted lines of a sailing ship floating across ocean waves. As Angel lifted the lid the smell of cedar drifted into the air. She reached for a white linen cloth from within and carefully unwrapped two earrings. I laid my necklace next to the delicate pieces.

8

Present Day
ANTIGUA

AS SOON AS I saw the two earrings, they spoke to me of mystery and the unknown. "May I hold them?"

Angel moved in front of the two pieces of jewelry that lay on the table as if they needed extra protection. "Of course," she said. She was so protective that I had to reach in front of her to pick them up. "They're so special to me and the whole family," she cautioned. "I feel obligated to make sure they're safe."

"I'll be very careful with them." My hands trembled as I picked them up. They felt light as a feather as I moved them back and forth from one hand to the other. They were so beautiful. My heart beat faster as I envisioned these delicate pieces in the hands of the pirate John Julian or an 18th century woman of means as she dressed for a special occasion.

When I placed them back next to the necklace, the design and color of both pieces of jewelry clearly indicated a matched set. I sat down to gather my thoughts. Brian and John moved closer to get a better look. No amount of doubt, if anyone had any, would sway me from my theory that the pirate John Julian indeed had access to Bellamy's treasure.

Angel glanced at her husband. "What do you think, John?"

The Antiguan said nothing. He stood quiet and focused his attention on his wife, as if he was unsure of us and what we were going to do with the information we were uncovering.

In soft-spoken words, Angel said, "John, I think that Brian's Mom should meet Old Sugar."

Old Sugar? My heart skipped a beat. Now we're getting somewhere.

"If you think that's a good idea." John waited for Angel to respond.

"It's fine with me."

We said our goodbyes and waited in the Jeep for John to lead us to his grandmother's house. "I still have enough time to finish packing for my flight tomorrow. I just can't leave until I get more answers."

Brian nodded in agreement.

We followed John around a large rotary and then turned down a densely packed street filled with houses, high fences, multiple cars, and trucks.

"I hope this little trip will be worth it," Brian said, as he kept close behind the Antiguan's car. "Once, when we were working at the orphanage, John said that his Old Sugar knew everything about their family history and could remember a lot of things…if she was having a good day."

I looked at Brian. "So you knew about Old Sugar?"

"Sure, but I've never actually met her."

We came upon a chain link fence surrounding a three-story cement-block house. It was built into a hill near the side of a gas station's retaining wall. I tilted my head over the side of the jeep's door to get a better look. "That must be Old Sugar's house. I hope today is a good day for her."

We watched John enter through the gate. He motioned to us where to park on the street of closely aligned houses. We squeezed in between two small trucks. I checked out the neighborhood. "Are we safe here?"

"I think so. I'll lock the glove compartment, but you'd better take your backpack in with you."

Once we gained entrance into the fenced yard, we only had to walk up a few steps to Old Sugar's doorway, which then took us down into a large basement room. The casement windows across the top of the walls were shaded and closed; the stale air added to the overall murkiness of the home.

John called out, "Grandma Sugar!" as he closed the door behind us. "Sorry about the condition of the place, but Grandma Sugar likes to keep the heat out the old fashioned way…by closing everything up."

A frail but clear voice came from another room. "Is that you, John?"

"Yeah, Grandma."

Grandma Sugar appeared with her walker under the archway of the kitchen. She was wearing a colorful housecoat and pink slippers, her grey hair perched atop her head in a bun. She stopped halfway into the living room to take a good look at her visitors. "Well, who are you?"

John smiled and introduced everyone.

She shuffled towards us, her head down, watching her every step. "I wish I knew you were bringing some company; I might have baked something." Old Sugar made her way to a well-worn rocker that was strategically placed in front of the television and beside a TV tray filled with tissues, a TV Guide, and several soap opera magazines. With a huff she took a seat. "Sit down, sit down. Tell me why you're here."

John took the earrings out of his pants pocket and unwrapped them in front of her. "Do you remember these?"

"Oooh, aren't they beautiful? I recall that I wore them on occasion. Doesn't Angel wear them now?"

"Yes she does, and they're the reason we've come today."

She took a tissue and wiped her nose. "Tell me more."

I opened my cosmetic bag that held the necklace.

"Brian's Mom has a necklace that seems to match these earrings."

Old Sugar leaned in to get a closer look at my jewelry and then she stared at the earrings. "Why yes, I think you may be right. Now what does it have to do with me?"

"Do you remember anything about where the earrings originally came from?" John replied. "What do you know of our earliest relatives?"

She mulled over her grandson's questions. "John, would you get me another glass of water?" she asked as she rubbed her chin. "And while you're up, go and get a box from under my bed. It's in a plastic bag. It might be dusty." She shook her head back and forth. "I just can't seem to get down there to clean."

We sat in silence. It was too quiet for me, so I started with small talk. "You have a very nice place here, Grandma Sugar. I understand that your daughter lives upstairs; how convenient for you."

"Oh yes." Her smile was broad and toothless. Contented, she rocked back and forth.

John returned with a dusty black plastic bag. He pulled a shoebox from within and dropped the dirty bag to the floor.

Old Sugar tapped her bony finger on the TV tray. "Here, clean this table off and put it right here." John did as he was told.

"Now open it, will you John?"

As he lifted the lid from the brown box, it made a swoosh as the bottom fell away to the tray.

We all craned our necks to get a better view of what was inside.

Old Sugar's arthritic fingers lifted out a book from within the cardboard box. It looked like a Bible. The bumpy black leather that encased its yellowed pages was devoid of any decoration. "This here's the family Bible," she announced.

I carefully placed the necklace back into my purse and sat next to Brian on a dark green polyester couch, directly opposite Sugar. John gathered the plastic bag into a ball and tossed into the kitchen's trash bin.

The old woman gestured to her grandson, "Come over here John." She carefully opened the Bible and pointed to its pages. "In here are your ancestors' names and dates." Grandma Sugar turned the stiff, brittle paper to get to the front. He knelt by her side. "When I was little, I remember my mother writing in the names of my brothers when they were born, and then my father's date when he died."

John looked at the written words that made a list on the beginning pages of the small book. He reached in front of Old Sugar's hand and pointed to the first name at the top of the page. "Old Sugar, is this our first relative?"

"That it is." She read slowly, "John Julian, Born 1692, Died 1740."

John read the next entry, "Elizabeth Thompkins Julian, Born 1701, Died 1735."

"May I see it?" I asked.

"Of course, help yourself," Old Sugar said with a smile.

As the old Bible passed from her hand to mine, its pages fanned open and a folded square of heavy vellum fell to the floor next to my foot.

"Oh, I'm sorry," I gasped. "I hope I didn't damage anything."

Brian carefully picked it up and handed it to me.

"May I open it?" I asked, holding the folded vellum over the open Bible.

Old Sugar waved her hand at me. "Go right ahead, I ain't never paid much attention to the scribbles on its inside. Never could understand them."

After closing the Bible, I attempted to separate the stiff sections of the folded square. After a few seconds, the vellum loosened and I was able to unfold it, exposing Old Sugar's 'scribbles', as she called them. "It looks like a drawing."

Everyone took a turn examining it.

I could clearly see what lay scribed before me. "It's a map of Cape Cod!"

Brian quickly added, "You're right, Mom; I can see the shape of the bent arm. See, there's Brewster, even though the words say Harwich. It's definitely the Cape." His finger moved close to the map's surface but drew back, cautious not to touch the vellum.

"Cape Cod?" John asked.

My eyes stared at the astonishing piece of evidence that had just been uncovered. My head was swimming with excitement. It was the clue that I needed. I kept my eyes focused on the remarkable drawing. "This clinches my theory that John Julian, your ancestor, has more than just a slight connection to Sam Bellamy and Cape Cod." I looked at John. "I think there's more treasure to be found. This map may just lead us to it."

John looked stunned. He sat down on a chair next to his grandma.

While I studied the map, I whispered as if I was having a conversation with myself. It was an old habit of mine. "Why else would there be a map in this Bible, if not to lead someone to something valuable?" I cocked my head to think deeper. "Bibles were safe places to put important things. This book is the Julian family's history." I glanced up at John. "Am I right?"

John and Old Sugar nodded.

By now it was 1:30 in the afternoon and I knew John had to get back to his sandwich shack. He'd already missed lunch and I assumed he didn't want to lose any more business.

I went right to the point. "I don't want to take up any more of your time. Would you allow us to take the map and make a copy of it? We'll return it to you as quickly as we can."

John rubbed his forehead to find an answer. He finally said, "I would agree to that."

"I promise I'll be very careful with it."

I placed the Bible on the TV tray next to Old Sugar and then asked one more favor. "John, do you think you could find a plastic bag to carry the map in for safekeeping?"

"Let me see." He looked pleased that I wanted to be careful with the old map.

Old Sugar spoke up, "Well, I'm not sure what's going on here, but I know my John will take care of everything. Won't you, John?"

From the kitchen, he returned with a small plastic bag, "Yes, Grandma, I'll return this evening and set everything back the way it was."

Standing up, I reached for the plastic bag. "Don't worry, Brian will drop the map off at your house as soon as possible." I slowly folded the vellum and placed it inside.

"I sure hope you're on to something." He looked at me with steady eyes. "Brian's Mom?"

"Yes?"

"If you find anything...don't forget us."

"I won't... I promise."

Brian couldn't drive fast enough for me as we headed to the Peace Corps office to find a copy machine. I knew flattening the relic was not the best idea as it was very brittle, but I needed a good copy and my phone wasn't the greatest for pictures. I stayed in the Jeep while Brian copied it for me.

Nick came from behind me as I sat outside. "Have a safe flight home, Mrs. C." He walked past me on his way into the office. I waved and wished Brian would hurry up. It was getting late and I was exhausted. My flight was at six in the morning and four AM would arrive before I knew it.

9

Present Day
ANTIGUA

THE COPY of the old map was slid into my journal. Although I was sad to leave Brian behind on the island, I was anxious to get home to Cape Cod. I felt sure I was embarking on a new adventure with this map, and the Cape was where I hoped to find the answers to the many questions filling my head. Besides, John is such a nice guy, if I actually found anything it would be nice to help him and his family.

My small writing book was zipped into the outside pouch of my backpack, which already puffed out like a fat man's belly from all my extra clothes. It looked even more cumbersome with the addition of the large grocery bag that held the six conch shells tied to the shoulder strap.

"Almost ready?" Brian asked, as he made sure everything was turned off in the little house.

"Yes, I think I am."

"We should get going; flights are erratic around here." He picked up my suitcase and headed down the steep stairway of the house.

"Okay, I don't want to miss my connection."

As the Jeep rumbled along the bumpy roads in the early dawn, I enjoyed the beauty of the island paradise one last time. If I looked beyond the poverty and discounted the fact that someone had broken into Brian's house, it really was a remarkable place.

"Your visit has been awesome," Brian said.

"It's been quite interesting." I could see the small airport's tower on the horizon.

Brian glanced over to me. "I was thinking this morning that it seems like fate connected you with a relative of John Julian."

"I guess there's more for me to find."

Clouds began to move in and the air grew cooler. "Will Nick be coming back to your place tonight? I feel uncomfortable with you alone in that house."

"You worry too much. Hey, I hope you don't mind, but Nick wanted a copy of the map for his pirate collection, so I made him one."

"You know, he seems a little too interested...all those questions."

Brian laughed my concern off. "He's okay."

"I guess so, just be careful." I checked one more time to make sure the copy of the map was safe in my journal.

Brian pulled up to the airport's sliding glass doors. "You know, finding that old map convinced me about your theory." He gave me a big smile then stopped the Jeep and got out to get my bags. He stared at me for a second then shook his head. "I still can't believe it."

"Me neither." I couldn't wait to get back to the Cape to investigate further.

He opened the door for me. "I've a meeting in around thirty minutes. Are you all right if I leave you here?"

"You know me better than that; I'll be fine. You should get going."

He gave me another hug. "I love you. I'll be home by Thanksgiving, if all goes well with the new orphanage."

I held him for a few seconds longer and then let go. "I'm so proud of you and what you've done. I love you."

He pointed at me from behind the wheel and said, "You be careful." Then smiled, "Watch out for pirates on the Cape."

I called after him as he drove away, "Be safe. God be with you and watch your back."

When the airport doors closed behind me I couldn't wait to call Paul. As soon as I checked in, the plane was ready to board for my first flight of the day to Puerto Rico. My cell phone showed only two bars for reception. I quickly tried to connect. "Paul?"

"Hi honey. It's good to hear your voice."

"I should be home soon, if there are no problems." I patted the backpack's pouch that protected my journal and the map. "You won't believe what I found."

"Nancy? You're breaking up. I can't hear you."

"Oh okay, I love you. See you tonight."

"Bye." Paul's voice trailed off into static as my cell phone decreased to no bars. Hopefully, in Miami, I'll have a better connection; if not, I'll try again in Boston.

Once I was settled into my seat on the first flight, I laughed, remembering how the plastic bag containing the conch shells proved to be no problem going through security. It was the walking down the narrow aisle of the plane that was difficult. Trying to hold the lumpy backpack ahead of me with one hand and the shells behind me with the other was daunting. The shells made clanking sounds as they hit against each other or bumped people in their seats. I'd smiled as sweetly as I could and repeated, "Sorry...oh, I'm sorry." In fact, as I weaved and bobbed down the aisle carrying my treasures, I thought I recognized one of the guys from back at the ocean bar, towards the rear of the plane. At least, he looked like he was one of them. As I passed him I accidentally gave him a good hit on the shoulder. He'd returned a half-hearted smile, so I wasn't worried that I'd really hurt him. I tried to be more careful on the next flight, knowing the kids would find the big conchs really cool.

It was almost six o'clock by the time I reached Boston. As the plane approached for landing, I could see the fall colors of the leaves. The air looked cool and crisp; a change from sandals to sneakers might be in order for the bus ride from Boston to Hyannis, where I expected Paul to be waiting for me. Once I land it should be less than three hours before I'm finally in my own bed ...and I won't need any netting.

* * *

1722
ANTIGUA

The sparse courtyard of Smith's stately house was void of life except for palm trees that lined the inside of the outer walls. A tall and well-built dark skinned man strode towards Davis.

"Mr. Davis, sir?" asked the young man.

"Yes."

A strong-looking hand picked up Davis's travel bag, "If you would please come with me, I'll direct you to your room."

"Why thank you, boy. I'm mighty obliged." Davis rose and followed.

The manservant led the Smiths' guest down a long painted hallway lined with rooms on each side. He opened the last door and placed the guest's leather bag onto the wooden-planked floor next to a small storage chest at the foot of a canopied bed. After opening the veranda's door, he politely said, "If you need anything, please do not hesitate to summon me. My name is Tobey."

"Of course." Davis quickly turned and called after the servant, "BOY! Tell the overseer that I want to speak with him as soon as possible."

"Yes, sir," Tobey obediently answered, swallowing his true feelings. He hated being called 'boy'. His name was Tobey. Someday he'd be able to correct rude people. He closed the door on Davis and rubbed his shirt, which hid a bumpy scar across his chest. It always ached when he found himself upset. A show of disrespect seemed to bother him the most.

Caroline passed him in the corridor. Tobey greeted the Smiths' new acquisition with a smile. Each year, the Smith family would buy three slaves from the neighboring Codrington Plantation on the Island of Barbuda. It was a stronghold of land and houses that had been bequeathed by Christopher Codrington upon his death to the Church of England in 1710. Now it was a place where slaves were held and 'seasoned'. The captured slaves became property of the Society of the Propagation of the Gospel in Foreign Parts (or the SPG) and branded with the word 'Society' across their chests. It was common knowledge that slaves in their first three years of captivity were fed well and given light labor. If they survived and did not commit suicide, they were destined for hard labor on other sugar plantations owned by the church.

Tobey touched the scar on his chest. He was restless. His life of servitude was becoming unbearable. He acknowledged that the Smiths had always been good to him but he wanted more; he wanted his freedom. As he searched for the overseer, John Julian, on the main floor, he held back the resentment for his state in life and followed through with his orders from Davis. When Tobey reached the second floor of the house, he saw John Julian close the door on young Isaac Smith, who was resting on the cool sheets of his bed.

"Excuse me, sir. Mr. Davis requests a meeting with you at your earliest convenience."

Julian whispered, "Thank you, Tobey. You may leave now."

"Yes, sir." Tobey lowered his head and turned to walk away. His face furrowed into a frown; he was worried about his future. He knew that Isaac Smith was here to sell the family plantation.

It was one of Tobey's duties to open and close doors and windows throughout the mansion to monitor its temperature. After dinner was over and the night air began to cool the many rooms of the big house on the hill, Tobey heard loud voices coming from Davis's room. He slipped into the vacant adjoining room and opened the veranda doors a crack to listen as two men argued. He heard Julian's voice yell, "I tell you Davis, it's there. You MUST do as I ask!"

Then Davis acquiesced. "I suppose I could help you, but how will I find it?"

"I've drawn a map."

Tobey stepped further out onto the veranda.

There was a slight hesitation in Davis's voice. "I don't know if I can do this for you. I have a wife now, and I'm well known in the community, I'm not sure…."

Scuffling broke the still of the night.

In a small window on the multi-paned door of Davis's room, Tobey could see Julian's reflection as he curled his hands around Davis's neck. There was a gasp then a gurgling noise.

"Remember, my friend," Julian said as he squeezed tighter, "I'm the only one who knows of your secret."

"You wouldn't, you swore to me," Davis pleaded.

Julian continued to threaten. "I won't hesitate to inform the authorities on Cape Cod about your part in the untimely death of Sam Bellamy…and whoever else happened to be in the house on the night of the fire."

Tobey pressed his back against the side curtain of the door. Curious for more information, he leaned forward again, beyond the dark room, for a better view and saw Julian push Davis up against the outside wall. With clenched teeth, Julian demanded, "Do you understand me?"

At that, Tobey retreated and quietly left. He wondered if he could benefit from this encounter between the two men. Closing the door behind him, he stood in the hallway. What was Davis's quest? After a quick knock on Davis's door, he entered and found the two men still struggling. They separated immediately and straightened their waistcoats. "Excuse me, sir," Tobey said, holding onto the latch of the door. "I need to ready your room for the night."

Julian glared at the servant. Davis looked relieved.

"If you don't mind, sir?" Tobey moved closer to them and began to turn down the bedcovers.

Julian headed for the door. As he passed the young black man, he ordered, "Tobey! Come to my house after you're finished here."

"Yes, sir."

Later, as Tobey followed the road down to Julian's house, he questioned the coming meeting between him and the overseer. He was prepared to defend himself if there was any confrontation other than the usual reprimand for the unexpected entrance to Davis's room. He hoped there would be none.

Meanwhile, Julian encouraged his wife, Elizabeth, to retire early. He explained to her that he had business to take care of and needed his privacy. Julian took a position outside on a bench and leaned back against the side of his house. The moonrise lit the dark night. He could see Tobey's approach.

"Mr. Julian, Sir?"

"Sit down, Tobey." He took out his pipe and waited for the slave to sit next to him. "How long have you been under the Smith family?"

"Eight years...since I was ten."

"You have learned your studies well and seem to have grown into a smart young man."

"Thank you, sir."

"I have a proposition for you." Julian glanced up at the moon and let out a long stream of smoke from between his lips. "Are you interested in improving your state of life?"

"What do you mean, sir?"

"I mean freedom. A new start."

Tobey remained quiet, holding onto the word freedom in his head.

"Well?" Julian persisted.

"I don't understand what you're asking of me."

Julian gave Tobey a knowing glance. "You were in the next room listening to my conversation...or you might say, persuasion, with Mr. Davis. Am I not right?"

"I meant no disrespect, sir." Tobey's posture was stiff next to Julian. He wanted to show he wasn't afraid of the man who controlled him.

"You show gumption. That I like."

Several seconds of silence passed before Julian spoke again.

"Mr. Davis and I knew each other a long time ago. Let's say we were partners."

Tobey stared straight ahead into the dusky night; his hands resting on top of his knees.

"I want you to sail to the Cape with Mr. Davis. You'll be under his care and will assist him in finding items that belong to me, whereupon you'll return with the found goods back to Antigua." Julian hesitated and then added, "I'm only interested in the safety of my property."

"How will this happen?"

"You'll carry papers that will identify you as a servant of the Smith Plantation, and it will explain that you're retrieving their possessions. When said items are delivered into my hands, I'll have the power to release you from bondage and reward you with enough coin to start anew."

Tobey stood now and faced Julian. "How do I know that you'll keep your promise?"

Julian reached into his vest pocket and handed him two gold coins. "If you are capable and complete your task, you'll have more of these. Trust me. You have my word."

Tobey held the coins in his hand. He mulled Julian's request over in his thoughts only for a short time and responded, "Yes, I'll do it." He was frightened but desperate for his freedom. "Did I understand you to say you care only for your property, and not for Davis?"

"That's what I said." Julian turned away from Tobey, entered his house and closed the door.

10

Present Day
CAPE COD

WHILE THE BUS sped along the highway from Logan Airport to Cape Cod, something kept bothering me. I unfolded the copy of the old map for the umpteenth time to study the crude lines of the drawing again. One landmark on the drawing looked odd to me. Even though it was within the mass of the Cape's land and I recognized the names around it: Harwich, Eastham, and Truro, I couldn't recall the identity of the lumpy round mark near the coast of Eastham. I knew the towns of Brewster and Orleans had not been incorporated until after the 1700s so almost the whole lower Cape was known as Eastham. This mark on the map had to be somewhere in present day Orleans.

It was almost dark when the bus pulled into the Hyannis depot. My heart skipped a beat when I saw Paul waiting by our white van. Even after 24 years of marriage, we were still passionate about each other. Of course, it didn't hurt that he was tall, lean, and muscular, sported a full salt and pepper beard and was born with beautiful blue eyes. I laughed to myself, he must have bought some new sneakers; they were stark white against his khaki pants and looked huge next to the black pavement. Everything about him was balanced, strong, and sturdy. Even his physical numbers were good, from his height of six feet to his shoe size of 12, all equal. Not like me, at five foot seven I wore a nine-and-a-half shoe…just a little bit odd. I was the one who encouraged the spur-of-the-moment decisions in our relationship and sometimes needed to be brought back into reality. But we're a good team.

I prayed a quiet thank you to Casey for watching the little ones at home. As I stepped off the bus, Paul quickly walked toward me with open arms.

I leaned in and smiled. "Hi, honey,"

"Welcome home." He kissed me on the cheek. "Everybody missed you."

His soft white whiskers mingled with my hair, instantly comforting me after my long journey. We held hands while the driver opened the bottom hatch of the bus so Paul could retrieve my bags. After loading everything into the back of our van, Paul pointed to the bumpy plastic grocery bag. "What do you have here?"

"Surprises for the kids."

He grinned.

I quickly got into the car, eager to get home. "I have so much to tell you," I said as I stroked his knee. "I missed you."

He leaned over to kiss me. "It's good to have you home."

The drive home flew by as fast as the lights from the oncoming cars as they passed us. We talked of Brian, the orphanage project and of course, the mystery map.

Paul looked over to me. "When you called from Miami and told me about finding a relative of John Julian I was hoping it wouldn't be anything that might prove dangerous." He shook his head back and forth. "Remember the night those guys broke in to our house? I can't believe this is happening to you again, I mean to us, to the family. Please be careful. We can't be getting involved in any more treasure hunting."

I pulled my hand from his leg and turned away to look out the window at the dark woods off the highway. "You know me...I'm always so curious." It was all I could come up with to counter his words. I decided to keep my thoughts of hunting for more treasure to myself. Maybe Paul doesn't need to know that someone broke into Brian's house. No harm was done.

*   *   *

1722
ANTIGUA

The lone figure crouched in the dark, pressing his shoulder against the massive twenty-four-foot facade of the rock. At its base, he patted the last of the loose soil flat then scattered stones across its surface. When he was satisfied his secret was concealed, he stood and wiped his mouth with the back of his hand, tasting the crunch of dirt. He looked around.

Grabbing the shovel, he smashed the rustic stretcher that had carried the now buried chest and threw the spade into the thickets surrounding the large stone. Securing the small bulging pouch under his belt, he tied its leather bindings secure. As he ran swiftly through the early dawn along a path that followed the sound of the crashing ocean, branches hit his face and stones twisted his feet. He pushed himself forward; all the while sensing someone was following him, searching for a safe hiding place where he could wait during the coming daylight hours.

John Julian bolted upright in his bed. Covered in sweat, he rubbed his eyes with trembling hands then breathed a sigh of relief that it was only another nightmare. He was tired of them.

Elizabeth stirred in her sleep next to him, but remained quiet. As he left the bed, his shirt clung to his clammy body. Wiping away the salty drops of liquid from his skin with the tail of his nightshirt, he shuffled to the sideboard for a drink of ale.

After the pungent alcohol soothed his nerves, he walked outside to sit on the bench. As he closed his eyes, his mind drifted back to Cape Cod. He remembered the grey color of the weathered shingles on the old house where he'd taken refuge that morning after burying his fortune by the rock. He had known the house was empty because there was no smoke coming from the chimney. Julian recalled thinking that he would be safe there until night came, but within minutes of his arrival, he'd seen the King's men at the neighboring property, searching for survivors from the wreck of the *Whydah*.

Another swig of ale passed over his tongue as Julian shook his head. Why couldn't he have gotten away with all of his treasure? He'd only had enough time to bury the extra pouch, filled with a small amount of gold coins, a short distance from the barn where he was hiding. He'd decided that if he were captured and, by chance, found innocent, he'd surely be able to retrieve the pouch later. It would be needed for his passage back to Antigua. The chest would have to remain hidden for a few years, until things calmed down on the Cape, and he could return for the real riches, unnoticed.

Elizabeth appeared in the doorway. "John, you ill?"

"No," he yelled. He was angry. Not with his wife, but at his past.

She knew her husband well enough to leave him alone to his thoughts.

Julian leaned back, his bare toes kicking at the dirt. He clenched his teeth and walked over to the side of his house to piss. The smell of urine and dirt evoked another memory; the dank and squalid floor of his prison cell where he'd awaited trial in Boston for piracy five years ago. It was also the day he thought he would be hung alongside Thomas Davis. Both men had sat on the putrid dirt floor that morning, with Davis penitently whimpering his sins aloud. 'I had wanted all of Bellamy's treasure,' he'd tearfully confessed to Julian. 'I followed Maria Hallett and Sam Bellamy to a house in North Harwich. I knew the wagon held Sam's treasure chests and had hoped for an opportunity to take it.' With wide eyes he'd continued, 'I grew tired of waiting, so I set the house on fire to ensure that no one would prevent me from gaining more gold.'

Before they were brought to trial that day, Davis had revealed to Julian that within minutes of the deadly flames consuming everything, a wagon had crashed out of the barn, driven by a dark figure. He'd also seen someone running towards the wagon as it drove away, taking the treasure with them. Davis had waited until morning, hoping to search for anything he could salvage.

Julian grinned as he flicked the last of his piss onto the sandy dirt, pleased that Davis had no chance to steal Bellamy's cache because he was captured in North Harwich the next morning.

11

Present Day
CAPE COD

THE SCENT of Murphy's Oil Soap tickled my nose as it drifted upstairs to my bedroom. My eyes opened in the morning light. The house was quiet. From the open skylight above my head, I heard gentle breezes rustling in the trees and traffic idling behind school busses along Route 6A. I rubbed my eyes clear, then stretched. Counting my blessings I whispered, "Good Morning, Lord. Thank you for Paul, Jim, Brian, Casey, Molly, and Danny. And thanks for getting me home safely to my own bed."

With feet planted on the carpeted floor, I stood to reach for my robe. Within a few minutes, I was padding down the steps and into the kitchen. Outside the window, leaves were falling across the driveway as autumn began to make its appearance on the Cape. The smell of coffee was satisfying; it was good to be home.

Paul appeared in the doorway of the kitchen. "Did you sleep well?"

"Wonderful. I forgot how great our bed is." Pouring some coffee I sat at the table.

He gave a gentle rub to my shoulders and sat opposite me.

I held his hand. "Did the kids get off to school ok? I missed saying goodbye to them."

"No problem. Martha was here bright and early."

I noticed Martha moving stealthily from room to room downstairs, trying to be quiet as she cleaned. "Have you given any more thought to my news about John Julian?"

"Yeah, you might be on to something there."

I perked up, pleased that Paul was agreeing with me. "I know I am. Of course, I still can't believe Brian never connected his buddy John to the Bellamy legend and the pirates who survived the wreck of the *Whydah*."

Paul stroked my hand. "So, what's on your agenda for the day, my lovely wife?"

"Not much, maybe a walk on the beach."

My caffeine jolt was already kicking in. I stood up with wide eyes. "Oh my God, Paul, I was so tired last night that I never showed you the map." I started for the door. "Hold on, let me go get it."

Paul grinned as he finished his morning coffee. "I have to get back to work. Show me later?"

My heart fell. Here we go again, I thought, no time for me. "Okay." I really wanted to share the map, but I knew he had some commissioned work that needed to be finished.

As he left for his studio he said, "I love you. I'm glad you're home."

I echoed back, "I love you, too."

I reminded myself that Paul's lack of interest in the map shouldn't bother me. He's the one earning the living for the family. I examined the calendar of appointments and events on the fridge and the reality of being home and being responsible grounded me. Rinsing my cup I went to find Martha.

As I walked through the front parlor's doorway, I found her leaning over, dusting the light green bookshelves. With red ringlets of dyed hair that fell alongside her face and partially concealing her wrinkles, she was not your typical housekeeper.

"Hi, Martha."

"Oh, hello." She straightened up, adjusted her top and wiped her brow with the palm of her hand. "Did you have a nice trip?"

"Yes, I did. Thank you."

The Murphy's smell emanated from her every move. The use of the old soap was one of Paul's weaknesses and requests. His mother had used it every day, so to him the smell meant a spotless home. I always thought I could fool him just by setting out a bowl of water with the oil soap in it, hoping he'd think I'd been scrubbing all day instead of shopping.

"Everything smells so clean. I'll be upstairs getting dressed."

"Okay," Martha said and turned her back to continue dusting the bookcases.

12

September 1722
YARMOUTH - CAPE COD

FELICITY DAVIS, six months with child, waited for her mother, Bethia Gibbs, to join her for tea. Outside, the clouds had thickened and grew dark. The few trees surrounding the Davis home bent over backward in the nor'easter that raged its fury across the Cape. Rain pelted its heavy drops against the paned window of the parlor where the ladies took their daily indulgence. Felicity looked uncomfortable in her skin and hated living in the Yarmouth house.

The new servant, Hephzibah, knocked before she entered the parlor; her tiny voice greeting her employer with, "Pardon me, your tea is ready." She carried a large shiny silver tray that held a blue flowered teapot, two matching cups with saucers, and a few tasty strawberry sweet cakes.

The sight of the blue tea set angered Felicity. This new face in her household was disturbing her afternoon with carelessness. She pursed her lips. "I don't want to use that blue flowered pot. Do you understand me?"

"Yes, ma'am."

"Take it away," she yelled at the young girl.

"Begging your pardon, ma'am. It won't happen again."

As Hephzibah retreated with the tray, Mother Gibbs flew in behind the hired girl before the door closed. Dressed in widow black, Mother Gibbs was also irritated on this bleak afternoon. Her satin skirts swished as she bustled over to a small settee and sat opposite her daughter who was resting in a straight-back chair. "I do not know why we need to live in such a primitive place."

Adjusting the cameo brooch that was pinned to her stiff neckline collar, Mother Gibbs looked over to her visibly upset daughter. Shaking her finger at her, she scolded, "I told you that this was a mistake… coming to this godforsaken place."

"I do regret agreeing to live in Yarmouth," Felicity sighed. "Boston was so much more civilized."

Their conversation stopped as Hephzibah returned with a rose patterned teapot.

"Will there be anything else, ma'am?"

Felicity glanced at the tray to make sure everything was acceptable and then dismissed the girl with a quick wave of her fingers. The unhappy wife of Thomas Davis leaned over the small table and rested her chin atop the palm of her hand. She grumbled, "Oh Mother, why did I not listen to you?"

Mother Gibbs poured the hot liquid into the delicate teacups, one for herself and one for her pouting daughter. She voiced another concern, "And now that you are with child, what are you going to do?"

A sweet cake seemed to calm Felicity. "I think I do love Thomas. I know he tries his best to provide, but I despise where he chooses to make his home…this no-man's land."

Mother Gibbs kept her eyes lowered and coyly asked, "Has he ever confided to you about where his fortune came from?"

Felicity reached for another cake with a confident air in her voice. "No, and I really don't care. I have the papers that say I will receive everything upon his death."

"Yes, of course you will." With another sip of tea, Bethia Gibbs added, "It was fortunate that your father was able to see you married before he passed and…" she glanced up, "…to have your husband's assets legally bound over to you."

Davis's pregnant wife gazed out to the storm ravaged landscape. "Thomas should soon be home from the West Indies."

Her mother reached for her piece of sweet bread and spoke the last word of the afternoon. "I wonder what Thomas will say after he discovers that he will soon be a father?"

*   *   *

Thomas Davis exited the ship in Barnstable Harbor with Tobey following him down the rain-sodden plank. Davis felt a few days of delay from the nor'easter that pummeled the whole New England coast would be an opportunity for him to find a suitable gift for his new wife. He turned and stopped, then ordered Tobey. "Hear me out, boy."

With rain dripping from the brim of his hat, the obedient slave stood his ground on the dock and listened.

Davis handed Tobey several coins. "Take this and find your own way 'til the ship sails again." He preferred to be separate from his 'appointed guard' and couldn't care less if he ever saw him again.

"Yes, sir."

Davis left Tobey in the rain and walked to the nearest inn looking for his own shelter. Tobey, alone and frightened, stayed where he was. It was his first time away from Antigua. He knew not where to go or what to do in this strange port, but he wanted his freedom, so he would make do.

The following morning, with rain still lingering, Davis went in search for a token of affection for Felicity. A woman walking towards him caught his eye as being familiar. When she approached and came closer, he definitely recognized her but could not place her.

No nod or greeting was passed between them and as he rounded a corner, he turned to look at her again as she crossed the street. She was so beautiful. Her brown hair hung in ringlets from under her cap, framing her delicate features. Very pleasing indeed, but who was she? He began to follow her at a safe distance. She led him to a side street where she entered a small printing shop.

Curious, he also entered the shop. The little black bell jingled as the door closed behind him. After Davis shook the rain from his coat, he found himself alone. Large iron printing presses occupied all the space behind a wooden counter close to the front of the room. To one side, a small hearth gave heat to the cramped quarters.

After several minutes, the woman that he'd followed came from behind a door. "May I be of assistance?"

"Yes. I'm looking for stationary, a gift for my wife. I need it before I sail home in two days."

"Let me check my husband's schedule book."

He waited for an answer, all the while studying her face. With lustful eyes, he continued to stare at her rounded bosom. "Forgive me, but you are so familiar to me." He raised his stare on her.

She looked up from her ledger at his face. "I'm sorry, I don't recognize you. If you'll excuse me?" Then she disappeared behind the door.

Davis scanned the counter and could not help but notice a blue flowered teacup. It resembled a similar pattern that was on the porcelain tea set that he'd given to his wife upon their marriage. He remembered the circumstances surrounding how he came in possession of the delicate china and began to make sense of whom this woman might be.

Maria Ellis held her forehead and sat down on the small bench next to her husband's worktable.

"Is everything all right, Maria?" her husband asked.

She was silent.

He came closer. "Are you feeling ill?"

"Matthew, I feel faint. Would you please help our customer? He's in need of stationary."

"Certainly, my dear." He kissed her on the top of her cap and did as he was asked.

Maria recognized the pirate Thomas Davis; his face was etched into her memory. Maria Hallett, as she was known then, had been the lover of Davis's pirate captain, Sam Bellamy. Her hands shook as she recalled how Sam had perished in the North Harwich fire, along with her dear friend, Abigail. The two other pirate survivors from the shipwreck, Davis and Julian, had disappeared from her world. She always prayed that they were dead.

Marriage to Matthew Ellis had made it easier for Maria to keep her past a secret. Building a life with her beloved husband was progressing well and now two children blessed their life together. If anyone knew of the things that she had done, they might take everything away from her, even her children. Young Matthew, only three years old, and two-year-old Abigail, were the beacons that lit her path to happiness. Determined to protect herself and her family, she would need to destroy any evidence that could lead to her true identity. Maria wrung her hands over and over in her lap trying to figure what to do.

"Are you better?" Matthew asked as he returned through the door to the rear of the shop.

"Better."

"That's good to hear. The gentleman inquired about you and thought he knew you."

"He did? What did you tell him?" Her voice quivered.

"Not much, my dear." He took her in his arms and held her until she stopped shaking. "The secrets of your past stop with me, my love."

The next morning, while the children played under the watchful eye of Anna, their nanny, Maria busied herself in the back parlor. Their living quarters were behind the shop and consisted of five rooms total: three below and two on top. She closed the door to separate herself from the kitchen and hurried to begin her plan. As young Matthew played with his wooden wagon in the kitchen, a loud crash came from behind the closed door and broke the tranquil setting. Little Abigail began to cry. Anna picked her up for comfort and then went to find the source of the noise. She discovered Maria standing over the broken pieces of her blue flowered china. A tray lay upside down over the shards.

Maria feigned surprise. "I don't know what happened."

"Oh my," said Anna. "Let me help you."

"No, you tend to the children. It was my mistake. I'll clean it up."

"Yes, ma'am."

Alone with the last of Sam's gift of china, Maria knelt down onto the wood planked floor and with great care she picked up the once cherished white and blue pieces. She reached for a large piece of material from her weaving chest. After she placed all the shards on top of the cloth, she folded the fabric over the pieces and tied its four ends together. Within seconds, she remembered the teacup from the front shop. She must retrieve it. In a few days, Davis would return for his order and must not see the china. Hurrying through the house to the shop, she grabbed the cup and, in an instant, thought of Sam and smiled. He had loved her in his own way, and she had loved him...at one time. Tracing the thin edge of the porcelain with her fingertip, she wondered if surely one tiny cup and saucer would not matter, if kept out of sight. Maria decided to keep the last two pieces. She looked around her bedroom for fear there was anything else that might incriminate her. The ring that Sam had given her on the night of their betrothal was safely stored in a tin box beneath her clothes. She and Matthew may need some extra money in the future.

Before the approach of dusk, Maria told Anna that she would be gone for a short time on an errand. Matthew was busy on Davis's order so dinner would be later than usual. She lifted the heavy cloth filled with the broken china into the children's wagon and pulled it to the harbor. As she walked the back streets, she comforted herself with the thought that what she was doing was necessary for her future. The remains of the china were the last of anything that pointed to her past. The gold coins were all gone. She fondly recalled the old leather chest that had safeguarded her riches for so many years throughout her exile on the outskirts of Eastham, where she had been banished for her supposed sins against the church. It too, was gone. The chest had been destroyed by accident when, filled with her treasure, it fell off their wagon the day Matthew and Maria arrived in Barnstable as husband and wife. As a wedding gift, Matthew had built Maria a new chest to hold her treasures.

By the time she approached the landing of the dock most people were home for their last meal of the day, affording her privacy to complete her plan. The wheels of the wagon rumbled against the black-tarred boards of the pier. When she could go no further, she untied the woven cloth and, with all her might, lifted it up and threw the shards from the material out into the bay as far as she could. The pieces sunk fast into the dark, blue green vastness.

Maria stood for a short while until the water settled smooth again, then she picked up the handle of the wagon and retraced her steps home. She hoped that young Matthew and Abigail were enjoying their evening meal; she could hardly wait to hug them, confident now of her family's safety.

13

Present Day
BREWSTER - CAPE COD

DANNY CAME HOME from pre-school around noon. He slammed the screen door, ran over to me and planted a big wet kiss on my lips. What a treat, I thought. He was my miracle baby. I'd had him when I was 40 years old, and he was the last of my five children.

"How was your day?"

"Great, Mommy."

He dropped his backpack on the foyer floor and took off for the kitchen. "I'm hungry."

When he ate the last bite of his PB&J sandwich, Sesame Street was just about over. I asked, "Want to take a walk on the beach?"

"Sure."

"Grab your pail and let's go."

* * *

The cool, shallow water lapped against my feet as we walked the expansive tidal flats on the bayside of Cape Cod. Danny was carrying his yellow pail and shovel, little toes patting the soft rippled sand just ahead of me. It was late September and one of the final days of summer.

The air was warm on my face but I could feel an underlying flow of cooler air, a clear signal of autumn's approach. To my left, a stone circle that I'd built a week ago had fallen apart from the tidal flow. I promptly found several rocks to fill in the empty spaces so the circle would be whole again. As I placed the last stone, I spotted a piece of pottery sticking up above the wet sand, among some broken pieces of quahog shells. I quickly picked it up and rinsed the creamy white piece in a tidal pool. It was curved on one edge and looked like part of a large dinner plate. A pattern of delicate blue flowers trailed across the surface of the old porcelain. Happy with my treasure for the day, I stuffed the chalky relic into my pocket.

Grey clouds had begun to crowd the western sky. I watched with awe as the dark mass gained strength above our heads. "We better get going." Grabbing Danny's hand, I ran to the safety of our car. As I buckled him into his car seat, I joked in my best pirate voice, "Sure looks like something's brewing up there." He giggled so I gave him a little tickle. "Now let's go see what your Daddy's doing." I touched my delicate 18th-century locket for good luck and hoped the weather would improve.

We arrived home just before the rains came pelting down. I emptied my pockets and put the newly found shard on my dresser before taking a shower.

After dressing, I put away all the travel lotions and creams. When the last of the little bottles was stored in the top drawer, for future travels, the pottery shard from the beach caught my eye. Sadly, the blue flowers had already faded across its now-gritty surface. The lack of seawater always triggered this natural process of drying after being left out of the salty water. Its simple beauty and where it came from began to speak to me. I wondered if I could locate the name of the pattern on this piece. Maybe an antique shop that specializes in ceramics and pottery could identify it for me.

I took out the map from my journal for another look and then refolded it. Both the pottery shard and map would be better off in the small safe stored in the back of our closet. A little key dangled from a chain on its brown handle. We never hid the key. The safe mainly served as protection against fire damage. I placed both items inside the safe, next to the cotton pouch that contained a dozen silver pieces of eight. I kept these small treasures at home for my own enjoyment, whereas the others were stored at the bank.

The thick steel box was closed with a quick turn of the little key. Suddenly a wave of sleepiness caught me by surprise, and I realized I was still suffering from jet lag. I knew I'd better get some more rest before making inquiries about the shard; my search would have to wait. Paul has got to see both of these, I decided. I'd show him after supper, when things are quiet.

As I turned the corner to go down the steps, I got a text from Brian.

Had small event for orphanage. John's house broken into. Earrings gone. Call you later with more info. Love you
Brian

14

September 1722
YARMOUTH - CAPE COD

FOR TWO DAYS, Tobey waited at the dock for the appearance of Davis. Nervous and unsure of what lay before him, he kept himself hidden from unfamiliar faces. On the third day, Davis finally arrived and said nothing to Tobey; only a glance was given toward the slave as he boarded the packet *Marie*. Tobey understood Davis's signal and followed behind him. Their destination was Yarmouth; silence between them remained through the rest of the voyage.

When news of the *Marie's* arrival spread through the small seaside village, Davis's manservant, Jacob, was summoned to pick up his master at the landing. Old Jacob, an Indian from Nantucket, tied his muffler tighter around his open neck as he set out for the sea's edge. He had several blankets in the wagon, knowing that his weary passenger would surely be cold and damp in the chilly fall air.

Jacob was surprised to see a black man accompanying his master but held his questions.

Tobey remained staid in his demeanor and undaunted in fulfilling John Julian's orders as their wagon rumbled along the cartway through the sparse forests of Cape Cod. In contrast, Thomas Davis whistled and looked forward to bedding his wife.

*   *   *

Smoke drifted from the main chimney atop Davis's house in Yarmouth, which fed several hearths on the two floors where they lived.

Hephzibah hurried up the winding back stairs from the kitchen to the third floor attic to change her apron. These sparse quarters were reserved for the live-in servants. The air was chilly to the young girl as she grabbed a clean covering; the room's warmth came only from the heat of the bricks that formed the chimney. She was going to meet Master Davis for the first time and couldn't bear for him to see her unkempt.

Felicity remained in the parlor, with her tea, and waited for her husband. It had been six months since he took his leave and she had news for him.

"It's good to be home," Davis said as he jumped down from the wagon's bench.

Hephzibah opened the front door and welcomed him with a curtsy. "Mr. Davis."

"Well, whom do we have here?" he asked surveying the young woman.

"Hephzibah, sir."

"I see," he said, noticing the shape of her body and comely features.

"Madam awaits you in the parlor," Hephzibah said keeping her eyes downcast.

Davis turned to Tobey. "Go with Jacob, he'll see to you."

Once inside, Davis passed his hat and coat to the servant girl and ordered, "Bring my ale to the parlor."

"Yes, sir."

He watched her walk into the kitchen until she disappeared behind the door. Aroused by this young beauty, he adjusted himself before entering the parlor. "Felicity, my dear. How are you?"

"As well as expected." Her voice was sharp and curt.

"Do I detect a slight bother in your voice?"

"I'm sorry, Thomas, but since you left me here in this place, some events have occurred that I'm quite anxious about." Felicity folded her hands across her stomach, over her unborn child, and looked straight at her husband. "Do you remember the day before you left for Antigua, when you forced your way into my bed?"

"Why, yes, it was quite enjoyable," he said, smirking with relish for the coming night.

"Maybe it was for you, but your carnal desires impregnated me. I am now with child and in my sixth month."

Davis knelt at her feet. "My good wife, your news brings great joy to me."

She looked away to the window.

He took her hands into his. "No matter what you may tell me, either by words or actions, I know that you're pleased, if not with me, then with the thought of a new life for you to love."

He was right about the child. Her features softened and she smiled.

Hephzibah entered the room carrying tea and a mug of ale. Davis rose from his knees and stood behind his wife.

After inspecting the tray, Felicity dismissed the servant with, "Leave us."

When they were alone, Davis took note of the rose patterned teacup and asked, "My sweet, do you not favor the tea set that I gave to you on our wedding day?"

"Oh, forgive me," she explained, "It's the new servant, I told her to always use that lovely blue tea set that you gave me. She never listens to me."

"I'll handle it," he said.

"No, I shall see to the matter myself." Felicity was determined to prove herself worthy of her husband's respect in managing the household. When the time comes for her to leave this awful place and return to Boston, he will surely accept her decision to leave as a wise one and in her best interest.

*   *   *

As Jacob steered the wagon to the rear of the house and into the barn, no words passed between Tobey and the old servant. When the wagon stopped, Jacob climbed down from his seat and led the horse into a stall. "Come wit' me," he said to Tobey. He pointed to a small room to the side of the barn where a single roped bed was positioned under a window. "That's where you'll be sleepin'." It had a blanket and a small pillow on its top.

"Yes, sir," Tobey said.

"How long you staying, boy?"

"My name is Tobey, sir, and I'll stay...'til I do my job."

Jacob understood the reference to the word, 'boy' and responded with a fatherly mockery. "Oh, pardon me...Mister Tobey." He spat some tobacco juice from his lips and waited for the young black man to react to his sarcasm. When nothing came, he shrugged and continued his chores of feeding and grooming the horse with no further conversation.

Tobey rose and began to help Jacob. He ignored the old man's remark, thinking Jacob may be his only friend in this new place.

"Been here long?" Tobey asked as he looked for more to do.

"Almost a year now. Got one more to go."

"You can't leave?"

"I be indebted to Mr. Davis."

Tobey found a pitchfork and threw hay to the horse.

Jacob was grateful for Tobey's help and began to feel at ease with the young man. He leaned against a barrel to light his pipe and then shook his head back and forth. "One day I woke up and was told I had to go with Davis."

Tobey looked over to the old man. "What'd you say?"

Jacob exhaled a long stream of smoke. "When I lost my wife and family to that sickness from the white people, I started my drink and couldn't stop, even after the money ran out." He squinted his eyes and curled his mouth up to the side. "My people are the Wampanoag, peaceful, strong and welcoming. Too welcoming, perhaps. We didn't deserve what happened to us. There ain't many of us left."

Tobey understood. He, too, had felt the meanness of those in authority. The strong heft of his next throw of hay almost hit the horse.

"Hold your temper, son." Jacob cautioned his charge and continued. "I owed to Mr. Cathcart, the tavern keeper, and was working off my debt. One night, he lost me in cards to Davis. It was a stupid game, and I was forced to leave my home. Now here I be." More puffs of smoke drifted into the air. "What's your story?"

Tobey wasn't keen on telling too much about himself. He was on a mission for his freedom and the sooner he returned to his island, the better. "I come from Antigua. Belong to the Smith Family and their sugar plantation."

"What you doin' here?"

"Business with Mr. Davis. As soon as I find what belongs to the Smiths, I go home. I can't say more."

Jacob tapped the ashes from his pipe outside on the barn doors. "I'll not be meddlin' then." He motioned to Tobey. "Come, I guess you be hungry."

The savory smells of clam chowder and fresh baked bread drifted towards the two men as they entered the kitchen from the rear of the house.

"Ma'am," Jacob greeted Hephzibah as she stood near the hearth.

Turning around, she answered, "Hello."

Jacob gestured to the tall black man. "This here's Tobey, from Antigua. He might be stayin' with us for a bit."

"Good to know," she said.

Hephzibah was used to men. The youngest in a family of four brothers, she knew how to handle herself in most any situation. She was not fearful of the stranger "Can I interest you in a pint?"

"Yes, ma'am," Tobey politely answered and stayed seated at the table. As he watched this attractive woman move back and forth, almost dancelike, attending to the final preparations of the evening meal, he wondered what it would be like to bed her, a white woman. Finding himself staring at her, he shook his head and rubbed his weary eyes, trying to rid any notions of this woman from his mind. It had been a long journey. He felt weak and exhausted. Best keep to himself.

15

September - 1722
YARMOUTH - CAPE COD

THE COLD NIGHT AIR crept in and around the Davis house. Felicity retired early, while Thomas finished his last ale for the day as he studied Julian's map. After securing the doors downstairs and snuffing the candles out, he went up to the second floor. Eager to pleasure himself with his wife, he stripped off his clothing, pulled back the heavy drapes around the bed, and slid in next to her.

"Felicity," he whispered. Not hearing any movement, he spoke her name again, "Felicity."

His wife kept quiet. Just as single-minded in his pursuit of getting his way, Felicity was also; she feigned sleep. He placed an icy foot against the calf of her warm leg that lay nearest to him.

She screamed, "Mr. Davis!" and sat upright. "Stop it!"

"Something wrong, my dear?"

"Yes, your feet are freezing. Get them away from me this instant!"

Thomas let out a quiet snicker.

Felicity adjusted her nightcap then turned to him. "Now that you have so rudely woken me, I have something to tell you."

"Is it that you desperately want me to ravage you?" he asked in anticipation of the coming events.

"Heavens no," she spat her words out at him. "I must return to Boston."

"What's that you say?"

"Mother Gibbs thinks it's best for my health and for the child that I reside in a place closer to civilization." She smoothed the coverlets with her hands. "And I agree with her."

Thomas lay back onto the bed, exasperated.

She waited a few seconds before continuing, "I'm not comfortable here, and distancing myself from the attention of doctors with whom I'm familiar is not in my best interest."

"Oh Felicity, must you leave me here all alone?" he grumbled.

"Mother Gibbs has already sent word to reopen our living quarters in Boston. We will leave in a few days." Her voice was firm and unemotional. She returned to her cocoon under the coverlet and closed her eyes, satisfied that the subject was finished.

Thomas remained on his back, not moving. He stared at the flower-patterned material that hung above his head across the bed's canopy frame. Rolling on his side towards her, he asked in one last desperate attempt to satisfy his needs. "My sweet thing, since I will not be enjoying your company for a while, may I create a memory of you that will tide me 'til your return?"

Confident that she had prevailed in her demands to leave Yarmouth, Felicity relented to his request, having decided that this was the least she could do for him. Throwing back the covers, she lifted her shift up to her neck, exposing her breasts, and invited him in.

Thomas formed a lustful smile as he rolled his naked body over hers.

While he enjoyed himself, Felicity closed her eyes and made mental notes of what to bring to the city and what attire would be the most flattering to hide her swollen stomach.

* * *

The sun had not yet made its presence across the land when Tobey rolled onto his side to face the opening of the barn stall. He pulled the coarse blanket up over his shoulders in the chilly morning air and tried to fall back to sleep.

Jacob entered and called out, "Tobey!"

The old servant stepped across the straw covered floor and over to the lone horse. He patted the gentle steed a good morning and gave him his feed. He called again, "Tobey! Get up!" After lifting the saddle over the horse's back he secured a strap under its belly. "Best you get up, boy. Mr. Davis don't like to wait."

Tobey sat on the edge of the roped bed, then got up and walked towards Jacob. "Where's Davis goin'?"

Jacob shrugged, "None of my business, but he said you was goin' with him."

Tobey stretched out his stiff muscles. As he scratched his head, his shirt opened to reveal the top half of a branded 'S' on his chest.

Jacob stopped and stared. He kept his gaze on the scar long enough to make the Antiguan uncomfortable.

The young man quickly tied his shirt closed, rifled through his hair to massage his scalp and said, "I'll be ready soon enough."

Jacob finished readying the old horse and rolled a short handled spade in a blanket behind the saddle. "Go on in and get some vittles from Hephzibah. It looks like you will be travelin' far today."

Tobey shook off the chill from the cool morning air as he took his piss behind the barn. He buttoned his pants and wondered what was ahead. Several days had passed without knowing what was expected of him. He reckoned he would find out today.

Jacob cautioned Tobey not to forget anything that he might need. He pointed to the bed. "Take that blanket with you for the nights. Carry your food safe…on your own person."

"Yes, sir. I'm grateful for your words." Then Tobey checked to make sure his knife was strapped tight to his calf and hidden under the bottom of his loose pant.

Within the hour, Davis and Tobey began their journey to Eastham. Tobey followed on foot behind the constant swish of Davis's horse. They stopped once for a short respite. Tobey relieved himself and crouched against a tree to eat, distancing himself from Davis. By evening, they reached Higgins Tavern, where Tobey found himself relegated to the barn behind the inn with the horse.

Davis went into the tavern for the night.

"Good evening, sir," Mr. Higgins greeted the weary traveler. "How may I oblige you this cool night?"

"A room, sir."

"That I am able to accommodate you with. Your name?"

"Thomas Davis, from Yarmouth. My servant resides with the horse outside."

"Follow me to your quarters. When you're ready, I'll provide a meal for you and your man."

"Thank you," Davis answered and trailed the proprietor up the narrow steps.

Soon he was enjoying a fine meat stew and a pint of ale. When near to completion, Davis asked Higgins, "Might I inquire your expertise in a matter that's a mystery to me?"

"I'm at your service."

"Do you know of a large rock or stone aberration close by?"

"Let me think, now." Higgins wiped the sideboard in careful thought.

Davis waited.

"I can think of only one place that holds such a description." He came closer to where Davis was sitting. "Not far from here, on the other side of our small settlement and near the shore, lies a large outcrop. You can see it from a distance." Higgins sat down on a chair opposite Davis. "The good settler, David Doane, named the massive protuberance after his ninth born son, Enoch. Some call it Enoch's Rock."

"Thank you for your kindness. I'll set out before the sun rises, as per your directions. I bid you good night."

"Best be careful. The land is private and belongs to Doane."

That night, Davis examined John Julian's map once more. What was asked of him seemed an impossible undertaking; but now, girded with the knowledge of the whereabouts of a large stone similar to the one on the map, his task was proving feasible. Davis retired with eagerness for the morning and foresaw a possible advancement for more riches in his life. He would need a new strategy.

*   *   *

By midmorning they arrived at Enoch's Rock, which rose eighteen feet above the ground and had a width almost the same. Only the eastern face was slanted for a safe footing; the southern–most facade was a straight vertical from top to bottom. Davis dismounted his horse and walked closer to further inspect the task before him. He placed his hand on the granite surface to steady himself as he kicked away leaves and sticks from its base. Then, walking around the rock's circumference, he glanced up and down, side-to-side, looking for any aberrations in the ground that would reveal where Julian's treasure might be located. Tobey watched and waited for word as to what his role was in this venture. As Davis rounded the southern side, he came across a pile of small rocks and called out, "Get the spade!"

Tobey did as he was told, "Yes, sir."

Standing over the mound, Davis directed Tobey. "Move away those stones and dig under them. Give me a hole two feet square."

The young man picked up the stones and put them aside, all the while thinking that what lay buried is, without doubt, what Julian sought.

Davis sat on a slope to the side. As he lit his pipe, he cautioned Tobey with, "Mind you keep a pace with your digging. We must leave here by sunset."

It wasn't long before Davis leaned back and closed his eyes. Tobey wanted to rest also, but as soon as his spade ceased cutting into the dirt, Davis sat up.

"Hear now, boy. Why have you stopped?"

Tobey had no reason but exhaustion. He continued his rhythm.

With one more hit into the black dirt, his shovel resonated with a dull thud. Davis looked towards the sound and then walked over to see what Tobey's shovel had found. As he came closer, Davis flapped his arm sideways, a clear signal to move away.

Tobey wiped his brow with the back of his hand and stepped back from the hole.

"Go further away to the horse; this is none of your business."

Again, he did as he was told.

Davis brushed away the dirt to reveal the top of a small chest. His past life as a pirate fueled his greed this day as his fingers furiously scratched at the dirt around its edges. He grabbed the spade and dug deep gouges along its sides. When the grooved line of where it opened was revealed, he scraped away at the center of the latch. With ferocity, he threw the spade to the ground behind him.

Tobey could see Davis's face turn crimson as he leaned further and lower into the hole. He hoped that he might be free of Davis if only the man's heart would give out. Maybe one hit of the spade over the man's head would be all that was needed. As his thoughts wondered about what was buried, they also encouraged him to step nearer to Davis and the sharp, flat tool on the ground now closest to his own foot. In silence, he reached for its wooden handle.

Davis opened the top of the chest, drew in a deep breath and closed it within seconds. Wiping saliva from the corner of his mouth, he caught sight of Tobey behind him with the tool in his hand. "Get back, boy, I told you once already." He struggled to lift himself up off his knees. "Best you get started filling in this hole," Davis ordered. "We have no need of its contents."

Tobey had seen a glimpse of what the chest held and questioned Davis's actions, but he kept his lips tight. He began to throw shovelfuls of dirt back into the hole. Taking note of the markings on the chest that was trimmed with leather, he tried to figure out what might happen next.

He stretched his arm out and held a fist to the late afternoon sun. Turning his palm toward his face, he counted how many folded knuckles fit within the orange ball and the horizon. All four fit squarely between; each bump signifying 15 minutes. He surmised that he had an hour to finish.

After a while, Davis grew impatient. "Replace the stones over the loose soil. We need to leave this place." He pushed the last remaining dirt over the covered hole with his own foot.

When Davis was satisfied with the Antiguan's work, the two men retraced their steps back to Higgins Tavern for the night. Tobey scrutinized the landscape, noticing any unusual tree or peculiar scape that would enable him to return, by himself, to the rock if needed.

The next morning, the travelers set out on their journey back to Yarmouth. It was dark by the time they reached Davis's home. Hephzibah had already retired and lay still under the covers listening to Davis rummage in the kitchen beneath her room. Felicity and Mother Gibbs had left for Boston earlier in the day and the young woman was uncomfortable in the house alone with Mr. Davis. She crept over to the door in her attic room, making sure the latch was secure. Hephzibah then placed the lone chair across its front and tiptoed back to bed. She would force herself to stay awake until there were no more sounds below her floor.

16

Present Day
BREWSTER - CAPE COD

BRIAN'S TEXT was a shocker. I stood for a moment, stunned, at the top of the stairs. My free hand flew up and touched the delicate necklace around my neck. I wondered if I should take it off. I shrugged my doubts away. How could there be danger back here on Cape Cod? Besides, I can take care of myself; I'm no dummy.

A gloom blanketed the inside of the house as the storm I'd witnessed from the beach turned into a nor'easter. Stepping down into the dining room, I turned on a few lamps. That's better. I decided to tell Paul about the break-in at Brian's house.

He was building a frame in our attached garage. I waited until he had joined all four corners. "We need to talk."

"Now what's wrong?"

"Well…before I left Antigua, Brian and I went to dinner at a café down on the beach. It belonged to his landlady. When we got back to the house, someone had broken in and rifled through my suitcase. Nothing was taken."

Paul looked upset.

"The Peace Corps office told Brian not to report it, but to be careful, and if anything else happens, he should move."

"So…what else?"

"I just got a text from Brian. Remember the earrings that matched this necklace?" I held it up. "Brian said they were stolen from John Julian's house."

Paul was quiet.

"I know I should have told you about the break-in, but I just didn't think it was important. Besides, you kind of yelled at me on the way home from the bus terminal about not getting involved in any new adventures." I went over and gave him a hug. "Forgive me?"

"You know, you're quite a handful but I still love you." He pulled back from me. "So what are you going to do now?"

"I might do some more research. I'm curious about what events spurred Bellamy to leave the Cape and sail to the West Indies. I don't think he was a pirate in the beginning." I turned to leave. "I promise to keep you informed of whatever Brian tells me."

*   *   *

Danny was folding clothes with Martha as I closed my office door and settled in front of the computer. The windy storm kept up its fury as rain blew sideways against the house. As I searched the internet, I found that there had been a hurricane along the Atlantic coast in 1715, the year before Bellamy left for the West Indies. In fact, there were several shipwrecks; one big one was Spain's treasure fleet, led by the San Miguel. The fleet consisted of a dozen or more galleons sent to the Americas by Phillip V to boost its coffers. Suffering from years of war, Spain needed money and bringing home the profits of its expansions into the new world was necessary. Besides, Phillip V was about to be married to his second wife, Elisabeth of Parma, and before she would consummate their union, she wanted a treasure trove of gifts and jewelry. I sat back in my chair. So…that's what Bellamy was going after…salvage.

*   *   *

The sky lit up with a flash of lightening then a thunderous boom shook the old glass in the parlor's bay windows. I heard a loud bang on the parlor door.

"Mommy?" said a frightened voice. "Are you in there? Can I come in?"

To be safe, I closed down the computer. "Sure, honey."

Danny pushed the door open and ran over to me. He wrapped his little arms around my waist. "I'm scared."

"It's okay. Let's go find Daddy." I felt relief knowing that, according to the weather station, we weren't in for another hurricane, just an ordinary nor'easter.

* * *

By late afternoon, the storm had stopped. The kids were settled in front of the TV, Paul was closing up the gallery, and I took out a frozen pizza for dinner. I remembered the old map and dashed upstairs to get it from the safe. The kitchen had the best light for what I wanted to see. I laid it flat on the small oak table. The familiar shape of a bent arm indicated that it was, indeed, Cape Cod. The names of the towns of Harwich, Eastham, and Truro were written across its surface. I could only estimate where the existing towns of today were located. The only other image on the map was an odd curved shape, just above the present town of Orleans.

Paul joined me in the kitchen carrying the mail. "Is that the map?"

"Yes. Isn't it beautiful?"

"It looks awful primitive," he said.

"When it fell from John Julian's Bible, back in Antigua, my jaw just dropped."

"Let me take a look at it."

I left Paul studying the map and went across the foyer to get a magnifying glass from the junk drawer in the laundry room. Within seconds, I was back at the table and gently pushed Paul aside. "I need to see what this little drawing is," I said, leaning nearer with the thick glass. "I think it looks like a big rock or boulder."

Martha came in to make a salad for dinner and stood at the table to see what we were doing. "What'cha lookin' at?" she asked as she craned her neck to see.

"It's an old map of Cape Cod." I kept my focus on it.

"Can I see?" Martha furrowed her eyebrows.

"Of course." I slid the map over to her view. "What do you think?" I pointed to the small little drawing. "The only thing I can't figure out is that." I leaned in next to Martha. Suddenly I noticed something under it. "Wait a minute, there's an x. See it?"

Martha got a better look. "Hmm…yeah, it sure looks like an 'x'. And that might be Doane's Rock. It's a huge boulder in Eastham, near the bike trail, on the way to Coast Guard Beach." She turned to reach for a large bowl and then took greens out of the refrigerator, unaware of her startling clue. "My children used to climb on it when they were little. It was great fun." She started to wash the tomatoes.

I felt as if I had just won the lottery, but grew cautious. "Paul? I want to show you something in the parlor that might need fixing." He looked at me funny as I folded the map and walked out of the kitchen. He picked up on my message of privacy and followed. Once out of earshot from Martha, I turned and faced him. "If that x marks where the treasure is hidden, then we know where to find it!"

Paul sat on one of the antique chairs that faced the front bay window and said, "It's too easy. I don't know."

I sat at my desk holding the map in my hands. "Martha has got to be right; she's lived here longer than us and boasts that she knows everything about Cape Cod."

"How about we all take a ride to find it, tonight, after dinner?"

"I think it's a great idea." Now I was extra curious. "The only way to find anything more about all of this is to go and see it for ourselves."

Paul cautioned me as we left the parlor. "Now, don't get too excited. Let's keep it to ourselves."

I held fast to the map and went upstairs to put it back in the safe until later.

After a few minutes, Martha left. I decided to set aside the salad and pizza for tomorrow night's dinner and instead grab some fast food on our way out to find Doane Rock. After eating, we were back on the road and driving past the National Seashore Visitors Center, off Route 6. I noticed Danny was looking at one of his pop-up books in his car seat. Casey was content in the rear bench to sip her soda; she only came along for the ride and some Wendy's.

Nine-year-old Molly asked, "Where we going?"

"Daddy and I want to see a big rock that someone told us about."

"Cool, can we climb on it?"

"I think so, but let's wait and see if we can find it first."

"Look, there's the sign." I pointed to a dark brown post with white letters that directed visitors to turn right for a picnic area. Paul eased the van to a stop in the small parking lot. A gray massive boulder shot up through the pines and scrub oak.

"That's it," I whispered.

We gazed at the rock from inside the van.

Molly called from behind, "Can we get out? Can we get out?"

"Sure," said Paul.

"Hold on a minute. Let me get Danny out of his seat." I was as anxious as Molly to get out.

Molly scrambled out of her seatbelt and waited for the okay to run.

"Go ahead," I said.

She took off and ran around the base of the boulder looking for a place to climb, while Danny followed after her. Casey stayed in the car listening to her iPod. After circling the gray mass once, we both stood still and watched Molly climb higher and higher out of our reach.

Paul called out, "Molly, be careful; don't go too high."

I pushed some dirt and stones near the boulder's base with my foot. Paul did the same over to the other side. We were both hoping there would be something that could give us another clue. But there was nothing. Too many years had passed to leave traces of anything buried.

He looked over to me and said, "Well, my dear, we seem to be as they say, 'at a rock and a hard place'."

"Crap, you're right." I looked up and around the boulder and then rested my open palm against its gritty surface. "Besides, we're on federal property. No one is going to give us permission to dig or do anything to this rock." Disappointed with the reality of the whole thing, we let Molly and Danny play a little longer until dusk began to settle in around us.

Casey finished the last of her soda and yelled out the window, "Mom, I've got a report due tomorrow. Can we leave now?"

"Yes, we better get going."

On the ride home, the sun set across the bay with beautiful reds and oranges. I refused to think that this would be the end of my search for John Julian's lost treasure and wondered when Brian was going to call again.

17

1722
YARMOUTH - CAPE COD

THE NEXT DAY, Hephzibah quietly greeted the man of the house with, "Good Morning, Mr. Davis."

"Humph," he replied as he passed her in the downstairs foyer on the way to his study.

"My tea, and be quick."

"Yes sir, Mr. Davis." Hephzibah curtsied, turned, and ran to the kitchen.

Davis stood by the window, contemplating where he could hide the found treasure of John Julian and how to accomplish this without Tobey's knowledge. But first all the papers and bills that were neglected while he was in Antigua needed his attention.

When he was finished, he decided to take a stroll outside to stretch his legs. As he rounded the house towards the rear, he spotted Hephzibah bringing in the dried laundry from the morning wash. She never noticed his presence.

Davis stood quiet in the shadow on the north side of the house, hoping for a chance to catch a glimpse of anything intriguing or pleasurable to his eye from Hephzibah's direction. He watched the young maid's skirts billow in the wind and strained his eyes for a closer view of her breasts each time she bent over to fold the clothes into the basket. He thought a bolder move was needed on his part. He straightened his posture, sucked in his stomach and walked towards the unsuspecting girl. "Hephzibah! 'Tis a fine day, is it not?"

Startled, Hephzibah dropped a coverlet on the ground. "Mr. Davis, you frightened me."

"Here, let me help you with that," Davis said and leaned over to pick up the material for her. He took his time to stand up so he could brush his hand against her ankle.

Hephzibah backed away from his touch. She looked to see if anyone else was near. Seeing no one, she feared her employer's kindness was a bad omen for her. Quickly, she gathered the last of the clothes from the fence.

He stood watching her every move.

She threw the dry clothes into the waiting basket then pleaded, "Please sir, I must get to my duties. If you'll excuse me." She bent over to lift the basket up.

Suddenly Davis reached for her wrist and pulled her close to him, forcing her to drop everything. "What's your hurry? We're alone; no one will know if you neglected your work."

"I beg you, sir. Let me be. It's not right."

With a quick maneuver he pushed her to the ground. Hephzibah fell on top of the strewn clothes and blankets. Davis dropped down onto his knees over her. He unbuttoned his pants and pulled at her bodice to expose one of her breasts.

She cried out, "NO! PLEASE NO!"

Tobey was honing his knife in the barn when he heard Hephzibah's scream. Dropping the sharpening stone he ran out the door, carrying his knife in an attack position. He saw Davis straddling the screaming girl. As Davis was about to bring his open hand against Hephzibah's mouth to stop her from screaming, Tobey grabbed his hand and threw him off the girl.

Davis roared as he fell onto his backside. "What are you doing here?" He sputtered, rolling over to his knees, trying to stand. "This here's none of your business. Get out of my doings."

Hephzibah tried to crawl to safety but her layered skirts stopped her from gaining any distance and she kept falling atop the grasses. With tears streaming down her face, she finally stood up. The frantic girl hiked up her skirts with one hand and ran to the rear of the house, all the while trying to cover her unclothed breast with the other.

Tobey ignored Davis's words and stood his ground. He cared little for this evil man and longed to vent his anger upon him. He could feel his scar burning, but this time it felt good. Tobey put his knife back in its sheath on his calf, knowing his bare hands could take care of this bag of bones with one hit to the jaw. Davis stood up and attempted to take a swing at Tobey. The young man blocked his clumsy attempt with his muscular forearm and then clenched his other hand into a fist that leveled Davis flat to the ground. Hephzibah watched from the doorway as her rescuer stood over her attacker. She wished Tobey would kill him, but knew it was not right.

Tobey thought the same and stopped himself. He had his limits. He could not bring any more harm to this man whom he detested. The force of his blow had satisfied a part of him that had been festering within his soul for years. Finally he had righted a wrong. He stepped over the unconscious body of Davis and proceeded to find Hephzibah. He found her cowering near the back door. Her back slid down against the rough wood of the doorframe to the ground. She cried with relief that it was over. Her instincts had been correct about Mr. Davis. He had every intention to harm her. She vowed to herself that by the time he wakens, she would be gone.

Tobey bent down to help her stand. He wrapped his arms around her shoulders, comforting her with a gentleness that she responded to.

"Are you all right?" he asked in quiet tones.

"Yes," she answered in between her sobs. "Please stay with me this night. I'm fearful of Davis's wrath upon his wakening. It's too late in the day for me to travel home to my father."

She turned to climb the steps to her room in the attic and held her hand out to Tobey. He took it in silence and followed behind her. Once the door was closed, he pushed the bureau against it, preventing Davis from entering, should he try to complete his evil deed. Tobey had no intention of taking advantage of their situation, aware that Hephzibah needed him for protection. That night, they shared the same bed, but only to comfort each other till early morning.

*   *   *

The evening sky had turned black and dew had formed on top of Davis's sprawled body. His clothes were wet through to the skin. A spotted garden snake slithered across his face in the night air. He flicked his fingers against his nose to stop the tickle and then slapped himself, thinking the problem was a pesky fly. He opened his eyes with a start then turned his head to see the snake's tail wiggling away, all the while he was wondering what was happening. He tried to move his body but the pain in his face kept him still for several more minutes. When he finally righted himself, his pants fell to his ankles. Unaware of his bound legs, he stepped forward and fell once more onto the damp grasses. Grumbling under his breath, he found his way into the house, where the discovery of a cold and empty hearth and no supper made him even angrier. His jaw was swollen and his mouth stiff; all he wanted was a pint of ale and his bed. He would tend to the whole matter in the morning. Not sure what he would do, he resolved to punish someone for this travesty.

18

Present Day
CAPE COD

AFTER LUNCH the next day, I secluded myself in the front parlor office. Maybe some writing would take my mind off the setback of not finding any other clues at Doane Rock. The manuscript that I'd been working on ever since I'd found the treasure in our backyard, four years ago was slowly turning into fiction. Although no one believed my theory that it belonged to the legendary Sam Bellamy, I eased my desire for credibility with my determination to tell a good story and let people believe what they want. Of course, I had the gold and jewels to back up all my assumptions. Bottom line, I thought, I'm sticking with the Sam Bellamy premise.

My eyes focused on the computer screen, and with fingers poised over the keyboard, I began typing, Chapter 15, *The gold and jewels....* I stared at the blank lines that followed the first four words for several minutes before I blinked. Sitting back in my chair, I thought of the phone call I'd made to a New York museum before I left for Antigua. I had left on my trip hoping they would be interested in a special exhibit of the gold and silver coins that I'd discovered. As of today, no one had returned my call. The museum should've jumped right on it, I thought. After all, one doesn't find pirate booty every day. Connecting with the museum curator was probably not going to happen.

My thoughts circled back to the old John Julian as I got up to get a cup of coffee. There were no other clues as to where his treasure could be found, or even if it existed. The one lead identifying Doane Rock had become a dead end after I realized that there wouldn't be any digging around it since it was on government property. I should have known better. With that and no response from the museum, I felt disheartened that my search was over. It seemed disappointment was now beginning to shadow my every move.

I finished my coffee at the kitchen table and thought about how much of a treasure I had actually found. The coinage was only valuable in its present stage, so to reap any substantial money, I would have had to melt the coins down. I promised myself I would never do that. It would be such a loss to history. The coins' heritage was more precious to me than cash; they were secure in a safe deposit box at the bank. The necklaces and gemstones that I managed to sell to different collectors and antique dealers were a real bonus. It felt satisfying to contribute to the kids' college fund and pay for some major repairs on the house. As a stay-at-home mom for most of my married life, adding cold hard cash to the budget was a rarity for me.

Martha sashayed past the kitchen on her way to clean the bathrooms. She was my one treat…a wonderful nanny and housekeeper.

As another load of laundry hummed through the quiet house, I thought of Brian back on Antigua and his yellow, stained clothes. He should've already called to tell me more about the robbery. Then again, I didn't know what to tell him except that maybe I was not pursuing the hunt for treasure. It sure would have been satisfying if I could've helped John give all of his kids a better future.

Within the hour, other responsibilities came running up the deck and into the house, one from the school bus and the other from our minivan in the driveway.

The children raced each other to the foyer door. Molly slid it open and then shut it with a bang and yelled, "Where is it?"

Danny struggled with the slider but managed to come in fast behind Molly. "Yeah, where is it?'

Martha had been hiding after-school treats for the kids for several weeks now. She coyly busied herself in the kitchen, pretending that she didn't know who left the little snacks of candy, pretzels, or chips around the house. I laughed as they dropped their book bags and lunch boxes on the foyer floor, eager to search under every nook and cranny for their surprises. Of course, the treats were easy to find and were discovered in lightning speed, then devoured instantly.

Paul walked into the house. "Did they find them already? They're getting faster each time."

I smiled at the thought that our little ones were developing into two great detectives.

Later, I found Martha in the laundry room. "Here, give me the clothes," I said, "I'll take them upstairs for you. Keep your eye on the kids; they seem to be a little wild today."

"Sure enough," Martha replied and went to make herself a cup of tea.

After dividing the towels between the two upstairs bathrooms, I passed my bedroom closet and the small safe caught my eye. I kneeled on the floor and revisited the old pottery shard that I'd found on the beach with Danny a few days ago. The delicate blue flowers were so interesting to me. Tomorrow would be a good day to visit a few antique shops to find out more about the shard. When I'm feeling discouraged, I only need a good adventure to recharge my batteries.

I headed down the stairs and into the dining room, looking for Paul.

I heard him call out. "I'm in the kitchen."

"Got anything going on tomorrow?" I asked.

"Nope. Why?"

"I'd like to find some background about this pattern on the pottery shard I found."

He looked at it with a quick glance. "Go ahead. Danny will be home but Martha's here to help."

With eager anticipation, I walked out of the kitchen planning my route for the next day.

*   *   *

I was up early, grabbed some coffee, and headed west on 6A. It was a few weeks before Columbus Day, the official end of the tourist season on Cape Cod, and I hoped that most places would still be open. To save time, I drove on the Mid-Cape Highway to the beginning of the Cape, just before the Sagamore Bridge. A quick turn around on Route 6A took me into Sandwich, a town with several antique stores to choose from as I worked my way back east and then home again.

Driving through the autumn countryside, the blue sky reflected in the water of the flooded cranberry bogs. I saw a couple of men in the water corralling the crimson berries into tight circles on top of the watery bog. The sight of those beautiful images reminded me of how lucky I was to live on the Cape.

My first stop was September Antiques, a large white building that sat close to the highway. It looked like it had once been an old gas station. Bentwood chairs, quilt stands, ironwork, and tables were lined up against its outside walls. The shop looked hopeful.

"Good morning," said the proprietor.

"Hello." I walked past a glass counter filled with jewelry and small collectibles. "I just have a question." I pulled the pottery shard out of my pocket and asked, "Can you identify this pattern?"

The elderly man took it from me and examined it under a light. "I'm afraid not. I get many old pieces in here but I'm no expert when it comes to china and porcelain." He handed it back and added, "I can't help you, but I know someone who can."

I perked up and took out a pad and pen.

"There's a lady over in Dennis, goes by the name of Agnes. She has a shop there and she knows her stuff when it comes to fine china and the real old ones."

"Where about in Dennis?"

"Well, I'm not sure, but the building is painted a pale yellow, right on Route 6A near Scargo Hill. You can't miss it."

"Thanks, I appreciate it." As a courtesy for the kind gentleman's information, I made a few passes down the rows of tables and shelves filled with memorabilia from times past. It's always a polite gesture when browsing to give hope for a sale, even if it is a false hope.

"Thanks again," I said on my way out the door.

"Good luck," he called back.

The next stops along the historic highway proved fruitless. By 11 o'clock I paused at a little convenience store for coffee and then decided to head straight for Dennis.

*   *   *

The old, buttercup-yellow building stood alone on the edge of the road and was in need of a paint job. Newer buildings connected to each other like a mini mall, surrounding it on three sides. The sign hung perpendicular to the front façade: *Antiques, will buy estates!*

There was no parking out front, so I looked for a driveway to pull into and found a good spot in the back lot. I followed a sidewalk alongside the building to the front, where a paper sign was taped to the locked door. It was handwritten in an old Spenserian style and read: *If you want to see this store, go over to Corabells across the street and ask to see the inside of this store.*

I laughed at the repeated words and its odd message. I peered to the other side of the highway and saw the sign for Corabells. It looked like a consignment shop. The door was open. I crossed the street and entered through the doorway. "Hello, is anyone here?"

After a few moments of silence, a middle-aged woman wearing tennis shoes, a white polo shirt, and a long denim skirt that molded itself across her wide hips emerged into the front area. She awkwardly moved past racks of used clothing. "Howdy. What can I do for you?" she asked with a smile.

"Well, I was over at the antique store and the sign said to come here if I want to see anything inside."

"Yup, you came to the right place, just a moment, I need to get the key," she said and disappeared into a back room.

From behind a flowered curtain strung across a doorway, I could hear, "Freddy, I'm going across the street. I'll be right back."

"Okay, Ma."

"Stop playing that dumb video game and get out here, in case we get some customers." She looked irritated but then she smiled and gestured for me to follow her out the door.

When we reached the yellow building and she opened the weathered portal, a heady, musty smell attacked our nostrils. Dirt, dust, and dampness emanated from the neglected old rooms that were once formal living and dining rooms. Contributing to its ancient aura were remnants of strong perfume and mothballs. It all combined into what I prefer to call an 'old-lady smell'.

"Sorry about the odor," she said and flipped on the light switch. "Poor Agnes hasn't been well lately. The shop's been closed more than open over the last year."

"No problem." I was confident it was the right place after hearing the name Agnes.

I began to browse up and down the dimly lit aisles looking for anything that would match the flower pattern on the beach find.

A cell phone went off to the tune of *Born Free*. "Howdy," my guide answered. Then silence. "I have someone in here now…sure," she said. "See you soon." The woman flipped her phone closed. "Well, you're in luck. The owner will be here in a few minutes."

"Thanks." I was hopeful that now my adventure would not be a waste of time.

I wound my way through the shelves of platters, bowls, plates, and tureens towards the rear, where one window opened to the outside. The sun's rays reflected on the floorboards in turquoise and rose from hobnail glassware that lined a shelf across a small window. I stepped onto the faceted reflections twinkling on the floor and noticed, out of the corner of my eye, a PT Cruiser pull alongside the building. Standing in the sunlight, I watched as the car door opened and the end of a cane appeared, followed by a bejeweled wrinkled hand that assisted a woman's exit from the cruiser.

Agnes, I thought, and then turned my attention back to my quest amongst the antiques. Lingering as I walked, I inched my way closer to the front, hoping to give the elderly proprietor enough time to settle in at the large desk behind the glass counter.

"I'll be with you momentarily," the frail antiquer called over her shoulder.

"Take your time," I said.

I pretended to be interested in a few etchings stacked against the back wall. As I made one more trip down an aisle, I heard Agnes call out with breathy words as she sat down to rest. "Now, what can I do for you?"

Hurrying up to the desk, I pulled the shard from my pocket. "Can you tell me anything about this pattern?"

"Where did you find this?"

"On the beach, about a week ago."

"I've seen it before but can't put my finger on it." She lifted her glasses, which were attached to a silver chain, up onto her nose.

I waited for her answer.

"The pattern looks to be from the Kangzi period. It was probably made in China between 1662 and 1722."

She examined it from all angles, and then held her chin, apparently lost in her thoughts. Agnes closed her eyes and looked like she hoped it would help in deciphering where it came from. "I remember," she said with a glint of success in her voice. She held the piece in her fingers and continued, "A while back, almost a year now, a young man came in and inquired if I bought estates. Of course, I said yes."

I stepped around the counter to get closer.

"He was a bit rough looking. Wore a black hooded sweatshirt with terrible looking figures on it and words that I dare not repeat."

The woman's reference was understood.

Agnes looked over to her friend and told her, "You can leave, my dear. I'll be fine. Thanks for your help."

"No problem," she said, leaving with a wave of her hand.

"Now, where were we?" Agnes looked down at the shard.

I chimed in with, "You were telling me about someone who wanted to sell some things from an estate."

"Oh, yes. Would you like a peppermint?" she asked, sliding a small crystal bowl filled with red and green mints towards me.

"Don't mind if I do." I assumed the cellophane wrapped candies were safe to eat.

The elderly woman swiveled around in her chair and reached down to a file cabinet's bottom drawer. "Let me see, it's in here somewhere," she said as she rifled through several manila folders.

The stale hard candy was refreshing even though it tasted like soft taffy.

"Here it is." The old woman pulled the file up and laid it on top of her desk. She scanned one of the papers inside. "It says here that the purchase was made last September and it included various tea bowls, saucers, and one teapot."

"So do you think the china shard is old?"

"Hard to guess. You see, there were more pieces made in later years, through the late 1700s and 1800s by English and American craftsmen, all copying the Chinese patterns."

"Was the estate from the Kangzi era?"

"Yes. I identified them by the marks on the bottom of one of the saucers," she said as she closed the file.

"Do you have one that I can look at?" Now I was intrigued.

"I'm sorry to say that I sold the set to a buyer in London soon after my acquisition from the young man."

"Oh, I see." Disappointed I started for the door and turned. "Thanks for your time." I thought maybe one more question wouldn't hurt. "Could you tell me the name of the young man who sold you the set?"

"Well...I like to keep my clients confidential." She busied herself with opening some mail from her desk. She paused. "You know, I think I may have something you'd like. Come with me, dear." She directed me to follow her to a small room in the rear on the side opposite the lone window. Agnes leaned her cane against a shelf of hurricane lamp parts and bent over an old box.

I stood quietly, wondering what the old woman was going to show me.

As she stood up, her face was bright red from bending over. In her hand the lid of a blue and white teapot peeked out from the crumbled newspaper that was wrapped around it. Agnes slowly unwrapped it. Its spout was chipped and the handle was broken away from the bullet shaped body. "The lid seems to be glued on. I could never open it and thus couldn't sell it," she said as she tried to wiggle the lid to prove her point.

"Is this from the estate?" I held the shard against the body of the teapot.

"Yes, it is."

"It looks like it matches my pattern perfectly." I could feel myself getting excited.

"It does look pretty similar to your piece." She held it out to me. "You can have the teapot for $5.00."

"I'll take it."

I carried the teapot back to the front and placed it on the counter.

It took Agnes several minutes to finally make her way to her desk and sit down. "Not as fast as I used to be," she said as she maneuvered her cane so that it wouldn't fall between an old bureau and a dark green metal cabinet. She opened the file once more and scrolled down to the bottom of her inventory sheet. "I can tell you the young man's name, but that's all I'll say. It's Tommy Chandler."

19

1722
YARMOUTH - CAPE COD

TOBEY HAD DECIDED the prior night that, if Hephzibah would allow him to accompany her, he would also leave the Davis household. He woke before dawn and gently shook the young woman's shoulder, hoping to awaken her without alarm.

Hephzibah turned onto her back, slowly opened her eyes and smiled at her guardian. Tobey's eyes reflected no evil and she felt no fear.

He whispered to her, "I want to go with you."

With relief, she said, "I would like that."

"Then we must leave before Davis awakes." Tobey rose and faced the brick chimney as Hephzibah dressed for travel.

Within minutes, the two were ready to leave. He slid the bureau away from the door and lifted its latch in silence. They crept down the stairs and into the kitchen, making no sound other than the swish of Hephzibah's skirts. She grabbed a small pint of ale with some day-old bread and wrapped them in a cloth.

Once outside, Tobey instructed her, "Go. I'll catch up with you. Don't worry." Then he disappeared into the barn to retrieve his belongings as she went ahead of him. He made sure his papers were concealed in a small pouch along with the gold coins from Julian. A blanket and extra shirt were rolled into a bigger sack, which he slung over his shoulder. He caught up with Hephzibah as she reached the end of the road that took her away from Davis's house. Together, they picked up their pace in the early morning light, each hoping to reach the open road before the townspeople began their day. Neither wanted to face the questions of those who objected to their differing skin color.

Tobey turned to Hephzibah and finally spoke. "I need to ask something of you?"

"Yes?" Hephzibah kept her eyes on the rocky, rutted road before her.

"I have decided to leave Davis for good. You say that your father is a kind man. Would he hire me?"

She looked over to him. "Now that my brothers are married and gone, he may well be agreeable to your request."

Tobey was relieved at a potential opportunity for work. He walked a little taller.

As they came closer to another village in the early morning, they walked apart again, keeping a distance between themselves until they once more reached its outer edges, and away from inquisitive eyes. Several hours and miles passed before they felt safe enough to sit and share the bread and ale that Hephzibah carried. Both travelers welcomed the rest and sat to the side of the road under an old elm tree. Tobey talked of the island of Antigua and the orders he was given by his overseer, John Julian.

"Was there really a chest filled with treasure?" Hephzibah asked.

"I saw it with my own eyes, and Davis knew I did." He bit off a piece of bread and took a swig of ale. Pleased that he had caught the attention of this young woman with his story, he smiled and continued, "Davis closed it so fast I thought he would catch the front of his pants or fingers in the latch."

Hephzibah laughed. "I wish that he did. It would serve him right."

The young Antiguan lay back against the trunk of the tree and admired her humor and beautiful smile.

* * *

DAVIS HOUSE, YARMOUTH

Davis lay sleeping long after the sun had risen. A loud knocking from outside roused him. Rolling over, he opened his eyes and winced with the pain from his swollen jaw. He tried to remember where he was and how he got into this predicament. As the memory of what had happened slowly seeped back into his head, he rubbed his cheek and cursed, "God damn, that girl is going to pay."

The noise grew louder and then he heard his name. "Davis! Are you in there?"

He didn't recognize the voice. "Just a minute, by God, I'm coming," he grumbled.

As his feet landed on the wooden floor he called out, "Hephzibah!" Standing up, he yelled again, "Where are you, girl? Answer the door."

Outside, Mr. James Baker was growing impatient. After hearing no response, the unannounced visitor walked to the rear of the house and headed for the barn.

Davis hobbled down the stairs to the front door. Seeing no one, he turned and proceeded to the kitchen for a drink. Both men swore as they continued calling out, each perturbed at the inconvenience of no response.

When Baker found the barn empty, he went to the back door of the house and banged his fist against it.

At the same time Davis, now in the kitchen, lifted ale to his lips. The loud noise startled him and he spewed his drink across the floor. "Gall darn it!" Ale dribbled from his lips and down his shirt. "Who's at my door?"

"Davis, is that you in there?"

"Of course it's me! Who else would it be?" Davis refilled his tankard and yelled out, "James Baker, is that you?" Without waiting for a response, he took another swig of ale, got up and unlocked the door. "Come on in."

James Baker pushed the door open to see his friend looking like he had been dragged through a field. His clothes were grass stained and dirty, while his cheek bore the colors of black and blue patches. "What have you been doing, man?" Baker asked with a sarcastic smile on his face.

"I don't want to discuss it."

"Is there no woman about the house?"

"No! And I'm thoroughly disgusted with the whole situation." Davis slammed his tankard to the board.

Baker laughed and sat down opposite his friend. "Well sir, I haven't come to question your personal life." Helping himself to some drink, he continued, "I have traveled here to ask if you'd be interested in a business proposition."

With these words, Davis grew more attentive. "Will it involve a profit for me?

"Yes, indeed."

"Then you have my interest." Davis stood. "I need to piss."

"Be my guest," he waved his hand, gesturing towards the door.

Davis leaned one arm against the outside shingles of the house to relieve himself. He called out over the dull thud of his bodily fluids against the damp mud. "Will it involve me doing any hard work?"

From inside, Baker replied, "Just your money, Thomas. Just money."

The two men sat by the cold hearth as Baker explained his venture, based upon the need of a mill to grind corn for the ladies of the North Parish of Harwich. It would be located near the natural ridge that separated Eastham from Harwich. He unfolded a paper with the words 'Baker Davis Mill' across the top as a heading, and a list of facts, expenses, and site directions underneath it. Baker added, "The Paine Mill, near the mouth of the Namskaket, is too far for the good Harwich ladies to travel."

Davis listened, allowing Baker to convince him that it would be a welcome addition to the commerce in the area. Davis knew of the location; it was not far from Enoch's Rock. This might be the answer to his problem of where to secure his newfound treasure. Being a part owner of the mill would also place him in a desirable position to hide his newly discovered cache in secret at the mill site. Control. That is what he wanted. It was all about control.

20

Present Day
CAPE COD

THE HIGHWAY was my best choice to travel home; it was quicker and would give me some extra time to visit Tommy Chandler at Tommy's Gaming in Yarmouth. A little guilt flickered through my head as I remembered how I'd secretly copied the kid's business address. I was sure Agnes wasn't aware of my snooping as I deciphered the upside down words from her open ledger and wrote them into my small notebook. It didn't seem that terrible to me; besides, it felt exciting, like I was a spy.

Right before Exit 10, I caught sight of a soaring hawk in the sky through the top of the windshield. "Wow, that's so beautiful," I whispered, until I saw the small chipmunk swaying in its talons. I took it as a warning. My instinct told me to be careful, reminding me that not all things are what they seem to be.

Once off the highway, a small open strip mall appeared on my left. The shopping area housed a variety of businesses, from medical practices to a hardware store and a pizza shop. I eased the van into the second row from the sidewalk in front of the gaming store. Its giant windows were covered with black paper and logos from heavy metal bands. It was not the most inviting place to me, but it definitely appealed to a certain few.

Cautious to go into the store at first, I made up my mind to go forward with my original plan of finding Tommy Chandler. I assumed that the game room was probably empty; kids would still be in school. With only phone and keys in hand, I started for the door.

It took a few seconds for my eyes to adjust to the dark interior and black lights, but because I was wearing a white blouse, I literally glowed and lit my own path to the back counter. Couches, beanbag chairs, and low tables lined up against the walls under several large flat screen TVs. To the right side of me were random sounds of binging and clanging coming from another room that housed pinball machines. A young man, slight in build, with long black hair that hung down around his shoulders appeared from behind the counter. "What can I do for you?" he asked, flipping one side of his stringy hair over his shoulder.

He took me off guard and I stumbled over my first question. "Uhhhh…."

He waited with an annoyed look on his face.

"Are you Tommy Chandler?"

"That's my name. Who's asking?"

"My name is Nancy Caldwell." I took a deep breath. "This is kind of an odd question, but, well, did you sell some china from an estate sometime last year?"

"Yup. What about it?" He stared at me.

His attention unnerved me. Not sure of what to ask next, I regretted not being more prepared. "I'm interested in the style of china that you sold. Do you have any other pieces for sale?"

"Nope." He began to look through some gaming magazines on the counter.

Now he was ignoring me. "I see." I sensed our brief conversation was coming to a close if I didn't come up with something more compelling. Perturbed with myself that I couldn't think of anything else to ask, I just stood there. As I started to say goodbye, someone called from the pinball room, "Hey, Tommy D! Got any more quarters for change?"

"Yeah, just a minute." He moved over to the cash register. "Lady, if you don't have any more questions, I got work to do."

I quickly reached into my pocket and handed him a card with my name and email on it. "If you find any more pieces of that china would you contact me? Here's my email."

He took the card and dropped it on the counter. "Yeah, sure."

"Nice talking with you." I turned to leave, but stopped and asked one more question. "I heard that man call you 'Tommy D', what does the 'D' stand for?'

He stood a little taller. "Davis." Opening the register, he started counting out quarters. "My dad named me after some dead relative... Thomas Davis."

* * *

I turned and hurried out of the store, barely believing what I'd heard. "Thomas DAVIS Chandler," I repeated under my breath. I knew from the Bellamy/Hallett legend that Davis was another survivor of the *Whydah*. Was this coincidence or fate that I'd found a shard of pottery on the beach that matched his family's china? I could barely contain my excitement as I made my way back to the van. Once inside, I repeated his name out loud, "*Thomas Davis Chandler*!" It pulled me right back into my quest. The question now was what to do with this new information? Could it be connected to where John Julian's treasure was buried? As I started the car, my cell phone rang. It was Brian.

"Mom?"

"Hi honey, I've been waiting for your call."

"Sorry, I got busy."

It was good to hear his voice. "Any news about John and the earrings?"

"Like I told you, they were stolen the day we were all at the orphanage reception. John and Angel seem a little nervous now because someone was in their house, and they're pretty sad they've lost a family heirloom, but they're doing okay."

"What do you think is going on?"

"I don't know. It does seem strange. This whole mess started with your visit."

"I don't know what to think." I felt bad and wondered if this could be my fault? But it couldn't be.

"I hope you put that necklace in a safe place?"

It was still around my neck. "Brian, there's no way I'm in any danger here on Cape Cod."

"I guess so." He was quiet.

"Did John go to the police?" I nervously fiddled with the necklace.

"Yeah. The police questioned him and wanted to know if he had any insurance on them. John was upset because they insinuated that he'd stolen them himself for the insurance money."

Brian's words surprised me. "I can't believe they questioned him like a criminal."

"Yeah, but that's what they do here."

"Oh my goodness," I said.

Brian continued, "Then they went around quizzing his neighbors for any information. But they still found nothing."

"That's too bad." My thoughts quickly changed to my son and when I would next see him. "When do you think you'll be coming home?"

"I don't think it will be for Christmas, too much legal stuff in turning over the orphanage to the local government. It's a slow process."

"Darn it." His news was disappointing. "Will you promise me that you'll be careful?"

"Yeah. Hey, you might be getting a visitor for the holidays."

"What do you mean?"

"Nick's getting some time off. He has no major projects that he's working on and has no family to speak of, so he asked if he could come to Cape Cod for the holidays, at least for Thanksgiving. I said it would probably be okay. Hope you don't mind?"

This was the last thing I wanted to hear, since it's our busy season, but I reluctantly agreed. "No, it'll be all right."

"I'll let you know if he's really going to come."

"Okay. I love you."

"Love you too. Tell Dad I love him."

*   *   *

All the way home, I began to go through the things that had to be done in case Nick was going to be in our house for Thanksgiving and maybe longer. Along with that, and what I'd found out today about the stolen earrings, the pattern on the pottery shard, and a kid named Thomas Davis Chandler, I hoped I could do justice to everything. I never even had a chance to tell Brian what was happening to me. Best to wait...so I can sort it all out first.

As I pulled into the driveway, rain appeared out of nowhere and came down in torrents. I threw my cell phone and keys into my purse then reached for the umbrella stored in the side pocket of the door and scrambled out of the car. With my coffee mug and purse in one hand, the umbrella in the other, I managed to open the back trunk, where the old teapot lay wrapped within a quilted blanket.

As the sky grew darker, I could see lights going on in every room of the house as the kids, already home from school, looked for their treats. I slowed my pace as I walked up the decking towards the foyer door. I didn't want to drop anything, especially my special purchase of the day.

Danny was the first one to greet me, followed by Molly chewing on a red licorice stick. Martha was occupied in the kitchen, unloading the dishwasher.

"Whew, it's really coming down out there." I shook the half collapsed umbrella outside onto the covered deck. "You guys don't seem to be very wet."

Molly spoke up, "Nope, we got home before it started raining," and then she sat down on the bench in the foyer. Pumping her right leg in a fast rhythm, she watched my every move.

"Where's Daddy?" I asked.

"Working," Danny said as he hugged my legs hello.

"I love you, honey. Did you have a good day at school?"

He nodded his head and then he and Molly ran to the living room to watch a TV show.

I positioned the wrapped teapot near the end of the bench, and then went to find Paul in his studio. While I passed through the living room, I pointed at Molly and asked, "Have you started your book report yet?"

Molly returned a wide-eyed stare and then ran to grab her backpack containing her new library book. Nothing more needed to be said; she got my message.

Paul was painting at his easel. I planted a kiss on his cheek and sat in the lounge chair. "Guess what?"

"Uh oh. What's up?" He made one more stroke with his brush and then stopped.

"After visiting a few antique stores, I finally found Agnes in Dennis."

"And what did Agnes in Dennis tell you?"

"A guy sold her some china from his grandfather's estate that matches my little shard."

"Keep going."

I pulled out the shard from my pocket, touched the blue flowers that decorated its surface and continued, "Agnes didn't have any pieces for me to look at but she said that the pattern looked familiar to her. Then she told me to follow her to the back of the shop." I looked at Paul with a big smile across my face and added, "When we got to the back, she reached down into a cardboard box and pulled out an old teapot."

"And?"

"It was chipped, cracked and the lid was stuck but it matched my shard. She sold it to me for only $5.00."

"That's great, but what does that have to do with anything?" Paul sat down at his drawing table and folded his arms.

"The teapot came from this kid's estate that Agnes then sold to a guy in London. Agnes would only tell me the seller's name, no address; client confidentiality. But as I was paying for it, I secretly copied the address from her ledger."

The phone rang, Paul picked up the receiver. "The Caldwell Gallery, may I help you?"

I grew impatient, waiting for Paul's attention. I wanted to finish my story and tell him that Brian had called. Twirling my hand in a circular motion, I signaled for him to hurry up. Paul nodded Okay.

*　*　*

Danny, engrossed with TV in the living room, reached for his juice box on the floor next to the couch and accidentally knocked it over onto the carpet. The red juice began to seep out of the plastic straw as the cup lay on its side. Instinctively, he ran to get something to wipe up his mistake. The first thing he saw was the small quilted blanket that lay jumbled in a ball on the foyer bench. A fast tug at a corner of the material was all that was needed. It came off the bench with a clunk against the tiled foyer floor. The sound of something other than the soft swish of material made Danny frightened. He stopped, quickly replaced the bulky quilt back on the bench and stuffed its ends into the corner. Then he ran into the kitchen calling, "Martha! Help!"

21

October 1722
YARMOUTH - CAPE COD

AFTER BAKER LEFT, Davis dressed and began his investigation into who was in his house and on his property. He climbed the stairs to Hephzibah's quarters to find them empty. Slamming her door, he walked with an angry foot down to the deserted kitchen. He then proceeded to look for Tobey in the barn. Having no luck in his search, he punched his fist into a hay bale inside the horse's stall. "By God, those two have not seen the last of me." He hissed, "I need a drink." As he walked back to the house, he rubbed his reddened knuckles. Once in the kitchen, he filled his tankard, emptied it with one lift of his hand, and filled it up again. Then he took his drink and Baker's information upstairs to his study.

Davis focused on two options: the up-and-coming business proposition and where to bury the newly found chest of treasure. Throughout the day he wandered aimlessly about the house until he finally devised a plan. He decided that he would remove as much booty as he could from Julian's cache and hide it in a safe place, well out of sight. He was confident that as he travelled to the Baker Mill site, he would figure out where that safe place would be. Besides, his journey would get his mind off the two scalawags who had roughed him up.

One of Felicity's kerchiefs lay on the floor at his foot. "Humph... insubordination, and from a woman yet." He mumbled, "Why did I ever choose her? Such a disrespectful wife." He shook his head back and forth in disgust and clenched his teeth. "Partying away in Boston, not caring about her husband." He grabbed the dainty linen square and threw it into the filled chamber pot. "She's a shameful wife and now she carries my only child in her womb." He collapsed on his bed. His eyes closed and he remained there through the rest of the day and into the night.

*   *   *

Davis rose early and secured the house. He stuffed Baker's paper detailing the mill site into his breast pocket, gathered a few garden tools, canvas sacks, plus several jugs of ale and then left for the barn. Finally, he strapped all to his horse and set out for Eastham.

Later that day, as he approached the crest of the dividing line between Eastham and Harwich, he noticed a man kneeling on the ground with his back to him. Coming nearer, he saw a circular stone foundation radiated around the crouched, solitary figure. The man seemed to be carving on a stone with a chisel and hammer.

"Good day," Davis greeted the lone carver.

The man kept quiet. He looked up and only tipped his hat to acknowledge Davis.

"Has Mr. Baker been here today?" Davis asked, dismounting his horse.

"No, sir." The carver continued his repetitive tapping of his hammer.

"Do you know when he'll be making an appearance?"

"No, sir."

"I see." Davis surveyed the land surrounding the mill site. The location was certainly suited for a mill, with ample wind coming from all directions. It would be a good investment. He took his ale and sat on a boulder off to the side to rest. Davis couldn't stop thinking about the treasure that lay buried only a few miles to the east. He stood and approached the stonemason. "Seems like you're near finished," Davis commented as he admired the man's labors. There were eight stones set in a circle, each one marked with the directional letters of the Compass Rose. The mason was chiseling the final seraph on the letter N. Davis ultimately inquired. "When will the carpenter come to frame the floor joists?"

The man kept his head down, concentrating on his work. "He took sick and near died, so they called in another man."

Davis stepped closer. "Do you think the new carpenter will be coming soon?"

The carver kept his eyes downward. "Not for a week. Too busy."

An idea sparked in Davis's head. Now that he was part owner in this enterprise, he probably could utilize the site for his own needs.

After the stoic stonemason packed up his tools in a sack, he went on his way without a goodbye. Davis mounted his horse and left in the opposite direction, following the ridge down to the path that led to Enoch's Rock.

The sun began to set as Davis neared the mammoth boulder that rose above the horizon. Looking around, he saw no evidence that anyone had disturbed the site since he and Tobey had last visited. Untying the spade from the back of his saddle, he began to dig under the stones and into the dirt that hid the chest. He laughed to himself. No matter how many times he set his eyes on gold coins and jewels, his mouth would salivate in lust for its possession. Spit now dribbled from his lips and into the open wooden box. Davis scooped as much of the treasure that would fit into three sacks, leaving a small layer on the bottom for John Julian. Greed clouded his rationale, making him think Julian would not remember the bulk of the chest's contents. He buried the near empty chest once more, placing a layer of stones over the freshly dug dirt.

*   *   *

That night, Davis slept under the stars nestled against Enoch's Rock, with three lumpy bags snuggled close to his body, his arms wrapped tightly around them. He woke in the early morning, stiff and cramped, but with a smile on his face. Pleased with his new fortune, he paid no mind to his aches as he threw the filled sacks over the saddle, tying them secure. Davis decided to walk, noticing his horse was already weighed down with the treasure. As clouds gathered above his head, he picked up his stride, eager to retrace his steps back to the mill site.

Davis made his way around the cove and up the ridge, finally arriving at the excavation. He stepped into the circle foundation and scanned the area within. The west facing stone was carved with a W, traditionally marking the door opening to the mill. It enabled the miller to watch the weather outside and the millstones grinding inside, all the while taking note of where to turn the arms for the most advantageous use of the wind.

When his work was finished and the three bags buried, he scattered stones over the loose dirt, noting the three steps that lay between the door's opening and the gold. Too tired to continue that day, he lay against a rock until the morning. Spent from the open road and longing for the comforts of his home, he tried to sleep but stayed restless. Before the sun made its rise, he pushed his weary body up off the ground and headed towards Yarmouth.

As the hours passed across the dusty roads, he grew even more fatigued until he at last reached his house, where, once upstairs, he fell into a deep sleep. Davis lay there through the rest of the day and into the night. When he finally opened his eyes it was almost morning. Still dressed in traveling clothes, his aging body cried out to stay sleeping. Exhausted atop the bed's coverlet, he slowly sat up. Feeling the urgency to relieve himself and in need of some more ale, he grumbled and winced from back pains as he made his way down the stairs and into the kitchen. The house was cold. As he opened the back door, a rush of frigid air pummeled his body, forcing him to stand in the doorway and not step to the outside left, as usual, for his morning constitution. The steam from his piss billowed into the atmosphere; it fell upon the hard frozen ground and lay atop the surface in a shiny puddle.

As soon as he closed the door, he found the last of the ale and proceeded to climb back up the stairs, drinking as he moved upward on his quest to find clean garments for the day's errands. He found a small amount of water in the dry sink bowl and managed to wash his face and hands. After spotting a dress shirt on the floor, he remembered it was only worn once and decided it would do just fine.

Before traveling to seek the discipline of Hephzibah's father upon his rude daughter and the authorities regarding the Antiguan slave, Tobey, he needed to do one more thing: secure John Julian's map in a safe place. He first went into his study to contemplate a suitable hiding spot, then he sat at his desk, pulling drawers in and out, trying to think of where he could hide the map. Davis pushed some books to the side of his desk and slid Baker's folded fact sheet into his ledger book for later. Finally, glancing around the small room for his answer to secrecy, he spotted the glass-fronted cabinet against the opposite wall. Behind its doors, the blue teapot that Felicity seemed to find distasteful sat elegantly on the wooden shelf next to the matching tea bowls and saucers. A broad smile beamed across his face as he retrieved the teapot from its perch.

Taking pen in hand, he drew a tiny windmill near the site of the proposed mill on the map and added the number 3 for his steps, along with a W for the directional marker. Folding the map in quarters and then once more, he fit the vellum into the opening of the ceramic vessel and sealed the lid with wax and glue. After latching the door to the cabinet, he stood back to admire his cleverness.

Before he left the house, Davis pocketed his pistol and grabbed his winter waistcoat. Throwing it over his shoulder, he reached for the latch and gingerly stepped outside. With the first step of his heel against the urine-coated mud, his foot slid from under him, sending his body and limbs flailing into mid-air. Within seconds, the back of his skull came crashing down against the stone threshold. As blood oozed from the open gash, Davis's life force seeped in an erratic pattern that encircled his head. While he breathed his last labored breath, the tiny snowflakes that floated gently throughout the winter landscape stole any warmth that lingered in his body.

22

November 1722
BOSTON

AN EARLY MORNING RAIN turned into sleet and stung the faces of the few people that ventured out onto Beacon Hill. A messenger approached house #35 and checked his ledger to make sure he was at the correct address. When he was certain, he lifted the iron circle attached to the door to sound his presence. The massive entranceway opened and a young employee of the Gibbs family appeared.

The young woman shielded her eyes from the cold rain. "Yes?"

"I'm looking for Mrs. Felicity Davis." Water dripped from the corners of the gentlemen's hat.

"Come in. Wait here, please."

He followed her inside. As the door closed behind him, John, the head butler appeared in the foyer and whispered to the maid to step back. She moved in front of the stairway leading to the second floor.

John turned to the unexpected visitor. With a somber face he asked, "What is your business with Mrs. Davis?"

"I've come from Yarmouth, Massachusetts with, I'm afraid, bad news."

"And?"

The messenger opened his waistcoat and produced a letter with Felicity's name on its front.

At that moment, Bethia Gibbs came into sight at the top of the stairs. "John, what is the disturbance?" Before he could answer, she descended down the steps to see for herself. The old woman wagged her finger and chastised her servant, "We must have absolute quiet in this house."

"Forgive me, madam, but there is news from Yarmouth."

Mother Gibbs showed no emotion as she instructed him further, "Show the man to the study and then leave us."

The sparse room was decorated with shelves of books, two lone chairs and a small desk. The three pieces of furniture were situated in the middle of the room. Atop the desk's wooden surface rested a quill pen with inkbottle. Mother Gibbs sat down and motioned for the man to also sit. "Now, what is your news?"

"I have a letter for the wife of Thomas Davis from the constable of Yarmouth, Massachusetts."

Mother Gibbs sat taller in her chair. "That is my daughter. I'll deliver it to her." She stretched her arm out to accept the letter.

Hesitant to give the missive to anyone other than the intended recipient, the stranger held it firmly between his fingers.

Mother Gibbs motioned with her hand to pass it over, but he held it fast. She grew impatient and raised her voice, "Give me the letter!"

"Forgive me, madam, the law states that the letter is to be hand delivered to Mrs. Felicity Davis."

She sat back in her chair and tried to soften her approach by lowering her head and speaking in quieter tones. "I am Felicity's mother and, at this moment, she is in her eighth month with child and beginning her travail." She stood and walked over to the window. "You must excuse me, but I'm quite worried about her health and I am not of right mind." She took out her kerchief and dabbed at her dry eyes.

The courier hesitated, but growing more convinced of the dire situation, slid the letter across the desk.

Mother Gibbs, out of the corner of her eye, could see it was free of his grasp and smiled, knowing she had won. She returned to the desk, placed her fingers on top of the vellum and coyly smiled. "I will see that my daughter receives this message."

He rose and gave the woman a slight bow, then asked, "Shall I wait for her response?"

"No, that will not be necessary. I am sure whatever the news is, we will take care of it in due time."

"Yes, ma'am."

Mother Gibbs rang for John to show the stranger out. Once alone in the study, she opened the letter.

Mrs. Felicity Davis,

I regret to inform you of the accidental death of your husband, Thomas Davis, which occurred in Yarmouth, Massachusetts on the eighteenth day of October in the year of our Lord, one thousand seven hundred and twenty two. Please be advised that his house and possessions will be secured until I receive further word as to your wishes.

Sincerely,

Constable John Maker

Yarmouth Massachusetts

Mother Gibbs was stunned, but she felt only a fleeting wave of sadness fly in and then right out of her heart. This was good news! She began to contemplate her options, and all of them began with the words that Felicity was now a free woman. Her status in society would be secured by this new increase in wealth. She decided to withhold the information until after the birthing of her grandchild. No need to bring more stress to her daughter. She folded the letter and locked it into a small drawer in the desk, made a quick adjustment to her bodice, pulled a few strands of gray hair behind her ears and stood tall. Bethia Gibbs looked happy for the first time since her daughter had unfortunately married Thomas Davis.

*   *   *

Ten days passed. Felicity still lay in her bed, unaware of her husband's demise and struggling with false labor pains.

Today, she screamed in agony as the child finally began to crown its head. Servants rushed about the house. Mother Gibbs paced as the midwife and doctor tended to Felicity's rants and tirades.

"He will never touch me again!" she screamed. "I hate him for doing this to me!"

"Try to breathe," coaxed the midwife.

Felicity thrashed about ignoring any advice or consolation. As the child finally made its appearance, Bethia Gibbs thought her looking glass would shatter with the pitch of her daughter's shrieks. When the drama was finished, the doctor checked the child's hands, feet, and little body for unusual markings or faults; the infant boy seemed perfect.

Mother Gibbs retired to the study. She sat at her desk and placed an apprehensive hand on the small drawer that hid the letter about Thomas Davis. She decided that she would inform Felicity of the untimely death of her husband in a few days. Determined to bring closure to her daughter's marriage and reap the benefits of inheritance, Mother Gibbs anxiously awaited the appearance of the family lawyer.

*   *   *

YARMOUTH, MASSACHUSETTS

Davis's employee, Jacob, had recently brought to Constable Maker's attention some interesting information about the relationships between Tobey, Hephzibah McCleron, and Davis. Seeking closure with the Davis death, he visited the coroner, Dr. Able. He wanted to be sure that the death was truly an accident. After a lengthy discussion between Maker and the good doctor, in addition to several pints of ale, they both decided that there should be an inquiry. Maker thought it best to pay a visit to the McClerons, in Sandwich, and talk to the man and woman involved, specifically the Antiguan.

*   *   *

Late November was not the best time to travel on Cape Cod. Constable Maker admitted this fact to himself as he rode along the new road to Sandwich, tightening his scarf against the strong winds that stung his cheeks. The Constable of Sandwich had given him directions, and he watched eagerly for a metal pig turning round and round atop the peak of the McCleron house. He was relieved to turn onto the path that led to the twirling pig.

Hephzibah looked through the one window in the front parlor. "Father, someone is coming."

"Daughter, to the kitchen, I will handle the visitor," John McCleron looked outside. "Go and fetch Tobey."

"Yes, Father," Hephzibah said as she exited the rear of the house towards the barn.

The knock on the door was determined. McCleron opened the door with caution. "May I help you?" he asked the stranger.

"John McCleron?" Constable Maker inquired.

"Yes."

"Do you have a daughter by the name of Hephzibah?"

"Yes. Why would you be asking?"

The only words from the chilled man were, "Constable John Maker of Yarmouth. May I come in?"

McCleron opened the door wider and then shut it quickly against the cold air, giving the man only a few seconds to enter.

Maker shook his hat, stamped his mud-caked shoes and then got straight to the business at hand. "Are you aware of the death of Thomas Davis?"

"Yes, news of that kind travels fast."

"There has been new evidence brought to my attention that your daughter and a certain black Antiguan had disagreements with the deceased."

Hephzibah appeared with Tobey in tow. Constable Maker took note of them standing by the hearth and smiled. "I see that my investigation has just become easier."

* * *

Bread, chowder, and ale were laid out across the sideboard as Tobey, McCleron, and Constable Maker talked and watched Hephzibah scurry around the kitchen. She spoke very little, trying to listen as her father explained what had happened prior to her returning home.

Tobey contributed few, if any, details of his last encounter with Davis.

McCleron asked Tobey, "Do you have papers?"

Tobey withdrew his identification from his vest pocket. It verified that the Smith family of North Harwich owned him and that he was not a runaway.

The Constable offered his sympathies to the young woman as he scraped the last of the hot white liquid from his bowl with a piece of bread. "I'm sorry to hear of your unfortunate and shameful experience with your employer."

"Thank you, sir," Hephzibah nodded.

Tobey sat quietly, wondering if he should speak. Thinking it best to explain things for his own survival, he uttered, "There is more."

All eyes focused on him.

"I want to tell you the reason why I joined Davis on his trip from Antigua."

Hephzibah stood next to him and placed her hand on his shoulder. "No, Tobey."

He looked up to the woman whom he had come to love and said, "Yes, I must."

The two older men at the table grew attentive as Tobey relayed the story of John Julian's request for him to find the treasure that was buried on Cape Cod. Maker interrupted only once with, "Do you know the whereabouts of this so-called cache?"

"I do."

Tobey leaned across the table and begged, "You must understand, I only sought my freedom and a chance to live with dignity."

The men looked at each other.

Maker asked, "May I speak with you, Mr. McCleron, in private?"

Tobey placed an arm around Hephzibah's waist as they watched the two men leave the kitchen.

Maker spoke first, "You are aware that no one needs to know of this new information...I mean about the cache?"

"I see where your conversation is going," McCleron replied. "But our options for retrieval must be within the law."

Maker added, "As far as the treasure goes, finding it may be advantageous for both of us. And if the Antiguan only seeks his freedom, I probably could arrange a meeting with Mr. Smith concerning his situation."

"Mr. Smith is fond of my pigs for special occasion feasts. I might be able to broker a trade of some sort for Tobey's freedom," McCleron considered. "Since my sons have gone, he has become invaluable to me on the farm, and I know that my daughter would be agreeable to him remaining here. He is a good man."

Maker smiled and added, "Let me think on this. Tomorrow we could go to find the treasure and, if we're lucky, all may play out in our favor. Contact with Mr. Smith will have to wait."

The next morning, Hephzibah watched the three men mount horses to begin their journey to Enoch's Rock in Eastham. Confident that Tobey would prove himself trustworthy, she returned to the house and her chores for the day.

* * *

The men traveled from Sandwich to Yarmouth, where they stayed the night within Maker's house. All three, anxious about what they would find the next day, encountered a restless night. When dawn broke, they left for Eastham, eager to continue their quest. Remembering the tension of his last travel, Tobey felt good to ride a horse instead of walking. By late afternoon, the gray crest of Enoch's Rock rose above the trees before them. Quickening their pace, they arrived at its bottom within minutes.

"Show me where it is," Maker ordered.

Tobey dismounted his horse with confidence. He went straight to the small pile of stones that lay to the rear of the enormous rock and pointed. "Here's where I buried it."

Hephzibah's father grabbed a spade from the back of his saddle and instructed Tobey, "Go and get yours and give me some help."

As the two men pushed aside the stones and dug into the dirt, their tools did not need to plunge very deep. The wood and leather bound chest showed through the loose soil within a few shovelfuls.

Once the chest was uncovered, Maker knelt on the stones and examined it with slow and determined actions. In an investigative manner, he scraped away the caked dirt around its edges, then brushed his hands of the loose soil, wiped them on his pants, and reached for the exposed latch. McCleron and Tobey leaned in. The lid opened.

Tobey gasped, "I don't understand." He knelt down next to Maker. His hands dove into the dark box searching for the gold coins that he had seen not more than a month ago. "Where are they?"

"What are you saying?" Maker asked. "There doesn't seem to be much of a treasure in here."

"Where's the rest?" Tobey yelled out. He sat back on his haunches, shaking his head in disbelief.

McCleron knelt to the other side of the constable. "Let me see." He put his hand into the dark chest. "There are coins at the bottom but not many."

Tobey stretched his hand down into the chest again. His forehead grew wet with perspiration and he felt himself spin into a panic. "It must be here! I saw it with my own eyes." He panted under his breath, "It can't be. It can't be."

The constable pushed himself upright, taking a position a few steps back. McCleron also stood and both men watched the young Antiguan frantically swirling his hand inside the near empty chest, banging his knuckles against the old wood.

"Mr. McCleron, it seems that we have a bit of a wild-goose chase on our hands." The constable stroked his chin trying to decide what to do next.

McCleron went over to Tobey and, with a sympathetic touch, tried to hold the black man's hands still. His voice was gentle. "Stop! You need to stop." He pulled back on Tobey's shoulders, forcing him upright. McCleron placed the handle of a spade in Tobey's palm and coaxed, "Here now, let's dig it out together."

When the chest was pulled from its secret grave, the gold coins were scooped out, filling only a small leather pouch. Tobey sat to the side and hung his head between his knees. Bewildered at the near empty chest, he shook his head back and forth in skepticism. "No one knew of the chest, it was just me, Davis, and Mr. Julian. I don't understand."

McCleron spoke up in Tobey's defense, "I can attest to the fact that this young man has been on my property since he and Hephzibah arrived weeks ago. He would not have had the resources nor the time to return here." He walked over to Tobey and placed his hand on the young man's shoulder. "Besides, why would he lead us to it, if only to prove his innocence? Freedom seems to be the utmost in his mind, not treasure. He's a man to be trusted."

Maker straightened himself and spoke with authority, "Let's finish here. No need to take the chest with us. Leave it."

He dropped the pouch into one of his saddlebags and motioned to the other men. "I know of a tavern not far from this place. We'll stay the night there and then home to Yarmouth to sort out the situation tomorrow."

McCleron and the Constable rode together with Tobey in the rear, out of earshot of the men talking. "Now what of Tobey?" McCleron asked.

There was no response from Maker.

After a short time, McCleron spoke again. "I know that the Smiths have just been delivered of a new child. Hephzibah aided in the birth and they have named her Lydia. They may be in for a celebration and interested in my meat."

Constable Maker glanced over his shoulder at Tobey. "My job is done here. You may contact the Smiths and arrange for his freedom."

23

Present Day
CAPE COD

THOMAS DAVIS CHANDLER tapped his fingers across the computer's keyboard, tracking an order from a game supplier. As he waited for the information to come up on the screen, he glanced at the business card that lay to his right: Nancy Caldwell, Gallery Director-Antiquities.

The word 'antiquities' caught his attention. He chose a new window and typed in her name. Up popped 50,000 entries, and #1 listed a Nancy Caldwell along with a caption in bold type, *'Brewster couple uncovers treasure'.*

He scrolled down the list of hits. Her name was highlighted along with other interesting words: Sam Bellamy, pirate ship, *Whydah*, gold, jewelry and untold riches. On the second page, at the bottom, he saw his own name. His eyes fixated on the bold letters. "What the hell?" A shot of adrenaline rose through his body. "Why is my name linked to pirates and treasure?"

Tommy called out to his buddy in the backroom. "Hey Silas, come on up front for a while, I gotta go home. I got some business with Sheila. I'll be back in a few. Keep your eye on things...okay?"

Driving the back roads to the house he grew up in, Tommy recalled hearing people whispering at his dad's funeral...'the last of the Thomas Davis lineage'...'too bad he's the last one.' Tommy mulled the words over in his head as he turned onto the neighborhood street. He was an only child and his father had no siblings, so he would inherit anything valuable. A smile curled across his face as he thought of what might lay ahead for him.

*   *   *

Silas Maroni played his last quarter. An old pinball machine known as the Black Knight clicked, binged, and flashed as he racked up points. When the last ball rolled down to the silver paddle, Silas spread his legs apart, determined to finish his game with a flourish. In a matter of minutes it was over. He watched the points tally to 850,000 across the multi-lit backdrop. He was now the top player at the gaming store. Fist pumping his hand in the air, he regained a normal stance then yelled, "Yeah!"

As he walked towards the front area of the store, all the chains that hung from his black baggy pants made a clanking noise. He eventually settled himself behind the counter to watch some TV.

*   *   *

Tommy kept the music turned up in his car as loud as the speakers would handle. He knew Sheila hated it and any chance to irritate her was good for him. It gave him some control over their relationship. He stayed in the car a little longer with the radio blaring.

Sheila Jenkins was Tommy's stepmother. He'd been comfortable enough to hang around at his dad's house but, after his father died, the new wife was meaner than ever to him. Unfortunately, she continued to live in the family house and his visits became fewer and fewer.

She shrieked from the kitchen as he entered the small ranch house, "How many times have I told you to keep your music down?"

"Yeah, I heard you," he said slamming the door behind him.

"What do you want?" she asked without looking up from her crossword puzzle.

He ignored the question, grabbed a beer out of the refrigerator and sat across from her at the kitchen table.

After several seconds, she lowered the newspaper a few inches, and in a sarcastic twang asked, "Aren't you supposed to be working at your little game store?"

He continued his sullen stare at her.

She went back to the puzzle. Finally, she took her cigarette out of her mouth and yelled at him, "What? What do you want?'

"What do you know about my family?"

"Not much." She leaned back in her chair.

"What about my Dad's grandparents or great grandparents?"

Sheila stood up, poured a cup of coffee and turned to face him. "Well, look at you. Little Tommy has found some adult words and he's actually using them in a conversation."

He took a drink then banged the bottle on the table. "Look, I just wanna know about the history of my family."

She sat down again and sipped her coffee. "All right, I'll tell you what I know, which isn't much."

Tommy leaned over the table.

"Remember the boxes of stuff that I gave you after the funeral?"

"Yeah, the old dishes and crap."

"Your father said that whatever was in them belonged only to you." She grew quiet.

"Is that it?"

"Yup, that's all I know."

"Shit."

Sheila went back to her crossword.

Tommy slapped his hand on the table, stood up and leaned his back against the sink.

Without looking up, Sheila continued, "If you're so curious, go up in the attic and look for yourself. Don't bother me with it."

* * *

Bored, Silas decided to busy himself with the computer. Sitting on a high stool, he wiggled the mouse to wake up the screen and took out a pocketknife to clean his fingernails while he waited. Whatever Tommy had discovered earlier was now in front of Silas's eyes and the same words that caught Tommy's attention piqued Silas's curiosity.

He began to move one leg in a nervous bounce as he read deeper and searched more pages. Silas ran his fingers through his curly red hair and scratched at his freckled cheek, trying to figure out how he could benefit from this information. He highlighted Nancy Caldwell's full name in the search box and added the word 'address'. Two hits came up from the Find People site. One Nancy Caldwell was from California and one was from Brewster, Massachusetts. He copied her address down and stuffed it in his pocket.

24

Present Day
ANTIGUA

THE CARIBBEAN AIR was steamy against the railing of the open veranda as the impatient caller waited for the voice on the other end to answer. He'd ordered a cold beer and could see it resting on the bar just under the palm-covered eve. He could almost taste its cool liquid. An elderly but distinguished voice answered, "Damien residence."

"Mr. Damien, please." Sweat dripped from the caller's forehead to the cell phone.

"Whom may I ask is calling?"

"I'm calling from Antigua. He'll talk to me."

"Of course, sir. Please hold on."

He couldn't stand it anymore; he hurried in under the shade and quickly grabbed the chilled bottle from the counter, then walked back outside.

A terse, accented voice asked, "Yes?"

"Mr. Damien, I've some good news for you. I have the earrings."

"Well, that is good news. What about the necklace?"

The sweaty caller hesitated. "Not yet." He wiped his brow. "I'm afraid I'm going to have to follow it to Cape Cod."

"If you must." An audible sigh could be heard.

"It's almost within my grasp. I'll have it for you soon, sir."

"I hope you will. We wouldn't want anything to go wrong, would we?" Mr. Damien sounded threatening.

"No, sir."

"I'm not paying you a finder's fee of three million dollars to find only two priceless items. I want all of them. I expect my employees to complete their assignments."

The cell phone clicked off, a sea breeze blew, and the nervous caller ordered another beer.

*   *   *

Across a continent, Mr. Damien took his afternoon tea in the solarium. He admired the blue flowers on his antique teacup, beautiful against the green of the delicate ferns, English ivy, and oriental lilies that surrounded him.

25

1746
BOSTON

"IF YOU CHOOSE to live in that house and defy me, you are dead to me," Felicity Davis screamed at her 24-year-old only son as he turned his back on her. In one last attempt to persuade him to stay, she changed her tone and begged, "Ezekiel, please don't leave me! I'm your mother!"

The door slammed shut and he was gone.

Ezekiel Davis found himself suffocating under his mother's roof. He could not put up with her whiney and dominating personality anymore. Now a successful lawyer, he was ever grateful for his education, but still felt compelled to leave and start his own life, with his own rules. Today he ventured out on a journey to claim his deceased father's house. Willed to him at birth, it had sat empty and abandoned for 24 years in the town of Yarmouth on Cape Cod.

Soon after boarding the ship on his first voyage unattended, he was confident that he would be fine. It would be a short sail, landing by late afternoon. The young man eagerly reached for the railing with anticipated excitement of being on his own. But his body cringed as thoughts of freedom and adventure collided with words from his dead grandmother: "You are just like your father, a boorish oaf." Ezekiel shook his head, trying to free his mind of these thoughts, reminding himself that he was a good person; he wasn't anything like his father. He never even knew him. The muscles in his neck tightened once more recalling his mother's threats as a child. "Behave yourself or your inheritance will amount to nothing." Ezekiel quickly regained his composure. He was determined to push on, be independent and begin a new chapter in his life. And what about his father? He was curious and wanted answers.

As the boat made its docking at Barnstable Harbor, Ezekiel stretched his body up and craned his neck to find James Twinning, his friend from Yale College. James knew of the location of the old Davis house and offered his assistance in guiding his friend around the small community of Yarmouth. When he caught sight of James, he bounded down the plank and shouted, "How goes it?" He shook his friend's hand as if he was pumping water from a well.

James returned the greeting with a one handed embrace and a pat on the back. "Good to see you, Ezekiel." With a wave of his hand, he said, "Come! Mother is waiting with dinner and ale." After climbing into the cart that would take them to the Twinning residence, James added, "First thing in the morning, you shall see your inheritance."

And once again, the young man from Boston enjoyed the sweet taste of freedom.

*   *   *

The next morning, the sun shone into the second floor bedroom where Ezekiel lay dreaming. The smell of spicy smoked meat woke him. He sat up in bed, happy and excited. After slipping on his socks, shoes, and breeches, he dashed down the steep stairs, ready for an adventure.

"Morning, Mrs. Twinning!"

"Morning, Ezekiel, I take it you slept well?"

Fastening the last button on his pants, he answered, "Yes, Ma'am!"

"James is already in the barn, tending to your rides."

He stood by the hearth waiting politely to be invited to partake of the delicious-looking biscuits and meat.

Mrs. Twinning gave a little laugh and said, "Go on, take what you like and get yourself out to the barn. You have a busy day ahead of you."

"Thank you, ma'am." He grabbed his breakfast and exited the back door.

Within an hour, the two friends found themselves on the winding highway laughing about their past school adventures. Soon the top of two chimneys on the bayside could be seen as they rounded a bend.

"We're almost there," said James and he flicked the reins of his horse to speed up. Ezekiel followed suit.

Brambles covered the stonewall that flowed across the edges of the property, separating it from the road. Thickets and wild bayberry bushes hindered their passage to the house, but the two men continued on undiscouraged. Ezekiel was first to approach the entrance to the old Davis estate. He was cautious, careful to sidestep a hole in the raised wooden landing of the threshold. The door was unlocked. He stepped in. There was little furniture throughout the house. The few pieces that were scattered about one room sat ghostlike in the dusty sunbeams that filtered through the dirty windows.

James smiled, "I thought it would be much worse."

Ezekiel covered his nose. "How could this have happened? It seems so depressing."

"Well, it's been abandoned for nigh twenty some years." James wandered into an adjacent room.

"Yes, but I thought...." Ezekiel's eyes caught site of a tall cabinet against the far wall, its filthy covering hung to one side. He yanked at the faded material. As it fluttered to the floor in a cloud of dust, a blue and white teapot and other small pieces of matching china revealed themselves behind the old glass. Surprised at the sight of these elegant pieces among such filth, he walked closer to the glassed enclosure to examine them. "James, come look.

His curious friend crossed the room and joined him. He shook his head. "I wonder what else is hiding in this wretched place?"

Behind them was a large rectangular shape with a rounded surface. James grabbed at its ashen cover and revealed a roll top desk. Ezekiel pushed past him and tried to open the drawers and topside but to no avail. The desk was locked tight with no key in sight. Ezekiel looked for something to pry it open. Also seeking a tool, James turned and walked past the main stairway and into the kitchen. Ezekiel ran his hands over the ridges of the top and then inspected its sides. He walked around its perimeter.

James called out from the rear of the house, "I found something," and returned with a poker in hand.

"That will do," Ezekiel said and took hold of the iron rod. "Could this hold any answers about my father?"

The desk opened with only a slight nudge from the iron wedge. Ezekiel dropped the poker on the floor, brushed his hands together, and slowly lifted the accordion shaped cover. Inside was a leather book, along with an inkwell and quill pen. He carefully picked the book up; its pages yellowed but not brittle.

"Is there anything written?" asked his friend.

"It seems to be a ledger for transactions, compiling everyday household activities."

James walked around the desk to have a look.

Ezekiel pointed to one entry and read it aloud. "September 5, 1721...10 lbs of flour...1 shilling."

Leafing through the rest of the journal, he scanned the pages for anything that would give him clues about his father and what kind of man he might have been.

Both men were so intent in their study of the ledger's contents that they never heard the swish of a skirt enter the open door behind them.

"Greetings," said a soft voice.

They turned together to see a beautiful young woman standing just inside the foyer.

James flew to her side. "Lydia! What are you doing here?"

"James Twinning, I might ask you the same question." She took his hand in a friendly clasp.

"Lydia Smith, I want you to meet a good friend of mine from school. He happens to be the proud owner of this dilapidated house."

Ezekiel closed the book and tossed it back into the desk, unaware of dislodging a folded piece of vellum from the tight hold of the pages. It stuck out from the bottom corner of the ledger. He closed the desktop and focused his attention on the lovely Lydia.

Walking over to her, he politely extended his hand, bowed in respect and introduced himself. "Ezekiel Davis, miss."

Lydia returned a curtsy. "Why, it is a pleasure, Mr. Davis." With twinkling eyes and a delicate smile, she asked, "Now tell me, what are you two doing here?"

James piped up, "My good friend plans on living here. After all, it's his family's house. We're all going to be neighbors."

"You jest, surely? This place does not seem habitable." She took her handkerchief and covered her nose.

"You may be surprised at what I can accomplish, once I put my mind to an idea," Ezekiel said as he glanced around at the empty rooms surrounding them.

James sat on the bottom step of the center stairway. "Lydia, you never answered my question. What are you doing here?"

"I saw your horses and my curiosity got the better of me. I've always wondered about this old house and who had lived here. My brother Isaac and I would explore this old place whenever he was home from the plantation." She looked straight at Ezekiel. "Of course, now I am privy to that very information."

Embarrassed at her question for not knowing the 'what and why' of his past, Ezekiel quickly changed the subject. "Some other time, Miss Smith. I must beg your leave; I have so many things to do before the week is finished."

He signaled James with his eyes that it was time for her to go.

"Oh, yes." James jumped up and headed toward their surprise guest. "Lydia." He held her elbow and began to usher the young woman out of the door, "I'm sure we'll make your acquaintance again. I'll see to that. Tell your parents I wish them well."

*   *   *

Ezekiel returned to his father's house alone the next day. Rain fell from the edges of its cedar roof like waterfalls as he ran to the safety of the open porch. He pushed in the heavy door to wait for the man who Constable Maker had retained to watch over the Davis house after the death of his father. From within his knapsack, he withdrew several candles and positioned them around the room. They cast long flickering shadows against the faded walls from the dark of the rainstorm.

His enthusiasm was not dampened by the gloominess that surrounded him. He smiled, thinking of the tasks that were ahead of him. He longed for doing good, solid work with his hands, far from the elitist society of Boston. As rain pelted the windows across the front of the house, his interest turned to the roll top desk. He was anxious to continue his search for any information concerning the father he never knew.

The rain slowed for a short time and a soft knock interrupted his scanning of the old ledger. An elderly black man appeared in the doorway. "Mister Davis?"

Ezekiel stepped towards the open door. "Yes."

"The constable said you wanted to meet with me."

"Come in. Come in." The new owner gestured for him to come in.

Brown, gnarled fingers took a strong hold around the young man's hand. "My name is Tobey, sir."

"Good to meet you, Tobey." He stood tall and with a broad smile across his face, entreated the old man, "Start from the beginning. Tell me everything about this wonderful house that will soon be my home."

Tobey took a deep breath and chose his words carefully, then motioned for Ezekiel to follow him. Ezekiel trailed Tobey up the stairs to the third floor, where Hephzibah had once slept and lived as housekeeper to the Davis household. Tobey gave what information Hephzibah had related to him and kept his personal feelings hidden. He talked about the structure of the house and the activities that had occurred in each room.

When they reached the study, back on the main floor, the rain finally stopped. The sun began its set in the west and cast an orange glow across the horizon and through the windows. The old man looked tired in the fading light. Ezekiel well understood the strain of travelling. He knew that Tobey had come from the western edge of Yarmouth, near Sandwich, to the Davis house, a good three-hour ride. Tobey stretched his arms up and rubbed his head and then his eyes. "Would it be to your liking if I sleep here till the morning?"

Ezekiel was beginning to grow fond of this gentle man and smiled. "Of course, I intend to do the same thing." Both eager to retire for the night, they started towards the door to retrieve their supplies that were tied to their mounts.

Tobey asked, "Shall I bed the horses down in the barn, sir?"

"Yes, let me help you." Outside, they walked together around the house to the back. "So you said that you slept in the barn when you first came here?"

"That I did."

"I hope they fed you well?"

"Yes, they did. That's how I met my Hephzibah. She worked for Mister Davis, your father. She's a fine cook." He opened the barn door, turned to Ezekiel and with a wink said, "Always had an eye for her and still do."

As night darkened the sky, the two men settled into their bedding. Tobey lay there, remembering the day he escaped from the Davis house with Hephzibah. Best keep those thoughts to himself, he decided; no need to stir up any resentment or anger. Mister Ezekiel seems like such a nice young man, not anything like his father.

The next day, Tobey left for home by early morning. It had been a good meeting between him and the young Davis. He could hardly wait to tell Hephzibah the good news. As he came close to the house, he rounded a bend in the road and could see her taking down clothes from the outside line. How he loved that woman.

Hephzibah saw her partner riding along the pathway out of the corner of her eye. She offered a welcoming wave but quickly returned to her laundry. The rain had left most of the clothes damp.

Once Tobey had settled his horse in the barn, he approached Hephzibah. Happy to be home, Toby moved nearer to her and pecked her on the cheek. "Always working so hard."

She returned a quick smile and continued checking the shifts and skirts for dryness.

"What's to eat?" Tobey asked.

"There's a stew simmering. You go on in, and I'll be there soon."

"Sounds delicious." He started for the door and then turned around. "I have something important to tell you."

Hephzibah stopped. "What is it?"

"Let's eat first. I'm sure you'll be pleased."

Eager to hear his news, she looked back to the rope that held the moist clothes then shook her head in disgust at having to prolong her chores. Most of the laundry will need to hang another day. After finding only a few more dry pieces for her basket, she followed Tobey into the house.

The hearty smell of savory meat and vegetables wafted throughout the kitchen. Before the bowls were placed on the table, Hephzibah asked again, "What's your news?"

"Well, my dear, our future is secure."

Hephzibah slowly sat down.

Tobey continued, "Young Mister Davis has asked if we would be interested in coming to work for him. Me around the house and you where you reign supreme…by the hearth."

She began to cry.

Tobey held her hand. "I hope those tears are for joy and not sadness?"

Hephzibah looked at him. "These past months I've been so worried about what was going to happen to us."

"I understand. I've been bothered by it too," Tobey said.

"I thought my brothers would let us live here after father's death." She got up to spoon the stew into their bowls. "And now they want to sell. I can't blame them." She sat once more at the table.

"I agree," Tobey added. "One can't forget that they were kind enough to let us stay for a while at least." He held both of her hands.

"I never thought father would do this to me, leaving me only the linens, bedding, and household items, as is the custom." Hephzibah shook her head. "It's a terrible practice in my eyes and a misfortune for any faithful daughter. Inevitably she is left with no place to put her cherished items."

Tobey leaned closer over the table. "We'll be fine." He touched her cheek. "These many years that we've been together have been such a time of love for me. We may not be sanctioned by a reverend but we're blessed with each other." He sat back against his chair, "I'm grateful for that," then looked eagerly at his bowl of stew. "Mister Davis has given us a month to prepare."

Hephzibah's shoulders relaxed as she pulled her plate closer and began to eat.

Tobey scooped up a tasty bite. "You need not worry. Mister Ezekiel is a gentle man, in the true sense of those words."

A smile of relief slowly grew across her face.

* * *

1749 - Three Years Later
YARMOUTH, MASSACHUSETTS

Lydia Smith checked the final preparations for her wedding day. She paused to admire a lovely silver tureen from her father. Hephzibah and Tobey had followed her instructions perfectly. Tomorrow was going to be the happiest day of her young life.

Ezekiel came into the front parlor where their wedding gifts were on display. "My darling, you're so beautiful."

"Thank you, my future husband." She threw her arms around his neck and kissed him.

"It was a lucky day when you wandered into my life, three years ago," he said and kissed her in return. "Soon we'll be together as one. I can hardly wait to hear the laughter and patter of little feet echoing through this wonderful old house. I love you."

Behind them, the delicate blue and white teapot, nestled on a shelf within the old glass cabinet, seemed to look upon them with approval. The leather books from Ezekiel's father sat next to the beautiful matching china pieces. They had become symbols of his past. It was all that was left of Thomas Davis.

As the two lovers held each other, Lydia and Ezekiel savored this special moment of complete happiness. Tomorrow would be a new beginning for both of them.

26

Present Day
CAPE COD

TOMMY PUT HIS BEER on the Formica countertop. The yellow speckles of the kitchen counter's surface matched the crumbs and dried food stuck to a stack of dirty dishes. He walked down the hallway past his old bedroom and reached for a chain hanging from the ceiling. A set of steps lowered from above his head. He grabbed the ladder's roped railing and climbed up. Too tall for the small opening, he ducked his head and stepped onto the plywood flooring that covered the open spaces between the rafters. Light from a tiny window vent lit his way as he swatted at cobwebs strung across the eaves above his head. A single light bulb hung from the center of the room. He pulled the chain that dangled under it and saw a cardboard box in the corner.

The last time he was in this attic, he'd found the china dishes that he took to the antique store. They were the only things that had looked valuable to him at the time, unlike the box that he was now staring at, filled with rags. Tommy bent over and lifted the yellowed material; and underneath he found two old books. He held the larger one closer to the light. Its crackled leather had separated itself from the binding. Tommy began rifling through the brittle pages for anything that could tell him about his past, at least more than he knew now. To his disillusionment, there were only lists upon lists of household purchases from the Thomas Davis household of Yarmouth, Massachusetts 1720-1722.

Disappointed, he tossed the book on the dusty flooring. A folded piece of paper fell out near his left foot. He picked it up and tried to open it but the fragile vellum began to crumble in his hands. Pulling out his knife, he carefully wedged it between the edges. When the paper finally separated, it broke into four pieces. He laid them atop the old ledger on the floor, matching words into sentences. Across the top, he read the heading out loud, "Davis Baker Mill."

The words below looked like they were directions: "*Follow the new road to the river of Namskaket. Travel to the southern ridge of where Harwich meets Eastham. The property of Baker and Sons will be marked with a stake ten yards from the corner of the oak. Follow the Magnetic North, parallel with the Cove's inlet.*"

Tommy scratched his head. "Harwich meets Eastham? I don't understand. Where's Orleans?"

He picked up the smaller book, which looked like a Bible. It had survived in much better condition. Inside, on the second page, a list of names was written in beautiful cursive.

Thomas Davis, Felicity Gibbs, m. 1721
Ezekiel, b.1722
Ezekiel Davis, Lydia Smith, m. 1749
Ezekiel, b. 1751
Lydia, b. 1752
Thomas, b. 1754 (stillborn)
Mary, b. 1756
Thomas, b. 1758
John, b. 1760

He scanned three pages of names and dates. The last entry was written in his grandfather's hand. It was his father's name and birth date: Charles Davis, b. 1959.

Tommy closed the Bible; his hand resting on the old leather. Under his breath, he mumbled, "Shit! What does this have to do with pirates and treasure?"

27

Present Day
CAPE COD

I OPENED the gallery door to the house. Danny was standing straight as a soldier. "Uh oh, what happened?" I asked.

I heard Martha close the dryer door and hurry into the living room. Danny was staring, head down, at a dark spot on the carpet.

"I'm sorry," he said with tears in his eyes.

"Don't worry, I'll be right back," Martha assured him and went to retrieve an old towel.

He stayed still, with his eyes glued to the carpet and the big red stain.

I walked a little closer to him. "Did you do that, Danny?"

He remained quiet.

"Danny?"

Just as I was about to begin a tirade about bringing drinks into the living room, Martha returned and hustled over to the spot. She threw a towel on top of it and told him, "Start dancing!"

Danny looked puzzled and so did I.

"Here, let me show you." Martha stepped on the towel and began to move her feet across it, pressing them into the carpet to absorb the liquid that slowly seeped deeper into the woven threads. Danny watched her body twist and turn; her large breasts jiggling back and forth.

She looked up and met his eyes, "Come on, you try it."

A smile grew across his face as he stepped onto the cloth dance floor. He went into a wild jig, kicking his feet up into the air. Martha went to retrieve a bottle of carpet cleaner. I could hear her laughing all the way to the laundry room. When she returned, she rubbed the clear liquid into the soiled carpet, trying to get it clean.

"Don't be too hard on the boy. It was an accident, Nancy. I think we got it just in time."

I looked directly at Danny. "Okay, but you need to take your drinks in the kitchen from now on." I re-stated the rules of the house and asked one more time, "Understand?"

He nodded.

I hurried over to the foyer bench, scooped up the teapot wrapped in the quilt and made my way back to Paul's studio to show him my new treasure.

*   *   *

"Here it is." I placed it on his drawing table and slowly unwrapped it. The pottery shard was placed next to it. "What do you think?" I stepped away so he could get a better look.

"Well, you're right, they do match each other," Paul agreed.

I watched him pick up the teapot and turn it over to see if there was any writing on the bottom. The lid dropped away and fell softly on top of the quilt.

"Oh my God! How did you do that?" I was stunned.

"I just turned it over," Paul said. "I didn't do anything."

I pushed him aside. "Let me see."

I replaced the lid atop the teapot then took it off again. I couldn't believe that it was loose. It had been stuck back at the antique store. I turned it upside down once more and noticed the edge of something peeking out of its opening.

"Wait a minute," I said and shook the teapot. I pushed my fingertips into the opening and began to twirl my fingers around inside until I was able to feel whatever was in there. Determined to get it out, I squeezed my hand in a little more. Finally grabbing hold of it and with a slow pull, I eased it out. It fell on top of the quilt next to the small lid.

"What is it?" Paul asked.

"Looks like some kind of folded paper." My heart was racing.

"Open it up."

"I'm too nervous."

"If you don't, I will," Paul gently coaxed.

"Okay...okay, give me a second." I wiped my hands on my jeans, picked up the delicate paper, unfolded it, and carefully laid it flat. There was a map drawn on it, with writing at the bottom. "How could this be? It looks just like the one that fell out of the Julian's Bible on Antigua."

Paul leaned in to me. "Let me see that." After a few seconds of examining the parchment he pointed to its lower right hand corner. "What's written down here?" We both looked closer.

I read, "Davis Baker Mill."

He added, "This fancy script underneath it looks like a description of a location,"

I pushed against Paul's shoulder. "Wait a minute, there's something else that's different here."

"What do you mean?"

"See this?" My fingers hovered above a small mark resembling an x over a small square and the number 3 with a W under it. "I don't remember seeing these markings on the other map."

He bent his head nearer to see it. "Looks like a little drawing of a windmill...maybe it's the Davis Baker Mill?"

"What do you make of the number 3 and the letter W?" I had an idea. "I'll be right back."

I rushed out of the studio and back into the house. The gallery door slammed shut behind me. Martha was in the kitchen peeling potatoes for the night's dinner. Danny, busy with coloring, listened to the sounds of the TV blaring the antics of Sesame Street. As I ran past them in the kitchen, I hesitated only for a second to wave at Danny. Once out of sight, I continued a fast pace up the stairs to the bedroom closet to retrieve the other map. Then I heard him downstairs scramble off his chair to see what was going on and run over to the bottom of the stairway. What a little monkey he is, I thought; he's always so curious and usually gets himself into trouble. With the map in hand, I traveled back down the steps where Danny was waiting for me. "Honey, I gotta go talk with Daddy. Stay with Martha."

I clutched the copy of the old map from Antigua as Danny began to quickly follow behind me. I turned around and firmly repeated, "Stay with Martha. You can't come with Mommy right now." I managed to escape through the gallery door by myself.

28

Present Day - Mid-November
CAPE COD

FINDING ANOTHER MAP was intriguing. Over the next weeks, I studied both of them every chance I could. They were of the Cape and the same hand had definitely drawn them. The only significant difference was the name, Davis Baker Mill, and the added directions to the site.

It was becoming increasingly difficult for me to keep my mind on being a good mom. According to the calendar, the holidays were fast approaching and the kids had so many parties, concerts, and programs to attend. I usually loved it all, including the decorations, but, at this moment, all I wanted was to solve a mystery. I sat at the dining room table adding to my list of things to do when my cell rang. It was Brian.

"Hi, Mom. Just a quick call to tell you that Nick is definitely coming to the Cape, but I'm afraid I won't be coming home yet. I just need a little while longer here."

I could feel a sadness begin to slowly rise up inside of me. "I understand," I said. Don't start to cry, I thought, no need to make him feel guilty. I swallowed hard. "It'll be good to finish up your project and get everything settled. Then you can leave on good terms."

"Gotta go. Love you and tell everyone I love them, too."

I sat there for a minute staring out of the window as my eyes started to moisten. Lately, my thoughts had been with the map, the news about the stolen earrings, and the fact that Nick might be coming for Thanksgiving. Brian's news had hit a nerve; I was upset. I missed him. The holidays were so special to me. I wanted him home with the family. Then I slowly reasoned that he did warn me about his not coming home. Besides, he'd be proud if we could give his buddy a warm New England welcome. I felt a little better.

I grabbed a tissue and made my way towards the studio to tell Paul that Brian wasn't coming home. It might even be nice to have Nick here with us, I rationalized, as he seemed like an okay guy, and he was so interested in what I had discovered. Brian would be home before we knew it.

* * *

Within the hour, I headed out to the grocery store. As I drove I thought it would be fun, before shopping, to stop at the library in Orleans to see if they had any old maps of the Lower Cape that I could research.

The library had burned to the ground around 1960, so I wasn't sure how far back their records went. The land where Orleans is now located was called the South Parish of Eastham in the 1700s. I promised myself that if no new information was found today, Eastham's library would be my next visit.

I parked opposite the entrance, locked the car, and walked toward its glass doors. As I entered the building, I noticed in the door's reflection an old maroon Toyota slow down behind my van. I could see there were no available spaces next to me so I continued to watch the car. It eventually backed into a space over to the side but close enough to see who came and went from the library.

Standing in the foyer, I pretended to browse some books that were for sale while I watched the car. I noticed trails of smoke coming from the half-open window. The driver sat very still. He tossed a cigarette butt out, reached into his black leather coat for another smoke, and then leaned back to continue his stare at the library doors. He almost looked as if he was watching me. Okay, stop it, I thought. I'm getting paranoid. Paul thinks I'm nuts because watching people is so fascinating to me. I'm always wondering what they're doing, or where they're going. I quickly realized that my curious nature was getting the best of me and reminded myself of why I was at the library in the first place.

Perhaps the guy was merely noticing our gallery's signage on the van's back window. Nothing to worry about, I decided.

One thing I was certain of, as I entered the main room of the library, was finding the big-framed map on the second floor. I wasn't sure if it depicted the Lower Cape but, when I saw it hanging in a dimly lit hallway, my phone's flashlight revealed that it was indeed of the Lower Cape. A grand piece of art, it was intricately drawn with names, dates, and places. I located Doane Rock, or something that looked like it. Curiously, it was labeled Enoch's Rock, but I knew it was right because the word Doane was written next to it as landowner.

My interest quickly turned to frustration as the flashlight illuminated the date of the map, 1856, later than what I wanted to see. I went back down the stairs in search of the reference desk and hopefully some answers.

"Excuse me. Do you have any old Cape Cod maps of the 1700s?" I asked the librarian.

Peering over her half glasses she said, "Let me see." And with that she swiveled her chair around to open a low file cabinet behind her and pulled out an old brown envelope. "We only have a few hand drawn maps from that time period."

I stepped closer as the woman rifled through the papers within the faded folder. One map was dated 1650, too early for what I was looking for, and the others were of the wrong locations.

I spoke up, wanting to show her that I also knew some facts. "I know Orleans was not incorporated until 1797, even though they wanted to be separate from Eastham in 1717. On many maps, the name of Orleans is not listed."

She smiled then turned away from me. "That's correct."

She must have felt I didn't need her help after my spouting information so I politely said, "Thank you very much for your time. Where are your historical books about Cape Cod?"

The librarian pointed to four stacks of books. "Some are reference and others can be circulated." She busied herself in another drawer at her desk.

"Thanks again."

Pulling down an old, worn black book I noted that the date of publication was 1919, not the right date but good for comparing. I turned to find a table to scan the book for any images of maps and walked right into a tall young man.

"Excuse me," I said and returned to the open book in hand. Then I stopped for a second to get a better look at who I had bumped into. I immediately recognized him to be Tommy D from the gaming store. I went back to my research but couldn't concentrate. When I'd met him earlier in the month, he didn't impress me as a frequent patron of libraries. Throwing caution to the wind, I walked over to him. "Pardon me, but aren't you Tommy D Chandler?"

"Yeah."

"I don't know if you remember me, but I stopped into your store a while back and asked you about the estate china that you had recently sold."

"Oh yeah. I remember."

"Have you found any other pieces?"

"No."

"Oh, I was wondering. Are you finding anything interesting here today?"

"Not yet."

"Well, it was nice seeing you."

Feeling my search was over for today, I decided to go home. I left Tommy D browsing the old books. The maroon Toyota was still parked in the parking lot with its driver still smoking. I unlocked my car and drove to the grocery store. Two unusual guys in one day, I thought.

*   *   *

Paul was getting the mail when I pulled into the driveway. He didn't look happy as he juggled a batch of letters and some trash from the road. I parked the van and opened the rear door to unload the groceries. He came over and grabbed a few bags to carry in.

"Hi, honey. Everything all right?" I asked.

"Yeah, I guess. I can't stand it when people throw things out of their car."

"Yeah, it's too bad."

Paul put the grocery bags on the counter, tossed the mail on the kitchen table and threw away the litter. "You know, it's getting worse across the street. That house is such a mess and now there seems to be a lot of crappy cars going in and out."

I hung up my coat. "I've been noticing, too. I think it started around the end of summer. They must be renting it out."

"I don't know how they got past zoning. Wonder how many renters there are?" Paul asked as he went to retrieve the rest of the bags.

I gave him a kiss. "Don't worry, it'll be fine. At least the winter snow, when it comes, will cover the trash so you won't see so much of it."

"How did the library hunt go? Did you find anything interesting?" Paul asked as we unpacked the food.

"No, not really. But I did run into Tommy D in the historical book section. Remember, the kid I told you about who sold his estate dishes? The ones that matched my shard?"

"You're kidding. What's he doing in the library? I wouldn't expect someone like him to be a history reader, maybe renting DVD's or something."

"I thought the same thing. It was kind of strange. But, of course, he is a bit of a strange character."

"Watch yourself, Nancy. Don't get too involved. I know how you're always looking for something mysterious in everything."

I raised my eyebrows and returned a little smile.

*   *   *

An hour later, on the way to his store, Tommy D had a hard time concentrating on the road. He turned down the hard rock music blaring from the radio and whispered to himself, "I don't understand why Harwich is next to Eastham. That stupid library was no help." At a traffic light, he rustled through the old papers that he'd found in his dad's attic. When the light turned green, he was able to pull into the parking lot of his store. There was a paper sign on the door that read, "CLOSED."

"Jesus Christ!" he yelled. "I ask that creep to do one thing and he blows it."

Tommy grabbed the two old books next to him on the seat and slammed the car door. As he ripped the paper sign down and entered the gaming room, a car pulled in next to his car. Within seconds, Silas walked in behind him. Tommy turned on his buddy and growled,

"What's goin' on, man?"

"Nothin'. I had to leave for awhile."

"Well, next time...don't! Or you're outta here."

Tommy settled in his back office with the old ledger and Bible.

By 3 PM, the game noises were blaring as kids poured in after school, pumped for the weekend. Silas stayed out front. Tommy hunkered in the back searching through the old books. Closing the journal with a bang, he held his head in his hand, looking disgusted. He wasn't getting anywhere with the books or on the computer. He wrote down the address of Nancy Caldwell and shoved it into his pocket.

29

Present Day
CAPE COD

THE NEXT EVENING, as I sat reading the daily paper, an article caught my eye on the third page towards the bottom titled, *Boundaries of Cape Cod*. I smiled when I read the last sentence: *"If you're interested in volunteering to search for the boundary lines of Olde Cape Cod, there will be a walk and explore on Sat. Nov. 11 (weather permitting)."*

"Hey, did you see this?" I asked Paul, who was sitting next to me on the couch, watching a woodworking show on TV.

"No, I didn't notice it."

"It's about a group of locals who are searching for the original boundaries marking the towns of the Cape. They're meeting this Saturday. I think I might go."

"I heard we're getting a snow storm this weekend."

"Maybe. But I'd still like to go." I laughed; Paul would never want to go with a group anywhere, anytime. He's just not like that. But I would. This sounded interesting.

* * *

My old blue snow jacket was zippered up as high as it would go. I patted my pockets for gloves, hat, tissues, phone, and camera. All set, I thought, as I walked through the gallery to Paul's studio. "Paul, I'll be back in a few hours."

As the car started, I felt ready for the challenge ahead of me. The thought of finding something that had been hidden for centuries always excited me. One thing this spit of land could boast was that there were houses and vistas that had not changed over the years. In fact, Paul and I chose to move our family from the Midwest to historic Cape Cod to experience history at its best. But Paul's free time was getting scarcer. Even if he didn't want to go, I bet he would have gone if I'd asked him. I waited patiently to turn out onto Route 6A, my head swiveling back and forth, looking for an opportunity to pull out among the cars racing by me.

Driving through the center of Orleans, I spotted a small inlet off to one side of Route 28. I made a note to explore it later. I knew that after a good nor'easter, remnants of shipwrecks and relics would suddenly appear on the beach and then be covered over with sand or water when the wind changed direction, not to be seen again till the next storm. An avid beachcomber like me never loses the desire to find treasures hidden under the ocean shorelines. I went over the directions to where the boundary walk was going to commence. According to the article, volunteers were to gather a few miles out of town, along Pleasant Bay. I should watch for a white van parked on the right side of the road.

I pulled in behind the van on a large patch of dirt that looked like people used it as a turnaround.

"Nancy Caldwell," I said, introducing myself to a group of ten people, mostly older than me, who were all standing in a semi-circle. Everyone smiled and said their names out loud to each other. I noticed there were a few rookies and some repeat explorers who were already acquainted.

"Ready? Let's go," said a hearty looking gentleman named Peter.

As we followed him in single file through a small opening in the woods, the brush and scrub swallowed us up. I looked back, trying to remember anything different that would point to the hidden entrance and took note of a twisted tree growing around a smaller one. Not to worry, I told myself, as long as I stayed close to the others. After all, I was smart and had to be the youngest among them.

"Isn't this exciting?" asked a tall man, wearing a stocking hat pulled close around his graying hair.

"Yes, I love hiking," I responded.

"How did you find out about this walk?" he asked over his shoulder.

"Read the article in the paper," I shouted to his back.

He waved his hand to the side acknowledging my answer, keeping pace with the others. I pulled my hat lower over my ears. The sun was out but the wind was now blowing hard. The temperature felt like it had dropped several degrees as we walked deeper into the woods. I tied my hood around the hat.

I couldn't believe how out of shape I was as we tramped over rocks and hidden bumps underneath the fallen oak leaves. After only ten minutes, I had to take some deep belly breaths to slow my heart rate, but I was determined to keep up with everyone. I followed behind the line of people snaking along a path that had been carved out over the years by the hiking of other nature trekkers. After another five minutes or so, we passed an old foundation set into an embankment, then ventured off the regular path uphill and pushed through a dense covering of prickers and fallen branches. When we finally stopped, I was ecstatic. As I stood still, my breaths started to come a little slower. I promised myself to exercise more.

Peter gave us a command, "Fan out in this area. See if you can see anything out of the ordinary. Keep within earshot though. If you find anything, give a holler." Then he cautioned us. "Don't forget that even in deep winter, mice, deer, and several other small animals that roam the woods carry the tick. And…please do not get lost."

People went off in all directions, studying the ground and looking for stone aberrations on the forest floor. I managed to keep a moving body in sight at all times so that I wouldn't get lost. At the same time, my eyes kept searching for anything that stuck out above the ground that looked interesting.

Snowflakes began to softly drift across the woods in the wind. The group, undaunted, continued to explore.

Peter yelled out, "Wah-hoo! Found something."

Five of us headed towards him. The others went a little further before turning around. We found our leader bent over a patch of forest floor, scraping off dirt and moss from three rocks that were laid in a small half-circle.

"What is it?" asked the tall man named John.

"I have a hunch." Peter straightened up, stood right behind the middle rock and stared out over the rough terrain.

We all looked in the same direction that Peter was eyeing. I laughed and asked him, "Are we supposed to be looking at something important?"

He smiled but didn't answer me. Then he called out to whomever was standing nearest to him. "A couple of you walk in a circle extending away from these rocks and see if you find more stones that might form a larger pattern."

I reached for a slender T-Bar that was leaning against a tree. Peter had brought it along for the hike. With slow and careful steps, I kicked up leaves atop the ground and poked the iron rod into the soil before me and on either side of my feet in search of other rocks. One woman went ahead, opposite my path, using her boots to uncover any odd protuberances that would mimic a circular stone formation.

After jamming the T-bar into the ground a few times, it stopped with a thud. "I found one," I cried out, bending over to pull at patches of green moss. There it was, a flat stone, just a short distance from where Peter had found the other rocks. My gloves were getting damp and black with the forest dirt but I didn't mind; I was on a hunt. I pulled more moss away.

Peter encouraged the others with, "Keep looking," before he came over to me. "Nancy, this is wonderful."

I was giddy about the stone that I had uncovered. I wasn't sure how important it was but it didn't matter. According to Peter, I'd found something noteworthy. People had presumably walked over it, time and again, paying no attention to its significance.

By the time the other trekkers came closer, seven more rocks, including mine were uncovered, making the rough outline of a complete circle. Intrigued, everyone gathered around, trying to guess at what lay before their eyes.

"A foundation to an old house?" one offered.

A man with ruddy cheeks added, "Pretty small house."

Laughter erupted but quieted in seconds as Peter spoke up, "I know we came here to find evidence of the boundaries of the first Cape Villages but I think we've just located the site of an ancient windmill."

We all stood quietly dumbfounded and thrilled at the same time. I hopefully wondered if the little windmill drawing on the old map could be connected to this. It was a stretch, but there might be a link.

Peter glanced at the sky then gave his last command as we all stood around the rough circle of stones, "The snow is starting to accumulate so let's disband until another day. Feel free to come back and explore the site but DO NOT touch or dig anywhere until we find some answers."

All agreed.

Peter tied a piece of yellow caution tape around a branch near the site and another where we'd veered off the ancient walking path. It was right near the old foundation. I wondered who would have built a house so far from the road. Our small group of explorers began to retrace their steps out of the woods, led by Peter.

As I walked to my van, I was silly with the idea that the group may have uncovered a foundation. I pulled off my gloves, which were all wet from digging. My numb hands fumbled through my pockets for the keys. God, it's cold, I thought, walking a little faster.

The car opened with a click. I looked behind me for oncoming traffic so I could open the door safely, then I glanced across the street from where I was parked. A maroon Toyota was at the convenience store opposite me. I slid onto the driver's seat and slammed the door shut. Waiting for the engine to warm up, I looked across the street again. The driver was taking a big drag on his cigarette.

That's weird, I thought, he looks like the guy from the library. I wonder if he's following me? Snowflakes started to stick to the grass and my windshield. My hands shook as I gripped the steering wheel. Was I cold or was it the sight of the maroon Toyota? A lot of things began running through my mind. Had I found another clue about the old map? Could I have located the Davis Baker Mill?

Once on the road, I pulled ahead to turn around, then slowly drove past the Toyota. The driver stared at me with a look that was almost menacing. I stopped for a red light and reminded myself to calm down…take a deep breath. It's just a coincidence.

As I sped along Route 6A toward Brewster, the car began to warm me up. I decided that the real news is that Peter's group might have discovered an archaeological site and maybe I could find a connection to the old map. I couldn't wait to tell Paul…it was probably best to keep the maroon Toyota to myself.

*   *   *

The Toyota reached its destination an hour later, turning into a long, winding driveway that led to the back of an old, run-down house. The driver parked his car near a wooden stairway, grabbed his backpack and climbed to the top of the stairs where he found a key above the side window. He entered the small studio apartment. After opening the vents on the heaters, he grabbed a cold beer from the tiny refrigerator and pulled a pair of binoculars from his bag. He had about 30 minutes before going back to work.

30

Present Day
CAPE COD

THE SNOW didn't let up for two days. After explaining to Paul we'd found the possible site of an old mill, he agreed with me that there was a good chance it represented the drawing on the map. I had a feeling he was just humoring me because he was busy with his painting. Then again, it didn't matter; I knew I was on to something important. I was also anxious to go back to the site, but there would be no exploring for a while. The storm had blanketed the Cape with its first snowstorm and Thanksgiving was next week.

I reached for my heavy coat and slipped on arctic boots to get the mail. With a dressing of new snow, even the messy house across the street looked picture perfect. The Christmas decorations would soon be up at our house. I relished what people would think as they drove past our front parlor bay window, where the multicolored lights of our Christmas tree always sparkled through the old glass, like colorful diamonds. The bucolic scene spoke of everything that's winter in New England. It was an old-fashioned image that usually brought a sigh from whoever saw it, reminding them of cozy families, traditions, and sweet treats. I try my best to make a wonderful Christmas for the family, but today, all I wanted to do was look for lost treasure.

* * *

The day after Thanksgiving, Nick showed up. "Mrs. C, it's great to see you," he shouted into the doorway as he gave me a big hug.

"It's good to see you, too." I hugged him in return.

Molly and Danny came running in from the living room to say hello, curious as ever.

Nick crouched down to their eye level. "You two look just the way your brother described you."

The kids giggled and ran back to their toys.

"Are you hungry?" I asked.

"No, I stopped at Burger King on my way here."

"Well, we're happy to have you with us."

"Thanks."

"Let me show you where you'll be sleeping."

I led him to the spare bedroom off the front parlor. "This is the best room if you want privacy. You'll be far enough away from the kids and all their noise." I watched him lift his suitcase onto the bed. "When you're settled, I've got some hot chocolate on the stove."

"Thanks again, Mrs. C."

* * *

Dinner was pizza and salad, nice and easy. Talk was all about Nick. When I was in Antigua his conversations with me were always questions concerning the treasure that I'd found in our woods. Now I wanted to know all about him. "What made you join the Corps?" I asked, passing the salad.

"I wanted to give something back. I'd graduated with a degree in archaeology and minored in math, but the higher-ups felt they needed a math teacher more."

"Minored in math?" Paul asked. "That's an interesting combination with archaeology."

"I always liked numbers, plus there's a lot of measuring and such with ancient discoveries. In the end, I liked digging better."

"So what's your project back on Antigua?" I started to cut Danny's pizza into narrow strips.

"Well, I'm not sure. The group I was working with disbanded. The Corps office said they would talk to me when I got back."

I thought this was an odd answer. The Peace Corps doesn't work that way; they always have schedules planned well in advance.

"Hey, Mrs. C, I was reading on my cell phone all about the *Whydah*, pirates, and your discoveries as I waited for my flights. I'm still so curious."

I smiled, thinking it was actually fun answering all of his questions.

He kept his stare on my necklace. "That's so beautiful, Mrs. C."

"Thank you, Nick."

I decided to bring out the coffee, cookies, and ice cream as soon as the last piece of pizza was eaten. Casey excused herself: she had plans for a movie with her friends. As Paul and Nick talked in the dining room, I began putting things away in the kitchen. I thought about sharing the new map with Nick and any details that I'd already found. Paul was interested, but he's always so busy. It might be fun to have Nick as a partner in solving these mysteries that keep appearing, like Holmes and Watson.

31

Present Day
CAPE COD

I WAS UP EARLY. By the time I reached the kitchen, Paul had finished reading the morning paper and was working in his studio. The sun sparkled through the bare trees in the eastern sky. Maybe some of its warmth would melt the snow and I could get back to the old mill site. The coffee tasted good as I checked my email. One message popped up from Brian. It had two attachments. What a good kid; he'd remembered my request to get pictures of the Julian family jewelry. Happy he'd photographed them before they were stolen, I opened the first image. They were beautiful. The second image was a close-up of only one piece to show the detail of its intricate flower design and color. I glanced up at the wall calendar and remembered my hair appointment, "Crap." I quickly printed copies of what Brian had sent and left them on the kitchen counter. I had fifteen minutes to get dressed and on the road.

Almost out the door, I stopped to take my necklace off, knowing the chemicals in perm lotions can wreak havoc on jewelry. I wasn't going to take any chances of ruining this special treasure. I promptly placed it next to the emailed copies of the earrings. I couldn't help but admire them again; they were such a perfect match.

* * *

A few hours later, as I pulled into our driveway, the sun was still shining. Perfect, I thought, another couple of days like this and the snow will be gone. Once inside, I found Nick hovering over the kitchen counter using his phone's camera.

"What're you doing?" I asked with my eyebrows raised.

"I didn't think you'd mind if I took a few pictures of your necklace and these photocopies of the earrings."

"I guess not," I said, hanging up my coat.

"Are these earrings from the treasure that you found?" He put his phone into his pocket.

"No."

"The patterns are almost identical to your necklace. They look like they could be a set."

"Actually, I think they are."

"Where did you find the earrings?"

"Antigua. You know Jim's friend, John Julian, who owns the sandwich stand?"

Nick leaned against the counter. "Oh yeah."

"The earrings have been in his family for centuries."

Paul came in and interrupted us. The perm smell always bothered him, but he tolerated it. He gave me a hug while holding his breath and said, "You look beautiful."

"Thanks, you're so loving. I'll be in the shower."

"Hey, Nick, I'll be out in the studio, if you need anything," Paul said as he headed out of the kitchen behind me.

Careful not to get my hair wet, I wrapped it with a towel and scrubbed my neck as well as I could. As the water fell down my back, I wondered if I should be worried that Nick was taking photos of the jewelry. I imagined he must have a pretty big pirate collection, but why was he so interested in the jewelry?

*   *   *

Nick closed the door to his room then checked his luggage to make sure the bundled sweatshirt was safe under his clothes. He sat on the edge of the bed and pulled out his phone as he stared at the detailed images of the earrings with the necklace beside them. After writing a short text, he pressed *Send*.

* * *

The next day, Paul, Nick, and I were having coffee at the breakfast table, enjoying the fact that the kids were off to the science museum in Boston with their friends.

"I'm going for a walk on the beach to find scallop shells," I said. "Anyone want to come?"

Paul stood up. "Sorry, I've got a frame that needs to be finished for my acrylic painting. A new client is coming tomorrow to take a look at it."

Nick turned to me. "I'd like to go with you, Mrs. C."

"Great. I'll be ready in about an hour." I glanced at the tide clock. "We have plenty of time; it's several hours before full tide. Do you need any gloves or a hat?"

"No, I came prepared. After all, we're in New England, and thought that maybe we'd go exploring. Brian said you were an adventurer."

What a nice compliment from Brian, I thought. He's right.

The sky was bright blue and there was only a slight breeze when we arrived at the deserted beach. The wrack line had crusted over in white snow that sparkled in the sunlight. The temperature, a chilly forty degrees, was bearable if you had the right winter clothes. Within seconds, however, the breeze turned into a gusty wind.

"Boy, Mrs. C, it's getting cold out here."

I picked up a few scallop shells. "Don't you just love to hear the sounds of the sea, even if it is a bit windy?" My hand struggled to deposit the shells into a plastic bag. "I can't get enough of it. I never take it for granted."

Nick zippered his jacket closed. "So, you want only the scallop shells?"

I nodded. "They're the only ones that don't break if you poke a hole into them. We use them to decorate our customer's packages in the gallery."

Nick walked ahead of me and stooped to pick up several large ones. I held the bag open and he placed them inside.

"After you found real pirate treasure what did you do with it all?" He asked as a gust of wind blew sand into our faces.

I quickly turned into the opposite direction and waited until it passed. "I'm happy you're interested." I picked up more shells from the wet sand. "But first, I want to tell you that I may be onto a new quest."

"Really? Fill me in," said Nick. He turned and started to walk backwards so he could face me as we talked.

"When I was in Antigua, I found an old map in John Julian's Bible."

"I know, I asked Brian for a copy the day you left."

"Oh that's right. I remember now. Well, I found another map that's very similar to it."

"What?" He stopped in his tracks.

"I may be on to something that might lead to more treasure."

Nick looked very interested. As we walked along the tidal flats, I told him everything I'd discovered. By the time we got back into the car, I could see that he was definitely excited about every word I'd said.

"Could you show me the maps?"

I smiled and nodded. "Sure."

Two heads are better than one.

32

Present Day
CAPE COD

WHEN NICK AND I arrived back at the house, the kids were jumping out of the SUV with their toys from the gift store at the museum. We all walked into the house together. "Who's hungry?" I asked.

Danny and Molly responded in unison with a loud, "Me!"

Martha thankfully took over the feeding frenzy, so I could show Nick the two maps and teapot. "Isn't it beautiful?" I held up the chalky beach shard next to the blue and white porcelain vessel. "Pretty good match, right?"

Nick smiled. "So, inside this was another map?" He touched the blue pattern on the teapot.

"Yes, I couldn't believe my eyes when they matched each other."

Nick took out his phone to take more pictures. Amidst the clicking of his camera, he asked, "You found the teapot in a local antique shop?"

"That's correct."

He quickly asked, "And the kid who sold this china to the antique store was named Thomas Davis Chandler?"

I lifted the lid and placed it back down on top of the teapot. "Yes... and Thomas Davis was a surviving pirate from the *Whydah* wreck."

"That's quite a coincidence."

"It did seem weird to me at first, but still plausible." I turned away from Nick. "I'll be right back. I want to show you the two maps."

*   *   *

We were sitting at the pedestal table in the front parlor, examining the precious finds and talking about all the clues I'd found, when the doorbell interrupted our cozy winter afternoon. Surprised, I looked over to Nick. "I didn't notice anyone pull in." I stood and called out to Martha, "I'll get it."

The kids had settled down to play with their toys and Paul was in his studio for the final hour of the business day. Nick followed me as I rounded the kitchen archway to see who was at the door. Both kids got up and met us in the foyer, equally curious. They looked out through the glass entry doors at the tall stranger. I recognized him; it was Tommy D. What a surprise to see him on my doorstep! Nick stood right behind me as I opened the door. "Hello, Tommy. How are you? Come on in."

The young man crossed the threshold with one step.

Danny and Molly couldn't take their eyes off his black leather clothes, long stringy hair, and the chains hanging from his pockets and jacket.

"Sorry to bother you." He kept his eyes glued to his feet, like he had done something wrong.

"That's okay," I said but remained cautious. I really didn't know much about this kid. "What can I do for you?"

Tommy D looked at me and then to Nick.

"This is Nick, a friend of my son's." Tommy fumbled to open a plastic grocery bag. "I wonder if you could answer some questions for me?" He pulled out two old books.

Intrigued, I reached out for them. "What do you have here?"

He let go of the large book first, keeping the smaller one in his hands.

The book was heavy and smelled musty. I was ecstatic to hold it. "Come on into the kitchen, so I can see what you have in a better light."

Danny and Molly were still wide-eyed. "Why don't you kids go into the living room for a few minutes?" No response. They just stared at Tommy D. I ordered them again, a little louder this time. "Go on, hurry up." I watched them until they were quietly settled in their chairs.

Tommy followed me into the kitchen with Nick behind him.

Martha had gone home for the day so the three of us were alone. The thought ran across my mind that I really didn't know this tall, strange kid and that something bad might happen, but I dismissed it. I would be able to handle this strange visitor if he tried anything; I knew where the knives were kept. Besides, Nick could be my backup. He seemed like he could handle himself if there was any trouble.

I set the book down on the table and opened it, careful not to disturb anymore of its unraveled binding. It looked like some sort of a ledger. I scanned the lists of household items.

Tommy placed the smaller book, which looked like a Bible, next to it. I watched him as he glanced around the kitchen. In a quick few seconds, I thought the cozy room must be nothing like what he's used to. Then I focused back on the old books and began to examine the significant pieces of history.

Tommy gestured towards them, "They were up in my father's attic. That's where I originally found the china you were so interested in."

My curiosity grew to a peak. I tried to remain calm. "Oh, I see."

"They have Thomas Davis's name in them," he offered.

"Well, what do you want me to help you with?" I ran my fingers over the yellowed pages, slowly turning them one on top of each other.

"I Googled you and found out that you'd discovered some treasure that belonged to the pirate Sam Bellamy."

"Yes, that's right."

"I also read that two pirates escaped from his ship when it sank. One was named John Julian and another…Thomas Davis."

Loud high-pitched voices came from the living room, interrupting our conversation.

Molly was screaming. "Mommy! Danny won't give me the remote."

"Damn it," I whispered under my breath. "I'll be right back."

"Okay," said Nick.

I didn't think Tommy D minded waiting; he looked relaxed in our welcoming kitchen. I saw Nick lean in to examine the pages of the old Bible.

After a few minutes, I returned and picked up the ledger. "You said that Thomas Davis's name was in here?"

"Yup, I'll show you."

Tommy D flipped the pages to where the name Davis appeared; it was on every third or fourth page.

"This is really interesting," I said as I sat down at the table to get a better look.

He pushed the Bible over to me and pointed to one of the first pages. "You can see that this one has listings of births and deaths, beginning with Thomas Davis marrying a Felicity Gibbs in 1721."

I was fascinated. The dates were all in close proximity to sometime after Julian and Davis were acquitted of piracy.

"My father's name was the last one written, and now that he's gone, I'm the only Davis left."

"No brothers or sisters?"

"Nope."

"Uncles or aunts?"

"Nope."

"What about your mom's side of the family?"

"Naw, she had one sister, but no one knows where she is. My mom died when I was ten." He spread his hand out on top of the table and moved his fingers up and down in a few nervous wiggles. "My stepmom lives in my...I mean, my dad's house...where I grew up. I guess it's her house now. We don't exactly get along."

I felt sorry for this poor guy and began to dismiss my fears about him. Nick pulled the Bible back over to his side of the table and browsed its pages.

"It's all very interesting, Tommy, but what do you want from me?" I actually felt a thrill to be in the same room with these early relics. I wanted to own them and craved more details; but I needed to go slow. There was no need to run this kid off with too many questions.

Tommy D was quiet, as if he was forming sentences in his mind before he spoke. "I found something else...by accident. It was inside the ledger."

I sat up straight, my heart racing.

He picked up the ledger and opened it to the back page then slowly pulled out the four vellum pieces that he'd discovered in the attic a few days ago. He laid them on the table, matching their written words into sentences. We all studied them for a few minutes.

Tommy D fidgeted in his seat. "What does it all mean?"

I pointed to the top of the page and slowly read, "Baker Davis Mill." Below the heading I read out loud the scripted words: *"Follow the new road to the river of Namskaket. Travel to the southern ridge of where Harwich meets Eastham. The property of Baker and Sons will be marked with a stake 10 yards from the corner of the oak. Follow a line along the Magnetic North, parallel with the Cove's inlet."*

"They're describing a location," Nick suggested.

"That's right, the Davis Baker Mill site." My heart was going so fast that I was almost swaying. I couldn't believe it. This was the same location that was written on the map from the teapot. But I still wasn't sure where it actually was.

Tommy D looked at us and then back to the vellum. "What does it mean...where Harwich meets Eastham...where's Orleans?"

I needed to remain calm and not give too much away...not yet. It was a struggle to hide my thoughts but I slowly explained, "The town of Orleans was not incorporated until 1797. This document is dated 1720, when the land was called Harwich, not Orleans."

"Oh."

In my excitement, I forgot myself and went further, "These directions mention the Magnetic North and a cove inlet. If I'm correct, they describe somewhere along Pleasant Bay Road, or Route 28 in Orleans."

I could sense that Tommy D was getting keyed up. His eyes grew wider. Now I've said too much, I thought. He must be thinking about how he could get his hands on whatever might be hidden, like treasure.

"I'm not sure if there's anything else I could help you with," I lied and returned my attention to study the words on the vellum.

Tommy looked at me. "I was wondering if there could be any possibility that Davis had treasure of his own. Maybe from the *Whydah* pirate ship?"

"Maybe." I lied again. I knew that Julian did, but I had to keep my theories to myself, for now.

"Okay." He picked up the pieces to put them back into the book for safekeeping. He then placed everything into the plastic bag and headed for the door to leave.

As he rounded the corner of the kitchen, I called after him, "Tommy?"

He turned around.

"If I think of anything that might explain more about your books, I'll let you know."

"Thanks," he said and closed the foyer door behind him.

Nick smiled. "Pretty smart, Mrs. C."

"Excuse me?"

"Best to keep it quiet. You know what I mean?" His smile made me feel uncomfortable. "Those directions on his paper were the same as the ones on your old map."

"Well, I need to think about all of this before I act on anything."

"Good idea."

We watched Tommy D get into his car. "He must be a pretty lonely kid," I whispered.

Nick straightened up from looking out the window. "Yeah, maybe." A serious look spread over his face. "I'm tired, goodnight." He disappeared into his room.

I headed for the kitchen to make some tea and sit for a while. I couldn't stop thinking about Tommy D. That kid probably just wants to know more about his past. Whether he's interested in finding treasure or just finding himself and his place in the world, it shouldn't matter. I had a responsibility to help him.

*   *   *

That night, after talking to Paul about what happened with Tommy D, I wrote everything down in my journal. I made a list of what was known in one column and what was still questionable in another. Everything seemed like a jigsaw puzzle. Once in bed, I closed my eyes and went over the facts several times in my head before I could finally feel myself dozing off. I got up at 3 AM to go to the bathroom, but once back in bed I started thinking again about Davis, Tommy D, treasure, and the old books. I tried to clear my mind by meditating. My quiet place or center was always in the woods, but my thoughts kept drifting. The old mill site that the cornerstone group found up in the woods, in Orleans, popped into my head. My eyes opened wide with the idea that the site was near the Cove along Pleasant Bay. Then I remembered Peter saying that we were standing on the Magnetic North...just like in the directions from Tommy D's old book and the map. I sat straight up in bed and shook Paul on his shoulder. "Paul, wake up." I had to push him again before he stirred.

"What's wrong?"

"I gotta talk to you."

"Can't it wait till morning?"

"I guess so." I lay back down but couldn't fall asleep. It was going to be a long night.

33

Present Day
CAPE COD

AROUND EIGHT O'CLOCK the next morning, a maroon Toyota idled in the parking lot of the Hyannis bus depot. Loud rap music and a thumping, deep bass masked any outside sounds for the driver. He looked content, nodding in time to the music, his eyes closed.

The click-clack of a metal knee brace rattled as a passenger from Boston made his way under the canopy and towards the parking area. People kept their distance from the strange looking man. His long, open, black leather coat revealed a black T-shirt and black jeans. He wore a black band around his head, which held in place a patch that covered his right eye. It made his long, gray, frizzy hair stick out on all sides. The older man limped over to the maroon Toyota and banged on its window. "You Silas Maroney?"

The driver jumped almost three inches out of his seat, dropping his cigarette ashes onto his leg. He swallowed hard. "Yeah, that's me."

"I'm your pick-up." The stranger walked around to the passenger side of the car.

Silas quickly flicked the hot ashes off his pants leg.

The unusual man maneuvered his body onto the torn bucket seat. "Your old man said to look for a crappy red Toyota and that you were a little shit." He looked the kid up and down. "I guess he was right."

* * *

The odometer ticked off miles in rapid succession as Silas drove his car along the highway to Brewster. His passenger never said a word to him during the twenty-five minutes it took to get from the bus station to the small apartment belonging to Silas's father. He pulled the car to the rear of the house. They both got out and climbed the back steps to the top of the landing. Peeling paint on the door reflected the condition of the dilapidated house.

Once the door was opened, Silas threw the key on the table. "So what should I call you?"

"The General."

"What?"

"The General. And don't ask me any more questions."

"No problem." Silas backed away. "You can have the bed in the back room. I'll sleep on the couch."

The General threw his duffel bag into the room. Under his breath, he muttered, "Suits me just fine."

"Uh huh," said Silas. "I got to get to work. Be back around nine."

"Don't care." The General turned on the TV and grabbed a beer from the fridge.

"You need anything?"

The General said nothing. He kicked off his boots and started to massage his knee.

"Right, then." Silas shrugged his shoulders and left, slamming the door behind him.

The General opened the window a crack, and then inspected the small apartment. There it was...his cellmate's prized possession. The Sylvania record console was piled high on one side with 33-RPM records. The General had become accustomed to listening to the jazz greats, courtesy of Silas's father. He selected a Benny Goodman vinyl, blew across its surface and placed it on the turntable. With a delicate touch of the diamond needle, the swinging sounds of a clarinet filled the dingy apartment. The old man's hips swayed a little as his hands moved behind the console. With his forehead touching the wall, he could just about see the gray duct tape. His lips curled into a smile as he peeled it off the wood. The Smith and Wesson .38 revolver attached to the back of the cabinet fit nicely into his hand. As he pulled three bullets off the sticky tape, he whispered a thank you to his old buddy, and then settled in front of the TV to clean his new weapon.

* * *

Present Day
THE CALDWELL HOUSE

"So you had another bad dream?" Paul asked as he dressed.

I was still in bed, looking out the skylight at the tops of the trees. They edged their skinny barren limbs across the window opening.

"Yes, but it wasn't terrible or anything too scary; it was more frustrating. But it also made me think about a new connection that might help me find Julian's treasure." I threw off the covers. "I'm going back to that old mill site," I said with determination.

"Nancy! What did I ask you before?"

"What do you mean, 'what did I ask you'?" I sarcastically repeated his words. I was a little upset. I'm not a kid.

"Maybe you shouldn't be going up there by yourself?"

"Oh? For heaven's sake, I'll be fine!" I ran into the bathroom to shower.

"You want me to go with you?"

He didn't sound very enthusiastic. "No, you've got that client coming over today. Maybe I'll ask Nick."

* * *

During breakfast, Nick said he wouldn't mind exploring the mill site with me. We were expecting rain in the afternoon but planned to be home before then. On our way into Orleans, I told Nick about my nighttime revelation and he seemed very interested in my theory about the location of the mill site. I felt encouraged that I might be right.

I parked the car at the convenience store across the street from the opening in the woods and looked for the twisted tree. Before we ventured too deep into the scrub's edge, I took a reading from the compass app on my phone to guide us out if we got lost.

The morning air was cold but, with the sun shining through the trees, we warmed up quickly as we climbed a short hill to get to the path. The brown forest smelled musty with a slight hint of burning wood from a nearby fireplace.

"If I didn't know it was late November, I would've thought it was almost spring," said Nick as he took off his knitted hat.

"New England weather is fickle. They say if you want a change in weather just wait a few minutes."

We both laughed as we waded through the damp oak leaves.

"What's that?" Nick asked as he pointed to a deep, hollowed-out opening with stonewalls on three sides.

I recognized it as the old foundation from the last time I was up here, with Peter's group. It was nestled into a high embankment to our right. "Looks like a partial foundation to a house or maybe the entrance to a walk-in basement."

Nick stopped at the top to get a better look down into it. "It's pretty deep on this end."

I continued ahead along the trail until I saw the yellow CAUTION tape. "Here's where we veer off." Nick scrambled to catch up. I was disappointed that nothing else looked familiar to me since the last time I was in the woods. I thought I was better at remembering details.

Another yellow marker waved at us as a burst of wind kicked up. The sun had disappeared behind some fast moving dark clouds, bringing a sudden chill to the air. I quickly pulled a hat from my pocket and found gloves in the other, then zeroed in on finding the old mill's stone foundation. "Try kicking around in the leaves and sticks. I know the stones are here somewhere."

Nick started to move his feet a little harder in half arcs.

A few flakes of snow began to drift through the woods so I buttoned my coat tighter. I kicked my feet a little higher into the air, but my disappointment of not finding anything was beginning to grow stronger.

Finally Nick called out, "I found something."

I turned to see him standing about ten feet from the yellow tape. "What did you find?" I forged through the brown oak leaves to get near him, not caring about the wild rose brambles that wrapped themselves around my ankles. I knew I wasn't crazy; those stones were here somewhere.

We both stooped down and began to brush away the forest litter. My gloved hands moved back and forth, trying to uncover the tops of the first three stones. Nick moved to the side of me to look for any other hard, grey surfaces. He discovered another three. I stood up and surveyed the shape that was forming. It certainly resembled part of a circular foundation, just like before.

"Check your phone," Nick said. "See if we're standing on or near the Magnetic North."

I stored my wet gloves in a pocket then activated my phone with a swipe of a fingertip. The app for the compass was a little slow to find itself. It felt like a long time, but after only about thirty seconds, there it was. I turned a little and the arrow pointed east. My body pivoted to the left and, according to the compass, I was now heading north.

Nick came closer to see the readings. "Press the Magnetic North button."

I was off by about thirty degrees, but I was definitely standing close to it. I clicked back to the compass screen, turned and stepped nearer to the stones. My foot landed in front of a particularly large one. I bent over to clean it. "Did you bring the water bottle?"

"Yes, why?"

"Can I have it a second?"

"Sure."

I unscrewed its cap and gently poured it over the gray surface. Some lines began to appear "Look! There's a W."

Nick bent over next to me to see for himself.

The lines were crude but resembled the directional symbol for West. I pulled out the old map from my inside pocket and unfolded it. We both stared at the tiny drawing of the windmill and the two symbols beneath it: a W and the number 3.

Nick whipped out his cell and began taking pictures of the map and stones. I traced the lines of the W with my finger. It gave me a good feeling; touching the past. My heart raced with excitement. Suddenly the snow turned to hail and began pounding our heads and backs. Disappointed, I yelled, "We'd better get going." I found my extra set of gloves, pulled them on, and quickly scrambled back through the woods and to the car with Nick close behind. I felt frustrated that we had to leave, but I knew for certain that I'd be back.

As we pulled into the driveway, the hail stopped and the sun came out. "What did I tell you, Nick? Our weather is so strange."

He laughed as we got out of the van.

A jazz melody quietly drifted in the air. "Do you hear that?" I asked.

Nick stopped and cocked his head to the side to listen. "It sounds like some jazz from the 40s."

I glanced at the house across the street, more curious than ever about its tenants.

34

Present Day
CAPE COD

MARTHA WAS READY to leave as soon as Nick and I entered the house. "Thanks for coming over today," I said as I took off my hat and coat. "Have a nice weekend."

Nick went to his room in the front of the house. As I washed my hands in the kitchen, I could see Molly in the living room decorating her new giant coloring book. "Where's Danny?"

"I don't know," Molly answered without even looking up.

I walked nearer to her. "What do you mean you don't know?"

I put my hands on my hips in a stern, motherly stance. "Where's your father?"

"I don't know," she said again.

Now she sounded snotty to me and I was irritated. I took off towards the gallery to find Paul.

* * *

As Nick rounded the corner to the guest bedroom, he noticed his door was half open. He grabbed the door handle, gave it a yank and saw the small figure hovering over his opened suitcase on the bed.

"What are you doing, kid?"

Danny jumped and turned around. If he weren't leaning against the edge of the bed, he would have fallen over.

"Get out of here!" Nick yelled as he grabbed Danny's arm then pushed him out into the front parlor.

Danny started to cry. Nick let go.

The little boy ran towards the living room. "Mommy!"

Nick quickly rewrapped the dark grey semi-automatic back into the thick sweatshirt. "Shit," he muttered and then checked to see if anything else was disturbed.

* * *

I opened the door to the gallery and called out, "Is Danny out here?" then closed the door behind me to keep the cold from entering the house. As I reached for the door to Paul's studio, I shouted again, "Is Danny out here?"

"No, I thought he was with Martha," Paul said, rinsing off his paintbrush in a stainless steel container. "What's wrong?"

"I can't find him." I turned and exited the same way I came without waiting for another word from Paul.

Molly was still on the floor coloring. I found Danny pouting on the big Lazy Boy chair on the other side of the room. His eyes were red and he was sniffling. "Where were you?" I asked as I squeezed in next to him on the chair. "What's the matter? Why are you crying?"

"Nick scared me."

"What?"

"He yelled at me."

"Why?" I pushed his hair back and kissed him on his head.

He whispered to me. "He has a gun."

"What'd you say?"

Danny repeated closer to my ear, "I saw a real gun."

"Honey, you stay right here. I'll go talk to Nick." I got up and started for the front parlor, then called out, "Nick? What's going on?" I kept walking toward Nick's room.

He intercepted me halfway through the dining room. "Hey, Mrs. C, everything all right?'

"Danny seems upset. He said you had a gun?"

"A gun? No way." He started to laugh. "I wouldn't know what to do with one if you gave it to me."

"He's crying. Did you yell at him?"

"Well, he was in my room going through my suitcase. I really didn't mean to yell at him. I think I may have scared him because I came from behind and called his name really loud."

"But he said he saw a gun in your suitcase."

"Maybe he saw my electric shaver. It's got a black handle." Nick's phone rang. "Hold on a minute, Mrs. C." He turned around and walked back into the parlor.

I was confused and upset. I went to get a snack for the kids and waited for Nick to give me a better explanation.

He came into the kitchen. "I'm sorry, but I'm going to have to leave this afternoon. I guess my Corps assignment's starting date has been pushed up to this coming Tuesday. My flight leaves tonight for Antigua." He stood quietly in front of me for a second.

I wondered if he was lying to me. He'd seemed like such a nice kid. I didn't want a confrontation with him, so I kept my eyes down toward the sink as I rinsed the dishes.

"Okay, I guess I better get packing."

I tried to make small talk as he left the kitchen but it felt awkward. All I could come up with was, "That's too bad."

I knew Danny must have seen something, but I just couldn't bring myself to believe Nick would have a gun. Little boys have such wild imaginations, especially Danny.

Within minutes, Paul walked into the kitchen to find out where Danny was. As he reached for another cup of coffee, I told him about what Danny saw in Nick's room.

"A gun?" Paul swallowed hard.

I dried my hands on the towel. "That's right, but I'm not sure what Danny really saw."

He put his cup down and turned to me. "You said Nick's leaving this afternoon?"

"Yes."

"Well, don't say any more about it. Let him go. We'll probably never see him again."

*   *   *

When Nick was packed and ready, we all stood in the foyer to say goodbye, except for Danny, who cowered behind the chair by the closet and waited. I gave Nick a half-hearted hug. "Have a safe trip."

Paul shook his hand and managed a stern goodbye. Molly smiled and waved at him.

As Nick walked through the doorway, he added, "Say goodbye to Casey for me."

We watched him put his suitcase in the trunk of the rental car and drive left out of the driveway.

*   *   *

Nick's car sped past the green highway sign pointing the way to Boston and continued up the road until he came to the first motel. He parked his car, checked himself in at the desk and settled inside the small room. After his shoes came off, he sent a short text: *Still on Cape. Little snag in plans nothing I can't handle.* Then he ordered a pizza and took out a file from under the old sweatshirt at the bottom of his suitcase. Inside the folder were papers printed with the words *1715 Spanish Fleet sinks – led by the San Miguel,* along with several pictures of jewelry. He sat down on the bed and stared at a newspaper clipping of Nancy Caldwell wearing a beautiful necklace around her neck.

35

Present Day
CAPE COD

THE GAME ROOM was already crowded by Friday afternoon, following Tommy's visit to the Caldwell home. Irritated with Silas's lateness, Tommy D yelled, "It's about time you got here."

"Sorry. I had some business to take care of." Silas sat down with a thump behind the register and waited for his boss to tell him what to do.

"See if you can get the Black Knight going. That old pinball has been jamming lately." Tommy D checked his pocket watch that was dangled from a long chain attached to his belt.

"Yeah. Okay." Silas sauntered across the room and plugged in the game. "Hey, I'm gonna be a little late on Monday. I gotta do a favor for my old man."

"Your dad? Isn't he doing time at Concord?"

"Yeah. But I owe him one. He made me pick up this creepy guy at the bus station in Hyannis a few days ago. I'm supposed to let him stay with me for a while at my dad's place in Brewster." The Black Knight started to clang and bing. "Now I gotta take him someplace else; he won't say where. I guess the dude has some unfinished business or something."

"You still sleeping over there?" Tommy D asked without looking up from his email.

"Just for a while, until I can convince my girl to let me move back in with her."

"Well, watch your step with that old guy. You don't want to end up in jail again." The young proprietor started to type.

"Hey...I may be short, but I'm a fighter. I'm not stupid." Silas bounded over to the counter and jumped up to sit on top of it. "I'm like a Berserker. You know? A Norse warrior who fights like he's in a trance. You can't stop them." Silas held his fists up in the air, as if he were a champion. His curly hair glowed fiery red against his wide blue eyes.

"Okay, okay, get off the counter. I'll be in the office if you need me." Tommy D sighed as he left Silas out front.

Opening the old ledger, Tommy D flattened the vellum with the written directions across his desk. He tied up his long black hair back and Googled, *Cove Inlet, Orleans MA, Magnetic North, Baker property Orleans 1722.*

Nothing appeared that seemed relevant to him. He held his forehead with both hands over the keyboard then leaned back in his chair and whispered "Crap. I don't know what I'm looking for." The noise of the games and loud voices of kids began to grate on his nerves; he couldn't think straight. Tommy D wondered why they'd never bothered him before, but then he realized that this was possibly the first time he'd ever tried to figure something out that was really important. He went out the back door into the alley and took a few deep breaths to clear his head.

Silas noticed his boss leave. He quietly slipped into the office and behind the desk. He refreshed the computer screen for anything important. Noticing the open paper about the Baker Davis Mill Site, he took a photo of what was written with his phone.

Tommy D re-appeared in the doorway. "What're you doing, man?"

Startled, Silas jumped. "Looking for a pen."

"I don't want you back here. Stay out front."

"Hey, take it easy. I'm not doing anything wrong."

"Just leave me alone." Tommy D moved quickly to close the tabs on the computer screen.

Silas started to leave but hesitated. "Hey, I was wondering. What's with that Caldwell lady?"

Tommy D gave him a strange look as he shuffled the papers on his desk. "What do you mean?"

"You know, she lives right across the street from my old man's apartment, in Brewster. I saw her name on your computer and looked up her address." Silas pointed to the old books. "And where'd you get those?"

"None of your business."

Silas came closer to the desk. "I read that she found treasure. She got anything to do with what you're searching for?"

"Listen, you leave her alone." He closed the books with a bang. "She's a real nice lady and has a family." Tommy D slid the old paper back into the ledger. "I'm only trying to find out who my ancestors are."

"So you're not looking for pirate treasure?" A sly smile grew across Silas's face.

"What? Are you crazy?"

The phone rang.

"Get out front and answer the phone. Make sure no one steals anything."

Silas left in a huff, slamming the door behind him. By the time he reached the counter, the phone had stopped. He mumbled under his breath, "The hell with it. I don't need him anymore."

*   *   *

Tommy D stayed in his office long after Silas closed up. He had nowhere else to go. The game room should pull in some good money through the coming holidays. He could use the extra income. He dreaded the long and quiet winter ahead of him.

*   *   *

Silas headed back to his Dad's place, hating the thought of spending any time with the old man. Hopefully the guy's not a talker. He couldn't believe that he had to get up an hour earlier next week just to take the cripple to some mysterious place. Silas liked his sleep.

36

Present Day - Saturday
BREWSTER

THE NEXT MORNING, Silas got up, showered, made some coffee, and was about to leave for Tommy D's when his roommate let out a loud yawn. Silas peered into the bedroom. He could see the General swing his legs out of bed and then heard him thump his feet to the floor. As Silas sipped his coffee, he watched him struggle to put the brace on his knee.

Their eyes met. "What are you starin' at?"

Silas quickly looked away. "I gotta get to work."

"Hey, hold on a minute. I wanna talk to you." The General pushed himself up off the bed and limped towards Silas. "Don't forget next week, Monday. I need a ride."

"Where we goin'?"

"Off Pleasant Bay. Near where the town wells are."

"You mean in the woods?" Silas looked nervous.

"Yeah, up the hill."

"I ain't going where there's any bugs or crap."

The General smiled. "You scared of the outdoors?"

"No. I just don't like to go into the woods. Not a fan of spiders."

"It's too cold for any of them to get you. Now ticks…that's different." The General started to laugh.

"What do you mean?"

"Nothin'" The old man took a bottle of pills from his backpack. Silas looked puzzled. He was going to be late, so he left in a hurry.

* * *

The General opened a Little Debbie cinnamon bun for his breakfast, poured himself coffee and swallowed a pill. On the small table to his right, Silas had left his laptop on. All he had to do was tap the bar and he was in. Just for fun, he checked Silas's history. When he clicked on some of the sites he found: Pirates-Treasure-Brewster lady finds cache in backyard. The General straightened in his chair and stared at the screen. "Why was the kid searching this?"

He stood up to put on an old vinyl record and get a refill of coffee. Then he settled back in front of the computer's screen and waited for his heart meds to kick in.

* * *

Later that same day
THE CALDWELL HOUSE

"Mommy, can we stay up late tonight?" Molly asked for the tenth time.

"We'll see."

Danny came running into the kitchen. "No school tomorrow, it's Sunday. Can we stay up late? Please?"

"I have a surprise for both of you. Casey drove over to her friend's house and is spending the night. How would you like to go see *Finding Nemo* at the theatre? It's a special showing."

Danny yahooed all the way into the living room then jumped onto the couch.

Molly's eyes opened wide, like saucers. "Are we really going to go? Tonight?" she started to dance in a little jig.

"Settle down or you'll be in bed early."

After Paul closed up, he cuddled in next to Danny on the couch and teased him. "Maybe we should all get to bed early tonight. Everyone looks so tired. What do you think?"

"Nooooo, " Danny cried out.

"I'm teasing. We're still going to the movie," said Paul.

Danny looked relieved.

Paul kissed his little boy on the top of his head. "I bet you a quarter that Mommy falls asleep first during the movie."

Danny shook Paul's hand and said in a tiny voice, "No she won't, you will! It's a bet, Daddy."

We hurried to eat our grilled cheese sandwiches and tomato soup. Just as we were about to leave, the rain came down in torrents. We left by way of the back door in the garage, which was closer to the car. The kids squealed with excitement as we ran through the raindrops.

The movie wasn't as crowded as I had expected. That was a nice surprise, a little less screaming. Midway through the movie, I looked over towards Paul. He was already asleep. I poked Danny and raised my thumb up to signal that he'd won the bet.

* * *

Silas, home early, drove to the back of the run-down house across from the Caldwell's. As he entered the small upstairs apartment he saw the General looking out the window through binoculars.

"What're you doing?" He reached to grab them from the General's bony fingers.

"Hey!" the old man snarled.

Silas walked over to the fridge to get a beer. "Stay out of my business."

"Well, you look like you're up to something...and I might want in." The General tapped his fingers across the Formica covered tabletop, waiting for a reaction.

Silas was quiet.

The General lit a cigarette. "You know, no one's home over there now. They all left. I've been keeping watch."

Silas looked out the window towards the Caldwell house. "Yeah. Their cars are gone."

The General casually brushed his finger across the open computer's keypad to bring up the screen displaying information about Nancy Caldwell. "So that lady across the street found pirate treasure in her backyard?"

"Yeah, I think so." Silas picked up the binoculars and stared at the Caldwell house. "I sure would like to get inside to see if there's any gold in there."

"Gimme your cell number, I'll watch from here." The old man took hold of his own phone and readied to add Silas's number. "I'll text you if someone shows up." The General seemed to enjoy himself as he subtly dared Silas to go into the Caldwell's house.

Silas hesitated for only a few minutes before he recited his phone number.

When the hard rain eventually stopped, Silas went down the back stairs and leaned against the outside of the house. He stared across the street for a few minutes, and then he ran across the road and onto the property. There were no lights on and it was almost dark. He walked up the decking to the main door, nervous, sweat beading on his forehead.

He was surprised to find the door was unlocked. Grinning, he slowly entered. A quick look around the semi-darkened home signaled that he was in the middle of the house. He headed towards the front, passed a stairway, doubled back, and then climbed the steps in search of the bedrooms. The flashlight app on the phone gave him enough light in the hallway to see what was in front of him.

After entering the first room on his left, he could see a large bed with two dressers. He straightened his shoulders and felt more confident. His phone showed no text from the General. A careful search through the drawers found nothing. He got on his knees to look under the bed. As he was about to leave for the next room, he noticed the closet door was open so he peeked inside. On the floor, beneath the clothes, was a small gray safe with a key dangling from its handle. Inside were some folded papers, a broken piece of pottery, and a small filled pouch. The little black bag felt heavy in the palm of his trembling hand. With hurried movements he quietly left the same way he'd entered. The only sign of Silas's illegal entry were the outlines of his wet boot steps left on the small tiled entry foyer floor.

*   *   *

Danny and Molly were dozing off on the ride home. Danny clutched the quarter he had happily won in the bet with his father. After pulling into the driveway, Paul carried him over his shoulder from the car. Molly held my hand as we walked up the deck. I waited for Paul to find his keys in his jacket pocket. Molly grew impatient and started to jiggle the handle of the door. It opened.

"Paul, didn't you lock the door when we left?"

"No. I thought you did. We used the back door, remember?" He carefully stood Danny in an upright position on the deck. "Stay here for a minute. Let me check if everything's okay."

I watched him enter and thought of Brian on Antigua. Our son did the same thing to protect me when someone had broken into his place.

The kids and I stood still, watching the lights go on, one by one, in all the rooms, upstairs and down. Thankfully, they didn't know why we couldn't go inside, and I wasn't about to tell them.

A few minutes later, Paul came out to say nothing appeared to be disturbed. The only thing I noticed was that our wet shoes had made a mess on the foyer floor. I'd wipe it up later. We guided the kids to their bedrooms, helped them get into pajamas and brush their teeth. Then we steered them into their beds and covered each one with their quilts. I lingered at Danny's bedside and watched his little chest rise and fall. If I hadn't been so strong and healthy the night of that terrible home invasion, four years ago, he might not be here tonight. My angel. I gently kissed his cheek.

Downstairs, I found Paul searching security companies on the internet. "Next week I'm going to call and see what we can buy for protection."

"Okay, don't stay up too late. I'm going to bed." I kissed him. "Love you."

Paul waved his hand good night.

I lay in bed thinking that we'd been lucky tonight. Nothing had happened. Then I remembered how I felt when I was tied up, in the front parlor, while two guys dug up our backyard looking for treasure. I was pregnant with Danny for God's sake. I could have lost him. I closed my eyes tighter, trying to rid my head of the whole thing. It could have been much worse, I thought. I've grown stronger since that night. I handled myself pretty well. Thankfully, the rest of my pregnancy with Danny proved to be very healthy. He was a beautiful baby and has grown strong. I could feel my body calming down and drifting to sleep.

* * *

The next morning, the little ones woke us up around 7:30. Paul was up before me, as usual, making the coffee. My mind haunted me with the idea that someone might have entered our house again, but I dispelled my insecurity with an admittance of being paranoid. A security system would be a great plan.

Paul kept the gallery closed and the day turned out to be very nice. I was happy to be thinking about the mill site, the number 3 and the letter W again. We had a great dinner of baked ham, potato salad, pickled beets, and fresh bread with a store-bought chocolate cake for dessert. Nice and easy. We were all together as a family and played board games with the kids. Then it was early to bed for Molly and Danny. After we blew the last goodnight kiss to the kids, Paul and I quickly settled in under the covers for a cozy night's sleep.

"Paul?" I whispered.

"What, honey?"

"Tomorrow, when Martha comes, would you come with me up to that old mill site?"

He was quiet.

"Almost all of the snow is gone and it's going to be sunny all week." I sat up to face him. "If we brought shovels, we could do some exploring around the site. I could use the muscle."

"I thought that guy Peter said not to disturb anything until he had a chance to investigate it further."

"I know, but I have an idea about something."

"Nancy, please don't go crazy."

"I won't. I'll be very careful. Besides, you'll be with me."

Paul pulled me closer.

"What could happen?" I said.

*   *   *

A few miles down the road from the Caldwell home, Nick was in the motel room studying all his notes and the images from his phone. He had transferred them to his computer so that he could blow them up on a larger screen to check for anything that he might have missed. He spotted the W and the tiny number 3 from the second Thomas Davis map.

His phone vibrated with an incoming text: *losing patience– you have 2 days to complete. A.D.*

"Shit!" He leaned back in the chair and decided he'd better get himself up to the mill site tomorrow. The snow had melted and there shouldn't be anyone around up there. He was running out of time.

37

Present Day
BREWSTER/ORLEANS

MARTHA ARRIVED EARLY on Monday morning. Around 7:30, Paul headed towards the garage to gather shovels for our adventure.

The coffee smelled good as I filled our travel cups and grabbed a few power bars. I hurried upstairs to take the map from the safe. When it was opened, I immediately saw that the pouch of silver coins was gone. I checked under our legal papers, twice. That's odd, I thought, but wanted to get to the mill site, so I just picked up the map and closed the safe.

Downstairs, I could see Paul was already outside. I quickly searched my pockets to see if I had my phone, a small notebook with a pen, and a copy of the teapot map showing the same directions from Tommy D's old vellum.

"All set?" I asked as I met Paul by the Jeep. "By the way, did you take the pouch of old coins out of the safe upstairs?"

"Nope. Why?"

"It's missing." I opened the passenger car door and jumped in. "Do you think that Molly or Danny took it out to play with?"

"I hope not. We told them the coins weren't toys."

"Well, let's get going. I'll talk to them when they get home from school." I climbed into the Jeep.

Paul slammed shut the rear hatch of the Wrangler and checked his pockets for his phone and gloves. "I've got as much as we can carry into the woods." Just as he climbed into the driver's seat, his cell rang.

"Paul Caldwell," he answered.

I waited, trying to sense who it was.

"Of course, I'll be here."

Darn it, I thought. Now what's going on?

He closed the phone. "Nancy, I need to stay home. Remember the new client that was interested in that big acrylic?"

"Yes."

"Well, they're leaving for Europe and want to see it one more time before they make their decision about buying it. They're flying out tonight." He gave me a sorry look.

I was angry. "Can't you be here for me just once in a while?"

"If I don't sell, we don't eat. We've been doing this for a long time. You should be used to it," he stepped out of the Jeep and headed towards the gallery.

I yelled after him, "I guess I'm just getting tired of it."

Over his shoulder, he said, "We'll talk later." He stopped and turned towards me. "You still going to go by yourself?"

"Yeah." I got out of the Jeep and settled into the driver's seat. "Just thought it would've been nice to go together."

He walked back towards me. "Be careful."

By now it was almost eight o'clock and I wanted to get going. I put the gears into reverse and gave him a half-hearted smile.

Before I turned left out of the driveway, I took a sip of coffee and adjusted my sunglasses. I'll be fine without Paul. I almost wish he had a regular, nine-to-five job. Then he'd have more time to be with me. Just forget it, I told myself. I'll be fine.

After a few minutes, I was in Orleans and getting close to Pleasant Bay. It's not too far, I thought, watching for the convenience store where I would park. Up ahead, on my left, I turned and parked in the rear of the store's lot, thinking I should be okay in the back.

As luck would have it, there was very little traffic on the road, which allowed me to cross the street with no problem. I studied the edge of the woods for the opening to the path, and remembered there was an interesting tree right along the road that marked the opening. I spotted it in a few seconds then headed towards the old fruit tree that had twisted itself around a little maple.

Shifting the shovel in my hand for a better grip, I stepped into the woods to follow the path. Hopefully the yellow caution tape was still marking the second path to turn onto so that I could see which direction to walk in to find the mill site.

As I passed the old walk–in basement foundation I'd discovered with Nick, the yellow caution tape came into view. I watched my footing up the sloped forest floor alongside the 8x8 foot opening. About three hundred yards ahead, the mill site's old stones were in front of my feet. I dropped the shovel and pulled out the directions on the teapot map.

I looked around for anyone else in the woods before I started talking to myself. It was an old habit that helped me think clearly. I read aloud, *"Follow the new road to the river of Namskaket. Travel to the southern ridge of where Harwich meets Eastham. The property of Baker and Sons will be marked with a stake 10 yards from the corner of the oak. Follow a line along the Magnetic North, parallel with the Cove's inlet."*

I checked a reading on my phone to make sure I was in the right place. "I'm standing on the southern ridge where Harwich meets Eastham." Scanning the ridgeline, I continued, "I'm also on the Magnetic North and parallel to Pleasant Bay's Cove. Now, where should I dig first?"

I looked closer at the map. My finger rested on the tiny drawing of the mill, then moved down to the 3W written under it. I stepped back from the stones and zeroed in on the ground to locate the stone displaying the carving of the W. After brushing leaves away from the ground's surface I saw it about a foot in front of me. Standing up, I looked at the stones to see the whole picture. Where does the number 3 fit in to all of this?

Could it be three steps? Of course, that's it! My shoe size was a good 10 inches long. If I step off and give myself an extra few inches…I walked forward, beginning with the W stone and then reached for my shovel.

38

Present Day
BREWSTER - SILAS'S APARTMENT

THE COLD, DRY AIR drifted through the old house. Silas lay still, not wanting to get off the couch where he'd been sleeping since the General moved in.

"Hey! Get up!" The General yelled from the lone bedroom. "It's eight o'clock. I got things to do today and you're my ride...wherever I wanna go." He limped into the bathroom. "So get your ass up and get dressed!"

Silas muttered under his breath after the bathroom door closed, "Shut up, you fuckin' old man."

The General came out of the bathroom to find Silas counting the pieces of eight from the stolen pouch. "Looks like you're still a sorry little shit, just like your father said you were. You should have looked around for more booty in the house. I would've warned you if anyone was coming."

Silas shoved the gold coins back into the cloth bag. "They might be worth something." He put the pouch in his coat pocket.

"Awww, I could've done better...." The General waved Silas off. "Found something valuable. Not that crap."

Silas headed for the bathroom and slammed the door behind him.

The General took his time going down the rickety outside steps that were barely attached to the dilapidated house. He carried a large, brown, leather satchel.

Silas trailed behind him with an exasperated look on his face.

"Where we goin'?"

The General said nothing.

When they finally reached the bottom, Silas quickly shoved the General aside to unlock the car. "Where we goin'?" he asked again.

The old man regained his balance, opened the car door and ordered, "Orleans, then get onto Route 28, by Pleasant Bay."

Silas pulled away from the back of the house and turned out of the driveway.

*   *   *

ORLEANS

After a mile and a half, the General barked, "Pull in over there. Park next to the chain-link fence."

Silas slowed the car. A small sign on the fence read: *Orleans Water Conservation Area.*

He turned right onto the dirt road and glanced down to check the gas gauge. "Christ, I'm almost empty. Maybe I should drive up ahead to that convenience store. Isn't there another way to get into these woods?"

"I don't know." The General adjusted his eye patch. "No time to get gas now. You can get it after we're done here."

Silas was out of the car first. He walked over to the edge of the woods and stared into the thick mass of trees and scrub.

The old man stayed in his seat. He sneered at Silas as he pulled out a plastic garbage bag and the Smith & Wesson from his satchel. Hiding the gun in the waistband of his jeans, he exited the car, carrying only the black garbage bag. "Hey, Silas! Carry this will ya?"

Silas reluctantly grabbed the bag and mumbled something, but the General never heard it.

"Did you bring the spade?" The General growled.

"Yeah." The kid opened the trunk to retrieve the pointed shovel.

They walked around the end of one side of the fence to follow the dirt road up a hill. The General stopped halfway, turned to his left then stepped over the brush and into the woods. Silas followed, carefully watching for any bugs or spiders.

The two unlikely partners trudged through the woods as the

sound of the General's metal knee brace blended in with the crunch of dead leaves and dry twigs.

The General stopped after about five minutes. "We got company."

Silas stared ahead into the brown forest. "I don't see anyone."

"Over there." He pointed to his left. "A woman. Looks like she's digging." He stood quiet to watch her.

Silas didn't care. His eyes were glued to the ground trying to see if anything had crawled up his pants.

The General motioned to Silas with his hand to keep moving forward, "Let's keep goin'."

* * *

Earlier that Morning
AN ORLEANS MOTEL

Nick woke early. The small round table next to the curtained window held his files and laptop. A photo of Nancy Caldwell's antique locket and paperwork from the Spanish Government about lost treasure were spread across the surface of his makeshift desk. On top of one of the files was a black velvet pouch; John Julian's heirloom earrings lay contrasted against the dark of the bag. A semi-automatic was nestled in a shoulder holster that hung on the back of a chair, within easy reach of where he slept.

Dressed in boxers and T-shirt, Nick sat on the edge of the bed looking at the piles of paper. The time on his phone was eight o'clock. He had just enough time to shower before the Army & Navy store opened.

After buttoning up his shirt, Nick strapped on the shoulder holster under his jacket then headed downstairs for the motel's complimentary coffee and Danish pastry in the lobby.

At the military surplus store, he bought gloves, a portable shovel, and some canvas duffel bags. After tossing them into the back seat of his rental car, he traced his route across a map of Orleans then headed south, for Pleasant Bay. Nick had a good idea of where he was going but he wanted to be sure.

39

Present Day
ORLEANS – CAPE COD

AFTER MY SHOVEL had gone down into the black soil only about ten inches, I heard some rustling behind me. Turning around, I saw two men in the distance coming towards me from the opposite direction of where I came in. My heart pumped faster.

Oh my God, someone else is here in the woods! I turned again to position myself so that I could face them as they came nearer to where I was digging, cautioning myself to stay calm. What if they ask what I'm doing? I'll tell them I'm researching something for the local historical society. Okay. That's a great idea. I continued my excavation.

I glanced up and noticed that the strangers were very different in age but both were dressed in black leather, like they'd just stepped off the city subway. I saw that the younger man was carrying a black garbage bag and a shovel. The other man had a limp and a black patch over one eye.

As the older man finally passed me, he lifted his arm up to wave, "Morning."

For a quick second, his ankle length leather coat flew open and I thought I saw the butt of a gun strapped to the side of his waist.

Maybe I should leave? I thought, as a cold chill climbed up my spine. The younger guy passed me at a distance, keeping his eyes on me the whole time. Yeah, I should get out of here. Then within seconds they both headed south and away from me. I relaxed a little, hoping to dig some more.

I watched until their backs disappeared over the ridgeline and out of sight. They seemed to be headed in the direction of where I'd entered the woods. Hopefully they'll be gone by the time I was finished here. I turned back to the pile of dirt by the stone featuring the W, concentrating only on my digging.

As I pushed the black soil around, I wondered how much deeper should I go. And where had I seen the younger guy before? Never mind, just do two more shovelfuls of dirt; then I'll leave. I plunged the shovel again into the black soil and hit something that stopped the blade. Determined to get through the blockage, I jammed the steel point into the ground a few more times, hoping to break past whatever was stopping my shovel. As the dirt flew up over my hiking boots, a tiny hint of silver appeared on the inside of the hole.

I knelt down to get a closer look. Using the shovel's blade, I picked at the speck of grey. My head filled with pressure as I bent my upper body downward so that my fingers could claw at the ground to loosen the dirt. Suddenly, several small discs began to fall onto the crumbling black soil, some silver, some gold. I reached again for the shovel to dig out more clumps of soil in and around the area. A flat, thin piece of what looked like bark fell away from one side. I quickly picked it up to learn that it felt like old leather. Oh my God! My head began to spin. I sat back with my hands resting on my knees and just stared at what I'd unearthed.

After rubbing the surface of one of the odd shaped discs, a faint crest was revealed. My body swayed as my heart beat faster. I realized that I was holding another real piece of eight: silver that was cut into an uneven circle then branded by a pirate as he divided up the stolen treasure.

The sun warmed my back and my emotions ran high as I dug deeper. As I unbuttoned my old winter coat, my antique necklace got caught on something around my neck. I should never have worn it today, I thought. I pulled at the silver chain, trying to get it free; as it broke loose, a few strands of my hair came with it.

I continued digging and could see various sizes of uncut gemstones also falling away from the sides of the hole and down onto the soil. Maybe I should get Paul. This is too exciting to keep to myself. Then I started to laugh at the whole situation and couldn't believe it was happening again.

I brushed a few strands of hair away from my face with the back of my dirty-gloved hand. Am I dreaming? No, I can taste the dirt on my lips. Stay calm, Nancy. My heart felt like it was going to jump right out of my chest. Take a deep breath and try to be sensible. The best thing to do now would be to cover up the hole so no one else would find it, and then return with Paul and some bags to carry whatever else we might find.

I shoved a few coins and some gems into my pocket, pushed the dirt back into the hole and smoothed it flat with the back of the shovel. After lifting the W stone back on top of the dirt, I scattered some leaves and twigs over the marked stone. It looked hidden from the average walker, but I knew where it was.

Storm clouds began moving in and the woods grew darker. A smile stretched across my face as I headed for the path marked with the yellow caution tape. This discovery was nothing like my first one. The treasure I'd found in my backyard yielded some gold and silver coins and only a few pieces of jewelry. Those artifacts belonged in a museum. This treasure was different. Gemstones! Diamonds! It presented me with an opportunity to reap profit for John Julian, back on Antigua, and also for myself.

I set my eyes before my feet so I wouldn't trip over any vines or branches as my hiking boots made their way across the forest floor. Paul and I were going to be millionaires!

The two guys I'd seen earlier suddenly crossed my mind. It'll be okay, I reassured myself, dismissing any sense of danger. They should be long gone by now and well out of the woods.

40

Present Day
ORLEANS – CAPE COD

NICK HAD PARKED right next to Nancy's car at the convenience mart and walked quickly across the street in search of the twisted tree marking the opening in the woods.

At the same moment, the General stood with his back to where Nancy had been digging, just out of her sight range. He leaned in over the deepest side of the old foundation to see that the bottom was about five feet down. The hole was relatively small and built into the side of an embankment that resembled a walk–in basement. He swung his head back and forth to scan the debris that covered its base. "It shouldn't be that far down under the dirt…maybe a foot or so."

Silas stood his ground next to the old man, not wanting to be any closer to the edge.

With a clack of his knee brace, the General stepped back, looked at Silas and ordered, "Get down there. Take the shovel."

"You're crazy. I'm not going in there."

The General opened his coat and pulled out the Smith & Wesson. "I didn't want to use this but you give me no choice."

Silas glared at him. "Take it easy. I'll do it." He cautiously walked towards the front of the foundation's edge where the dirt was almost level with the forest floor. Straddling a few rocks that had been part of the original stonewall, Silas's shoe sunk into the muck about two inches. "Shit." He brought the other leg over so he could get a better footing.

The old man looked impatient. "Keep goin'," he growled, now waving the gun at Silas to hurry up.

"Fuck you," Silas whispered, and then he slowly walked straight back to the rear of the hollowed-out ground.

"Over in the corner, on your right." The General's gun pointed to the same direction.

Old stonewalls surrounded Silas on three sides. Flashing a disgusted look toward the General, he jammed the shovel into the black dirt then quickly turned and asked one more time, "Come on. Do I really have to do this?"

Silas heard the General pull back the hammer of the gun; a clear signal the old man was serious. He continued to dig, cursing with every lunge of the spade. It wasn't too long before he heard a dull thud. He stopped and knelt on one knee. As he brushed dirt away, the top of a brown backpack appeared. The bag loosened only half way from the soil as he pulled at it. Silas quickly unzipped the exposed top half. "Holy shit! There's money in here."

"That's it," the General urged, stepping closer to the edge to get a better look at what Silas had uncovered. The heel of his leather boot accidentally slid against a moss-covered rock, catching him off guard. His finger squeezed the trigger. The gun went off.

The old man fell onto his back, knocking the wind out of him as he dropped the gun. He scrambled to his feet only to see Silas laying face down over the opened backpack. His gnarled fingers reached for his pills from the inside of his coat, flipped the lid off and swallowed one. The General's hand trembled as he reached down to retrieve the gun.

41

Present Day
ORLEANS - CAPE COD

A LOUD BANG stopped me in my tracks. I listened but the woods were silent again. My pulse increased. Was that a gunshot? Oh my God! Why didn't Paul come with me? Damn it! I need to get the hell out of here. I kept the shovel in my right hand so that I could use it as a weapon if I needed to. *Hail Mary full of grace….*

As I scrambled through the dry leaves I kept turning my head back and forth and behind me, in search of anything out of the ordinary. Take it easy, I told myself, I'm the one who loves to walk in the woods. Everything will be okay.

After another couple of steps, I saw the old man in the long leather coat. He was still in the woods and it looked like he was hiding something behind his back. As I came closer to him, he turned and stared at me with his one eye. A low growl echoed towards me as he muttered, "God damn it."

With no other way out of the woods I knew I had to walk right by him. I wondered where the other guy was. I slowed up a little, trying to give myself a few moments to calm down.

He was looking right at me. "Hello…again."

I forced a smile but kept my head down and said nothing. As I approached him, he looked even more menacing with his wild gray hair and black eye patch. He turned towards me and in a garbled voice asked, "I was wondering if you could help me out?"

Oh no, I thought, as I cautiously slowed down to pause near the edge of the hole. "What's wrong?"

"My friend seems to have hit his head and isn't answering me." He pointed to a body lying in the hole.

"Holy crap!" I swallowed hard.

"I'd go down there myself, but my knee isn't very good." He gestured to his knee brace. "I'd really appreciate it if you would check on him."

"Maybe you should call 911?" I suggested, hopeful that would end our exchange.

"Well, I've got this old phone...but it doesn't get any of those little lines. That means no reception, right?" He showed me a flip phone that looked to be about ten years old.

I nodded in agreement then slowly took a few steps away from the edge of the hole. Turning my back to the old man, I prepared to leave.

He asked again, "Sorry to bother you, but could you go down in there and see if he's okay? I'm getting worried."

I spotted a cell phone tower on the horizon and wondered why he wasn't getting any reception. I turned around, quickly slid my finger across the bottom of my phone to unlock the keys. Just as I tapped in 911 and pressed SEND, the old man slapped the phone out of my grip with one hand and shoved me backwards with the other.

The skeleton-like branches at the top of the bare trees were the last things I saw as I fell backwards, down into the dark hole. I let out a quick scream, but in the few seconds that it took for my body to slam onto the dirt, my head filled with a barrage of words, begging and pleading with God to not let me die. I saw Paul, Molly, Casey, and Danny's faces flash through my mind. Then I got angry. I will not die here!

I buffered my fall by curling my legs up and trying to land and roll. My lower back hit the ground first. On impulse, I rolled onto my right shoulder, but the force of the impact took control and pushed my upper body to the other side, like a pinball. The jagged stones in the dirt jammed their sharp edges into my back. The pain took my breath away. With a dull thud, my left shoulder finally slammed against a large boulder. I felt my body rock back and forth a few times before I blacked out.

42

Present Day
ORLEANS – CAPE COD

THE GENERAL STOOD watching the woman fall into the hole, waiting to figure out what he should do next. When she finally lay still, he looked around the woods to see if he had any other company. There was no one. With the click of his knee brace, he limped down the embankment to where the ground was level then slowly lifted his good leg over the stones so that he could swing the bad one next to it. He pushed his ratted hair back under the band of his eye patch to get a closer look at the situation. The woman lay a little to the left of Silas. The kid was still face down over the half buried backpack.

"I can do this," the General grunted. He winced in pain as the heels of his black boots sunk into the dark soil. "Fuck!" Determined to retrieve the backpack, his body swayed back and forth as his big boots, caked with mud, clumsily made their way to where the two bodies were lying. When he finally stood over the woman, he swiveled her upper torso further away from where Silas was lying, "Sorry, lady." The General then pushed Silas's body closer to the stone wall and onto his back. He was surprised to hear his young accomplice moaning. So he wasn't dead after all.

With a few awkward pulls on the strap, the dirty nylon bag popped out of the dirt, sending the old man onto his butt. He sat with his legs outstretched, going through the contents of the bag, like a little kid playing in a sandbox. It was all there, just as he had left it three years ago. His eyes moved swiftly over the fifty packs of small bills that were bundled with rubber bands. Under each band was a square piece of paper with the number 2000 scrawled across it.

Intent on making sure all of his money was there, the General never noticed the approach of someone else in the woods.

*   *   *

Nick grinned when he spotted the yellow caution tape up ahead. His presence in the woods was non–intrusive; he'd been trained well. The stones of the old foundation appeared in the distance on his right, confirming that he was on the correct course to the mill. He stopped a few feet from the edges of the crumbling stonewall and stared down into the hole.

An old man was sitting on the dirt between what looked like two dead bodies. "Now what?" Nick sighed. The unexpected scene took him off guard and his foot stepped onto a dry twig instead of over it.

The General heard the crack. He stopped rifling through the bag and cocked his head to listen, his hands curled around a bundle of cash. He sat motionless until his attention was diverted to a gold coin in the dirt next to the woman's side pocket. Shoving the cash back into the bag, he reached for the yellowed object. Then with one hand holding the coin and the other gripping the strap of the backpack, he tried to push himself up to stand. He fell backwards. Next he rolled over and balanced on his knees in another attempt to get up, but with no luck. He did manage to lift his head, only to see a stranger looking down on him.

"What're you doing, buddy?" Nick came closer to the old man who was on all fours now. Nick reached for an elbow. "Let me help you."

The General swatted at the intruder who was interfering with his plans. "I don't need no help."

"You sure?" Nick grabbed at the half-open backpack and spotted the cash inside.

The old man wouldn't let go of it. "Don't touch that. It's mine!"

Nick raised his hands in mock submission. "Take it easy, I just want to help you out." He watched the leather coated geezer eventually stand. Peering beyond him, Nick recognized one of the bodies as

Mrs. C. "What'd you do, old man?"

The General clutched the backpack against his chest and turned to get away. Nick knelt down next to Mrs. C. He felt her neck and found a pulse, then he awkwardly reached behind her to unfasten the antique necklace. The clasp wouldn't open. He fiddled with it for a few seconds before it came free. He shoved it into his coat pocket.

By this time, the General had already started to walk up the slope of the embankment to head out of the woods with his found money.

"Hey, where you going?" Nick yelled out as he hustled after him.

Just as the General reached the high point of the hole, he fumbled for his gun under his coat. Nick took the opportunity to land a solid right onto the old man's chin, sending him to the ground…out cold.

Nick picked up the bag filled with money and checked the old man's pockets for anything else that looked interesting. He found a gold coin, a bottle of heart pills, and the Smith & Wesson. He took the gold coin plus the backpack and continued up the path to the old mill site, a sinister grin now darkening his face.

43

Present Day
ORLEANS – CAPE COD

MY EYES SLOWLY OPENED to see gray sky. For a moment, I wasn't sure where I was. I turned my head slightly to the left, then right and up a little...nothing but dried oak leaves and dirt. My left hand lay listless by my side. Lifting my right hand, I rested it across my stomach then wiggled my feet up and down. I could feel my legs...a good sign. My body started shivering and shaking as shock took over.

I remembered the old man who'd pushed me down. Where's my phone? Shit! He'd knocked it away from me. I turned my head to the right and gasped when I realized there was a body lying beside me. It was the creepy guy who'd been with the old man. His eyes were closed. Was he dead? Oh, dear God, what have I gotten myself into this time? I looked above me, through the tree branches, where a bird flew across the sky. I had to get out of here.

My body didn't listen as I tried to sit upright. Each time I thrust forward, I fell back in pain. Maybe I could roll to the side and get up on my elbow; that might work. I took some deep breaths then slowly raised my upper body onto my right elbow and forearm. Everything started spinning. Rolling backwards, I tried to breathe. I felt sick to my stomach. After a few seconds, I rolled over again and managed to stay put, but as my injured left shoulder sagged, its weight pulled my left side closer to the ground. It felt like someone was yanking my arm right out of its socket. I thought I would pass out from the pain. Trying to hold still, I didn't know how long I could stay on my side. It hurt too much to breathe deeply, but my lungs were screaming for air. An aching pain began to crawl up the side of my neck. I rolled onto my back again.

Dizzy as I was, I coached myself to keep going. It was almost more than I could bear but I was determined to get up. I unzipped my jacket and put my wrist inside of the opening. It acted like a sling and enabled me to try again. Finally once on my side, I pressed my cheek against the ground, then my forehead, turning, pushing, and trying to maneuver myself up so I could sit back onto my legs. With my arm stabilized, the pain subsided long enough for me to think a little. I must stand up, I told myself. The stone walls that surrounded me seemed insurmountable, but maybe they could offer leverage to help me get off my knees. But first I had to roll flat again. I hit the ground with a cry of pain then caught sight of the guy opposite me. He was still not moving.

Moving my upper body closer to him, I gripped my jacket tighter and wiggled my torso nearer to his side. After a deep breath, I was able to roll over just enough so that I could lay my good forearm across his chest to reach the wall. It was agony. I stretched as far as I could for any stone that stuck out from the rest. He groaned a little and I noticed a small amount of blood by the zipper of his jacket.

My fingertips finally found a grip across one of the stone edges. With all my strength, I started lifting and pulling my body up to a sitting position, keeping a hold of the gritty surface. Wet sand crumbled as I clawed up the gray bumps, trying to gain some more height. It felt as if my fingers would break away from my hand. I felt two fingernails split under the pressure but my body was finally rising up. Don't stop…keep going…pull up! I was able to place a knee on the guy's upper thigh. This gave me a chance to get my other knee closer so I could stand up. Another groan came from the still body.

Once upright, I peered over the old wall; my head almost level with the ground. I'm going to be okay, I assured myself, only to come face-to-face with the old man, who was lying on his stomach. His eye patch had flipped to one side, revealing a large mottled scar that should have been an eye. I recoiled at the horrifying image. The position of his body gave the impression that he was sleeping. His arm was oddly stretched out beyond his head across the forest floor, as if he was pointing to something.

I heard my cell phone ring to the tune of *Pirates of the Caribbean*. But where was it? I couldn't see it anywhere. Just as I took a step to start walking out and away from the old walls, I felt something latch onto my foot. I panicked and almost fell over, but grabbed onto the wall again. Turning, I realized the guy on the ground was holding my ankle.

He pleaded with me, "Lady, don't go. My name is Silas. Please, help me."

"Let go!" I screamed back at him, shaking my foot with enough force that his hand broke loose and he fell back to the ground.

He moaned as he closed his eyes. "The General shot me."

"The General?" Who's he talking about? I looked down at the scared kid, "I'll get some help, I promise." Why the hell did I tell him that?

The old man was still laying on the edge of the hole with his face towards me. He looked like he wouldn't be doing any more harm to me, but I certainly couldn't be sure. I decided to come back and help Silas later, but right now I need to save myself.

I was able to regain enough strength to slowly walk to where the ground was level and lift my feet over the rock foundation. My shoulder hurt like hell, but I continued up the embankment and past the old man's body in search for my phone. It was too painful to bend over, so I kicked my foot around, trying to uncover it. I heard it go off again. I listened for it, but still couldn't locate it.

I glanced around the woods to get my bearings and to see if anyone else was nearby. There was a body on the ground and a body in the old cellar. What a predicament! I wasn't sure what to do.

The sound of a shovel slicing into dirt caught my ear. I didn't have to walk very far before I saw someone digging near the old mill site. I shuffled towards the hunched-over figure. He heard my approach and looked over his shoulder. It was Nick! But I thought he'd left the Cape already.

"Nick! Is that you?" I tried to walk a little faster to get to him but my breathing became labored and I had to stop. The pain in my shoulder was returning with a vengeance and I could feel my strength growing weaker by the second. The surprise of a familiar face lowered my defenses and everything began to move in slow motion. My eyes wanted to close. I felt faint. No! I'll be okay, I thought, now that I know Nick is here. He'll help me.

Nick stood up and came towards me. "Mrs. C, you all right?"

His arm was strong around my waist as he helped me over to a large boulder. I couldn't even talk. I just wanted to sit down. When my hurt arm finally rested across my lap it actually felt comfortable.

I looked up at Nick. "What are you doing here?" My eyes moved away from him for a second so that I could settle my bottom to a flatter part of the boulder's hard surface. "I thought you left the Cape."

Nick picked up a trowel. "I was on my way over the bridge when I got a call from the Corps. My assignment was delayed again." He knelt down and continued digging. "I decided to hang around a bit; take in some of the sights."

Questions flew into my head, but every time I moved, even slightly, the pain shot up into my neck and clouded my reasoning. I asked again, "But what are you doing here?"

He didn't answer. I could see the W stone was moved to the side and he was digging deeper than I had gone. I began to feel uneasy about his coincidental presence in the woods and the fact that he was digging under the W stone.

"Nick?"

He slowly met my eyes with a look that sent a chill up my back. "Look, you bitch, just sit there and shut up!"

44

Present Day
BREWSTER/ORLEANS

PAUL HUNG UP the phone and threw the client's information into the trash bin. "Boy, that's disappointing." He started to leave but stopped to massage the back of his neck and think a minute. Leaning over to retrieve the paper from the trash, he smoothed it out on his drawing table then placed it in the file labeled 'potential sales'.

The wall clock hadn't reached 10:00 AM so there was still time for him to join Nancy up at the mill site. He grabbed his phone, pressed Nancy's number and waited for her to answer. He slid it back into his pants pocket when she didn't pick up. Once inside the house, a quick peek at her desktop revealed notes as to where the site was located. Paul jotted the directions down and signaled to Martha, "I'll be back in a few hours." He went to get his camera in the studio.

"Okay, Paul. No problem." She glanced up from emptying the dishwasher to look out the kitchen window. A black sedan slowly pulled into the driveway. "Someone's here," she called out before he was able to close the door leading to the gallery.

Paul turned around and headed back to the glassed foyer door. He saw two men dressed in black suits get out of the car then walk toward the deck that led to the house, avoiding the path to the gallery. He noticed the closed sign was still out and visible from the street. He opened the door with caution before they could knock on it. "What can I do for you?"

A man with a crew cut asked, "Mr. Caldwell?"

"Yes?"

"We're from the FBI. I'm Special Agent Clark." He showed his ID card with badge.

Paul stood taller and stepped back but kept his hand on the door's handle, holding it open only half way.

"Is Mrs. Caldwell available?"

"No...." Paul's face paled. "What's wrong?"

"We have reason to believe that your wife may be in danger. May we come in?"

Paul swallowed hard before he let them in.

As they crossed the threshold, Martha peered out of the kitchen to stare at the two strangers. Paul looked visibly upset. His chest heaved up and down in short panicked breaths.

The agent with glasses asked, "Is there somewhere private we can talk?"

"Of course." Paul led them into Nancy's office.

Martha met her employer's wide eyes with a questioning glance as he passed her. He ignored them and ordered her, "Stay in the kitchen, Martha."

With only a few long strides, he reached the parlor door in seconds. The agents followed him in, and Paul slid the pocket door closed behind the three of them.

Agent Clark located a picture on his cell phone and showed it to Paul. "Do you recognize this man?"

"That looks like Nick," Paul said with alarm in his voice, "but with the black hair, I can't really tell if it's him or not." He kept studying the image. "What does he have to do with the FBI and with us?"

Clark tapped his phone closed and looked to his partner. "So that's what he's calling himself this time...Nick!"

Paul grew anxious, his voice rising. "What do you mean 'this time'?" He clasped his hand over his mouth, trying to calm himself.

"Take it easy, Mr. Caldwell. We're aware that he's used several names over his young career, but his legal name is Quinten Sulicci. A known associate of the New England Mafia, he turned rogue and has been working on his own for a few years now."

"What?" Paul looked startled then angry. "Tell me what's going on...now!"

"Where was your wife going this morning?"

"Orleans. I was supposed to go with her but couldn't." He pulled the paper with the directions to the mill site out of his jeans pocket and handed it over. "This might help you find her. What kind of danger is she in?" He pulled his phone out and pressed in Nancy's number again. He looked over to Clark. "I tried to call her before, but she didn't pick up." Paul's hand was shaking as he shut the phone down and shoved it back into his pocket. "She's still not answering!"

Clark checked his watch. "We don't have a lot of time to explain any more to you right now. We're meeting Lieutenant Gale over at the Orleans police station in about twenty minutes."

"Well, if it involves my wife, I'm coming with you." He stood in front of the closed door in a feeble attempt to prevent the men from leaving the office if they wouldn't agree to his tagging along. "You can't stop me from following you in my own car."

The two FBI men took a stance, shoulder-to-shoulder, legs spread in anticipation for some trouble. "I'm afraid you need to stay here, Mr. Caldwell."

There was a two second standoff before Paul slid open the pocket door, stepped aside for them to leave. He followed right behind them through the house, past Martha in the kitchen. They went out the main door without him. He stayed inside and watched the men get into their car and drive away. With a quick twist of his head, he gave Martha another order. "Stay here and wait for the kids to get home. I'll call you with any news as soon as I know myself."

"But...?"

"Just stay close to the phone and keep the doors locked." He slammed the door shut behind him.

The Orleans Police station was not far from the Caldwell house. He knew a short cut and arrived at the station within minutes. Once inside, he found the FBI men standing in the entranceway, talking with a policeman.

"Mr. Caldwell, I thought we asked you to stay home," said Agent Clark.

Paul looked him straight in the eye. "Yes, you did, but I need to know what's happening with my wife." He stood defiant, waiting.

The policeman stepped between the FBI men and came closer to him. He put his face a few inches from Paul's nose. "Mr. Caldwell? I know you're worried about your wife, but you need to let us do our job. Understand?"

Paul stood his ground.

"If you'd sit down for a minute, we'll be able to assess the facts that we do know and then get back to you."

"Not good enough."

Lieutenant Gale spun around. "What'd you say?" He placed one hand on his holstered gun and the other on his leather belt.

"Don't worry," Paul said with resignation as he backed up onto the bench and sat down. "I'll stay put."

The three men looked at each other then disappeared behind the closed door.

Within seconds Paul got up and left.

As he drove toward Pleasant Bay he tried to recall the directions that Nancy had left on her desk. He fumbled around in the glove compartment, looking for his Leatherman, the multi–purpose knife with a lot of tools attached, which he kept in the car for emergencies. The convenience store came up on his left. He spotted Nancy's car in the rear parking lot. After pulling in beside her car, he opened his trunk and grabbed the tire iron.

Once across the road, he looked for the twisted trees. According to Nancy's notes, they marked the entrance to the path. With the marker in sight, he headed for the hidden opening. Rain started to drizzle, dampening the leaves and forest floor.

45

Present Day
ORLEANS – CAPE COD

AS A CHILD, if I was in a nightmare, I could just stop, turn away from whomever or whatever was chasing me, place my forearm over my eyes and escape. It always worked. I wanted to do that now, but I couldn't lift my arm and I wasn't dreaming. I felt sick. Rain began to drip onto my jacket from the trees above my head. I wondered if I was going to die.

Nick never lifted his face to look at me as he continued digging. I wanted to know why he was here in the woods, but I didn't want to make him angry, so I kept quiet.

He must be after the treasure. If I could keep him talking maybe someone will walk by and see us. I took a chance and whispered, "Nick...what are you looking for?" I remembered we'd talked about finding something valuable, based on the old map, when we came up here together. I never expected he would turn on me like this and steal whatever was buried. I kept watching his hands as they sifted through the gold coins and pieces of eight that were slowly being uncovered. God, what a find! These artifacts have not seen daylight for hundreds of years. As much as my arm hurt, I couldn't take my eyes off of the strange scene unfolding before me. "Nick?"

Paying no attention to me, he stopped digging. Then he picked up a thin, narrow object that resembled a dagger, or letter opener. I squinted to focus better. It looked like a hairpin. The decoration on top of it also resembled the design on my necklace. I went to touch the good luck charm around my neck. It was gone. I looked to my left, where the old man was lying. I must have lost it somewhere in the leaves when he pushed me.

Suddenly the kid Silas appeared over the ridgeline. He was limping towards Nick and me and looked like he was carrying a gun. His red hair literally glowed against his pale face. Is this good or bad for me? God, I don't know what to do. I prayed that he was going to help me.

Big raindrops collected from the branches and dropped on my head. Thank goodness my coat was waterproof. I flipped up my hood. Why was I thinking about keeping dry instead of figuring out how I was going to make it out of here?

Silas's footsteps across the forest floor were muted as the leaves became wet from the rain. Nick didn't hear or notice his approach; he just kept admiring the object in his hand. The kid hobbled faster towards us. He carried a gun and it was pointed directly at Nick. When Nick finally turned his head to answer me, he saw Silas coming up on his side.

Silas yelled out in a high-pitched voice, "I want the backpack! Hand it over."

Nick dropped the hairclip into the hole and swiveled his upper body to face him. Within seconds, he pulled his gun out and shot my potential rescuer. Silas's body fell forward.

"Nooo…." I cried out. "Why'd you shoot him?" My eyes started to tear. "He's just a kid."

Nick's face twisted into a sneer. "Look, I do what I need to do."

I was in so much pain. I didn't want to die now.

Nick finally looked at me. "You know…I really liked you, Mrs. C." He bent lower to pick up what he'd found and held it in his hand, admiring its beauty. "You've got a real nice family." He casually blew some particles of dirt from the hairpin. Then he studied the ornamentation on its top.

Maybe I could talk him into letting me go. "Please, Nick. I'm not going to say anything. You seem to have found what you were looking for. Won't you please let me go? Take the treasure. I don't care about it anymore." I looked right at him, hoping he'd listen with whatever decency he once had inside him.

He ignored me and started to scoop the coins into the canvas bag that lay next to his feet. "You know, you made my job so easy." He picked up the backpack. The bundles of cash were stuffed into the bag on top of the coins. He held up a stack of bills. "This was a nice bonus." Then he let out an evil laugh.

"What're you talking about?" I asked, trying to stall him from completing whatever he was planning to do to me.

"Curious?" He stopped and looked over to me. "Mrs. C," his voice was sarcastic now, "not so smart are you? Interested in what's going on here?"

I nodded and prayed…please take a long time to tell me.

"I was hired to find the missing jewelry from the *San Miguel*. You know, the Spanish treasure fleet that sank off the coast of Florida; the wreck that Sam Bellamy was going to salvage." His shovel dug a little deeper and began to unearth the vivid colors of multiple gemstones. "A discreet collector was very interested in your necklace, which I learned about courtesy of your first adventure. Then you blabbed on about a matching pair of earrings, which I of course stole from Julian on Antigua. And then you led me right here, for the *piece de résistance*; this priceless hair pin." He put the hairpin into his coat pocket, scooped up a handful of gems and threw them into the bag.

I watched him kick dirt back into the hole to fill it in. Some of the gold pieces were still lying there as he carelessly tried to cover everything up.

"You won't get away with this, Nick," I warned him, hoping to keep him talking.

He just smiled. "I already did."

46

Present Day
ORLEANS – CAPE COD

PAUL FOLLOWED the dirt path until he saw a yellow caution tape blowing in the wind. He heard a shot and slowed up, scanning the woods for any sign of Nancy. A line of old stones appeared on his right. He stopped to look into the partial foundation but saw nothing out of the ordinary. As he turned back onto the path, he spotted a glimpse of red in the far corner of the foundation. He stepped over the small wall of rocks and hurried towards it. Taking a quick breath, he picked up Nancy's phone.

Paul rushed out of the foundation and started up the sloped path, only to trip over the old man's prone body. He found an orange bottle of pills, didn't recognize the name but knew they were for the heart. He felt for a pulse but found none. As he crouched near the body, he looked up and spotted a man kicking his feet in the dirt. A woman was sitting on a nearby rock. It was Nancy. She looked hurt. As his eyes focused on the strange scene, he noticed the body of another man, face down on the ground, a few yards up ahead. He stared for only a few seconds and then crept to his left, silently crossing the wet oak leaves.

47

Present day
ORLEANS

I COULD SEE Paul sneaking through the woods out of Nick's sight. My heart felt like it was going to jump out of my throat. He was getting closer. Keep asking questions, I told myself. Keep Nick's attention on me. I quickly uttered, "Nick, could I please see the hairpin?"

"Why not? It may be the last thing you see." He took a step towards me and, from his pocket, he pulled out the pin and held it within my clear view. Attached to the top of the silver pin, a delicate oval piece of ivory was carved with scrimshaw and tinted with blue. Tiny diamonds surrounded its edge. It was the same design as the earrings and my necklace. Beads of sweat dripped from his forehead as he held it nearer to me. The hairpin was exquisite.

Paul was coming closer, carrying a metal bar in front of his chest. Please be careful, I silently prayed.

Nick withdrew a velvet pouch from his pants pocket. He opened it onto the palm of his hand. I could see Julian's earrings and my necklace. "Beautiful, aren't they? My client will be psyched to complete his collection."

"Please, Nick, let me go," I begged.

He filled the pouch with all three pieces. As he tied it shut, he said, "You've been a great help, Mrs. C, but I really should get going now. Sorry I can't stay and chat."

I needed to keep his deadly eyes focused on me. "Nick, please tell me, how'd you find me?"

He pocketed the pouch. "Well, that was easy. You're all over the internet; lots of images showing you and that necklace. You shouldn't have worn it so much." He leaned over to brush the dirt from his knees.

"And what about Antigua? Surely you didn't find out from the internet that I was going to visit my son in the Peace Corps?"

He laughed. "My client has very high connections. People owe him a lot of favors."

"But you were Brian's roommate."

He laughed even louder now, his eyes betraying an evil heart. "I was an imposter, Mrs. C."

My heart went cold. "Then who was my son's roommate? Where is he?"

"He was just in the way. That Devil's Bridge, back on Antigua, sure comes in handy when you need to cover up incriminating evidence."

Nick grabbed the duffle bag in one hand then slowly turned to face me, a relish for murder on his face as he pulled out his gun.

"Nick, don't," I cried.

I saw Paul behind him. Within seconds Paul swung a tire iron across the back of Nick's head. My attacker arched his back up as his body fell to the side. His gun dropped to the ground. Paul rushed over to me still clutching the tire iron. He was breathing heavy as his arm encircled my shoulders: my knight in shining armor.

"Ohhhh, I winced in pain. My left shoulder. I don't know what I did to it."

He quickly withdrew his arm but stayed crouched by my side. "I'm so glad I found you."

"I love you," I whispered.

"The police should be coming soon…I hope." Paul stayed near me.

I breathed a sigh of relief, but it was short lived. Nick moved his leg and started to lift himself, as if to stand.

"Paul!" I screamed. "Nick's moving. Grab his gun."

With a twist of his body, Paul lunged for the semi–automatic and wrestled the gun away from Nick's hand. The gun was now pointing at Nick. With a nimble shove of his foot, Paul pushed Nick, or whatever his real name was back to the ground then took a protective stance between us.

I started to cry with joy at seeing the creep flat out again. The roar of motorcycles rumbled in the distance. We looked at each other simultaneously in amazement. "Do you hear that?" I asked. Paul looked puzzled.

Two warning shots rang out and echoed through the trees as several men, dressed in black and blue nylon jackets, came running across the wet forest floor towards us. Some were police and others were FBI agents.

One policeman yelled to Paul, "Stand down! Drop your weapon!"

Paul dropped the gun and raised his hands high above his head.

I sat there in astonishment. Then I raised my voice, "He's okay! He's with me."

The policeman crept nearer to us. He seemed to ignore my words and kept his gun pointed at Paul. He slowly bent down to pick up Nick's gun, never once taking his eyes off Paul.

Paul recognized one of the FBI men and called out, "It's me, remember? Paul Caldwell?"

The FBI guy shouted out to the policeman in front of us, "He's okay, Lieutenant. That's his wife."

With my good hand, I wiped away tears of relief and looked around at the scene before me. Three bodies were on the ground: one dead, others...not sure. The treasure I was seeking for John Julian had been found. I was alive and my dear, sweet husband was standing next to me.

Another FBI agent approached me. "Mrs. Caldwell, how are you doing?"

His face looked somewhat familiar. I thought for a second. He was the guy at the bar on Antigua, talking to Brian, and the same guy from the plane I'd bumped into with all of my shells.

With a smile, he asked, "Did your children enjoy the conch shells you brought home from Antigua?"

I half-heartedly returned a smile. "So you were following me?"

"Yes, ma'am. I'm Special Agent Clark. We knew you'd made a key discovery four years ago that would enable us to catch one of the biggest smugglers of lost treasure. His name is Alexander Damien."

"I've never heard of him."

He looked over to where poor Silas was lying, signaled to someone to check him out and then continued explaining. "Damien hired the man you know as Nick to find the priceless Spanish Queen's jewels, valued at almost ten million dollars." He walked over to Nick, who was stirring again, and rifled through his pockets. The agent pulled out the velvet pouch and held it up. "This is what he was after, part of the lost treasure of the San Miguel Treasure Fleet."

He shouted another order. "Lieutenant Gale, get one of your men to handcuff this one." He pointed to Nick.

I wanted to get up and punch Nick but my arm was still hurting. It wouldn't do any good except maybe make me feel better. I sat there with a smug look on my face, knowing he was going to jail and I had the treasure. The officer pulled my attacker's hands behind his back and cuffed them, and then he hauled him up to a standing position. Our eyes met and a low grumble rolled out of Nick's mouth as he passed me. "Fuck you."

A grin grew across my face as I watched him leave. "The same to you," I called after him.

A policemen kneeling over Silas yelled out, "This one's alive."

Paul helped me stand up. I was hurting, but it was different now that I knew I was going to be okay. He held onto my good arm as we walked past Silas and then the old man. There was no easy way for anyone to get out of the woods except to walk, that is, if you were able, and I was able. ATV rescue vehicles began to appear, crashing their way through the underbrush.

"There's our motorcycles," I said. One of the three wheelers stopped next to Silas's body.

"Poor kid, I hope he's okay."

As Paul and I passed the old foundation, we stopped and looked down into it. It really didn't look that menacing now. I guess it was deep enough to do some damage though. Feeling secure with Paul's arm around my waist, my senses began to restore themselves and I remembered the reason I was in the woods in the first place. "Paul, what about the treasure I found?"

He gently touched my cheek and tucked a few strands of hair under my hood. "Don't worry, Nancy, I'm sure the police will take good care of it."

"But...," I pleaded.

"No buts, I need to get you to a hospital and check out that arm of yours."

"Please. I'll wait here while you go and talk to Clark. Tell him to be careful with everything. Make sure they understand that it belongs to John Julian, on Antigua."

He looked at me with such care in his eyes, but I could tell he was also really listening to me, which is why I love him so much.

"You sure you're okay?" he asked.

"I'll be fine. Just go." I waved him on with my good arm and followed him a few steps back up the slope to survey what was going on.

Paul walked over to Agent Clark and pointed to the hole that held the artifacts. I watched them talk for a few minutes; then they shook hands.

"Did you tell him that it belongs to someone on Antigua? I hope the government doesn't confiscate everything."

"It's okay. He said he would personally monitor whatever else was dug up. He'll call us tomorrow at home. If you're able to go home."

"I'm sure I'll be fine. I have so many questions." I felt Paul's strong arm again. "What about the money in the backpack? Where did that come from?"

As we made our way ever so slowly out of the woods, I kept talking and Paul just listened. "And what's with the old man and Silas? I think the poor guy on the ground in the leather coat must be the General." By the time we arrived at the cars, our eyes had adjusted to the darkening skies. I looked across the street. Lights began to glow inside the woods, where, I assumed, men would be working to gather up the buried treasure of old John Julian. I still had so many unanswered questions.

48

Present Day
BREWSTER - CAPE COD

SURGERY FOR my torn rotator cuff was scheduled for the Tuesday following my fall into the old foundation. I knew something was terribly wrong with my arm or shoulder. The doctor said I was lucky that I hadn't broken anything. Snow blew sideways outside the bay window of my office. Another storm was upon Cape Cod. I hoped we wouldn't lose power in the frigid temperatures.

Thank goodness I didn't hurt my right arm; I could still function and type at the computer. I would have plenty of time to finish writing about my first adventure and the treasure of Sam Bellamy while I recuperated from my injury. I decided last night that it would definitely be a mix of fact and fiction. Right now, the completion of my novel awaited me. I sat at the computer with one hand hovering over the keyboard.

Molly and Danny ran in. "Mommy, can we help you?"

My arm felt secure in a sling but I was cautious. I held my other hand out, palm up. "Whoa...go a little slower, guys. Mommy needs to be careful so that she doesn't hurt herself any more than she already has."

They came to a halt a few inches away from me. Molly spoke first. "We're supposed to ask if you need something."

I laughed. "Give me some kisses first, right here," I pointed to my left cheek and then to the right.

They asked in unison. "Want some hot chocolate and ginger snaps?" They both beamed as they waited for my answer. Danny latched onto my good hand with his and spoke very seriously. "Sure glad you're okay, Mommy."

"Alright, who's ready for some hot chocolate…and I need plenty of whipped cream on mine."

As I followed the kids into the kitchen, the phone rang.

Martha answered. She peeked her head around the corner. "Nancy, is it all right if an Agent Clark from the FBI comes over tomorrow to talk to you? He wants you to sign some papers."

"Tell him that's fine."

*   *   *

I was up early and eager for more information. Martha said he was coming around 10AM.

At 9:55 I glanced out the window to see a black car pulling in to the driveway. It was special Agent Clark.

The door opened with a blast of cold air. "Come on in," I said.

"Good to see you up and around, Mrs. Caldwell."

"Yes, I'm happy to see you, also. I've so many questions."

Clark stomped his shiny black leather boots on the welcome mat. "Let's go in my office," I said.

I settled at my desk and he in the antique fireside chair. He put his glasses on and pulled out a file from his briefcase. My shoulder ached a little with the tension that was building up inside of me for any news but I waited patiently for him to speak instead of blurting out my questions.

"Let me begin by telling you that, at this moment," he looked at his watch, "Alexander Damien, the international smuggler and collector of rare antiquities, whom I mentioned to you before up in the woods, is being paid a visit in London by Scotland Yard, along with our department, and will probably not be happy with his future situation." He shot a sly grin across to me. "By the way, Damien was Nick's, I mean Quinten Sulicci's, employer. Sulicci was hired to find the Spanish wedding jewels of 1715 Elizabeth of Pharma."

"You know, before all of this happened," I interjected, "I'd read about those wedding jewels when I researched why Sam Bellamy went to the West Indies."

Clark took off his glasses. "Now all we have to do is figure out whom the rightful owners are of the treasure we found."

I sat back in my chair. His statement took me off guard. Surely the earrings belonged to John Julian and the necklace was mine? I quickly asked, "What do you mean…who owns the treasure? Don't the earrings belong to Julian?"

"Well, because he and his family have had them in their possession for so long, they do belong to him but…they were originally stolen."

I knew that if you find anything on your land, then it's yours, no matter what. Of course, this new treasure was found on public land, so that could be a problem.

He added, "I'm working with our legal department concerning all the parties involved with the items recovered at the mill site."

"Well, I trust your judgment. You've been great so far." I still couldn't wrap my head around the idea that there was even a question as to who owned what.

He stood to leave. "Mrs. Caldwell, here are some papers explaining the events that have occurred. I would like you to read them over. There's a place for you to add anything else you feel is important at the end. Then I need you to sign them."

The stack of papers could fill a small binder. "I hope I'll have time to finish reading them before my surgery next week."

"I would appreciate your quick response in this matter." He started to close up his briefcase. "Call me when you've signed them, and I'll send someone to pick them up."

I took the papers and placed them on my desk. He took a step to leave.

"Wait," I said. "What about the money that was in the backpack? And who were those two guys?"

He turned around. "The money was drug related, so it will be forfeited back to the local police department."

"Really?"

"Yes, Gerard Simpkins, or as you heard him being referred to as 'The General,' was part of a drug network here on the Cape a few years ago. He evidently buried his profits up there on the conservation lands before he was captured. He did some time but not for long; they only had circumstantial evidence against him."

"Who was the young kid? And is he going to be okay?" I was curious about poor Silas.

"Simpkins and the kid's father were cellmates in prison. That was their connection. The kid, Silas Maroney, was Simpkin's driver." He started for the door again. "Oh, I almost forgot." He took out a small pouch from his jacket pocket. "Do you recognize this?" he opened the bag and out poured the pieces of eight.

"They're mine. Where did you find them?"

"In Maroney's pocket, at the hospital."

I couldn't believe what I was hearing. "Right before all of this happened, we took the family to a movie one night and forgot to lock the door. We suspected someone had entered our house but nothing seemed to be missing at the time. Now it all makes sense."

The last thing Agent Clark said to me was, "Mrs. Caldwell, you really should be more careful."

I held the oddly cut coins in my fingers and then spotted the cracked blue teapot on my bookshelf. I stared at its beauty and wondered how many miles it had travelled and how many people had touched it over the centuries. I got up and moved closer to the relic. With my good hand, I removed the lid and placed the pieces of eight inside its rounded body.

"Hide these for me," I whispered. "I know you can keep a secret."

EPILOGUE

Five months later

THEY SAY THAT a good man finishes last…but maybe not always. In my journal, I wrote:

> *Quentin Selucci, the bad guy, was never found guilty of murdering the young Peace Corps volunteer he had impersonated. But they did get him on several counts of manslaughter from previous crimes, so he received a minimum of 20 years. More charges are being discovered against him as I write this.*
>
> *Did the good guy win? I think so. When John and Angel Julian graciously gave up the rights to their family earrings, and I relinquished my good luck antique necklace, everything fell into place. The queen's jewels were going to be returned to the Spanish government as a matched set. After several meetings behind closed doors with a judge, the treasure was equitably divided up between John Julian and Tommy D. I had decided that because there were two maps and two owners, Tommy D was entitled to a share; after all, his map was the one clue that actually led me to the mill site. Details about the young man searching for his past were added to my signed papers.*
>
> *I can only wonder and guess at the changes that are about to*

happen to these two men, who, at one time, were thousands of
miles apart and now are so close. And what a surprise I had
when I was awarded a finder's fee in the tens of thousands.

Spring breezes filled my office with the heady scent of lily-of-the-valley that was in full bloom under the bay window. I contemplated my life; here I was, in the middle of May, with Brian returned to the states and living at home while he planned his future. My physical therapy for my new shoulder was almost over and I was feeling pretty good.

Brian walked into the office. "Mom, did you see the news feed on the internet?"

"No. What's going on?" I closed my journal, wiggled the mouse and woke up the computer screen.

Brian pointed to the headlines about Antigua that popped up across the screen. "Look! It's John Julian with Tommy D."

The image almost made me cry with joy. John Julian was shaking hands with Tommy D, except the caption said that his name was Thomas D. Chandler. His hair was cut short and he was wearing a nice white sport coat, light blue dress shirt, and jeans.

The headline read: *Cape Cod Man Opens New Youth Center!*

I looked at Brian. "I'm so proud of that kid."

"Isn't it great? It says the two men have formed a philanthropic partnership for the benefit of troubled youth in the West Indies. They're going to help the local island kids through a program using video games and interaction with the community."

"I don't know what to say."

The story went on to report that *"Thomas D. Chandler left Cape Cod to permanently make his home in the West Indies, so he can be close to his work."* I was speechless.

Brian leaned over my shoulder. "Mom, you did it again." Then he stood by my side and faced me. "Ever wonder where I got my perseverance and determination? My will to push on where all else fails?"

I smiled and with a wink, I said, "Mmmm...I wonder."

"Gotta go, Mom. I'm meeting some friends for lunch. Talk later." And with that he was gone.

I watched his car pull away then continued in my journal:

Since Brian's return to the states and his official termination as Peace Corps, he's decided he wants to take a few months off to rest before he ventures off again. First up might be a Master's degree in Public Health, and then he thinks he'll be off to Alaska, the Last Great Frontier, to follow his dreams.

Jim, our wanderer, has been going from job to job since college. Now, after finally opening and closing a small bistro here in Brewster, he's decided to try his talent in Hollywood. He's not sure if he wants to be behind or in front of the camera. He's been in LA for the last few months. I'll be flying out to visit him in a few days…some quality mother-and-son time.

Casey will be entering her first year of college and is very involved with the theatre arts. Molly and Danny are simply growing up too fast.

By nine o'clock, I was tired. Bedtime couldn't come soon enough. My flight to California was fast approaching. I could feel an ache starting to creep into my shoulder from too much packing. Almost finished, I pushed my suitcase to the side of the dresser for tomorrow's final items.

I walked into the living room. Paul looked over to me from the couch. "Almost done?"

"I think so."

He patted his hand on the sofa next to his side. "Come here. Let me rub your feet."

I willingly surrendered to the soft cushions and his gentle touch as he massaged my tired feet. I could feel myself dozing off.

Paul stopped his hands. "I hope, this time, you're finally going to get an uneventful vacation with our son."

Even with my eyes closed, I could sense a slight tease in his voice. I just smiled, remembering what had happened when I visited Brian on Antigua.

He covered my legs with a fleece blanket.

"Don't stop. It feels so good," I begged him.

He continued without hesitation. "Nancy, I'm serious, don't you think you've had enough adventure? I don't want to lose you. I love you."

"Don't worry." I sat up next to Paul and snuggled with him under the blanket. "All I want to do is roam the beaches, visit with Jim, and just relax."

"Great idea, but don't pressure him to do too many things if he's busy."

"I promise. I'm going to LA with no expectations. If Jim has to work, I'll take in the Hollywood sights by myself and just have some fun. After all, it's only Jim and me, what could possibly happen?"

The End

Map of Cape Cod by John Julian 1722

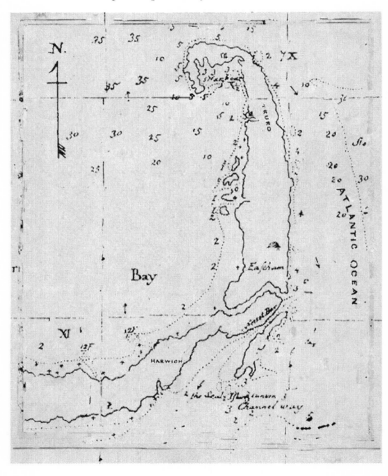

Additional Markings by Thomas Davis 1722

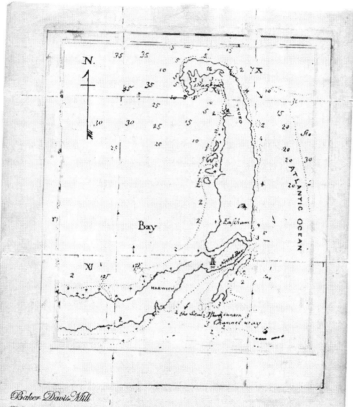

Baker Davis Mill

Follow the new road to the river of Namskaket. Travel to the southern ridge of where Harwich meets Eastham. The property of Baker and Sons will be marked with a stake 10 yds from the corner of the oak. Follow the line along the Magnetic North parallel with the cove's inlet.

ACKNOWLEDGMENTS

Following your dream is never easy but with the help and encouragement of family and friends it becomes less maddening.

So, I would like to first thank my husband, Timothy, and all my children and their spouses, especially my son Tim, who gave me the inspiration to write about a Peace Corps experience.

Next in line for thanks are my two writing groups.

The Monday, Tuesday Group That Meets On Friday: Anita, Joan, Barbara#1, Yvonne, Jerri, Pat, Nikole, Iris, and Carol. They've been listening to my words for over eight years and still keep coming back for more.

Writers In Common: Katrina, Jason, Debbie, Diane, Barbara K, Greg, and Susan always catch what the *Monday, Tuesday…*group misses. Between the two groups there is quite a unique set of talents for critique.

My early readers were astute in their evaluations of the manuscript: Barbara#1, Pat M., Maryanne, Jennifer F, Charlotte, and my daughter Heather.

My editor, Nicola Burnell, who always had the kindness and foresight to argue with me about getting rid of my favorite words, all for the flow and success of my writing.

I can't forget Michael Farber, who led an eager group of explorers, including me, looking for the cornerstones of Cape Cod.

And finally, without the expert advice on weaponry from my son–in-law Eric, the bad guys wouldn't have been so nasty.

.

ABOUT THE AUTHOR

When the author and her husband Tim, a professional artist, turned forty in the late 1980s, they moved from Ohio with their three teenagers to an old 1880 house in Brewster on Cape Cod. The Cape's history and brilliant natural light drew them in; this was a place where Tim would paint and Barbara could write.

A storyteller at heart, Barbara's imagination took flight after she unearthed a mysterious pattern of red bricks under ten inches of soil behind her barn and found a beautiful blue-flowered pottery shard on the tidal flats of Brewster. She conjured up a connection to an old Cape legend about Maria Hallett and her pirate lover Sam Bellamy, captain of the wrecked ship The Whydah.

These unanticipated events catapulted Barbara onto a journey that led to the writing of a series of old Cape stories featuring contemporary character Nancy Caldwell.

She is currently a Member in Letters of the National League of American Pen Women, International Thriller Writers, Sisters in Crime, Board Member of Cape Cod Writers Center and belongs to two writing groups. Always a journal writer, she is fascinated by history and writes a blog about the unique facts and myths of Cape Cod.

ALSO BY BARBARA STRUNA

The Old Cape House (Historical Fiction) Contemporary Nancy Caldwell relocates to an old house on Cape Cod with her husband and four children. In her backyard, she finds an old root cellar and at its bottom is evidence that links her land to the 18th century legend of Maria Hallett. As you follow the lives of these two women, a Cape Cod secret, hidden for 300 years, is uncovered.

.

Made in the USA
Middletown, DE
23 May 2021